STRIKE WHILE THE IRON IS HOT

a fiction story,
written and illustrated
by
Guy Lautard

"Did you ever go after Thatcher!"

"That's right. I did. No sense in fooling around with him. If you want something, you've got to strike while the iron is hot," John said grimly.

Published by Makerworx, LLC

Strike While the Iron is Hot. Copyright © 1983 by Guy Lautard.

Published by Makerworx, LLC, Ann Arbor, Michigan, USA. Previous edition published by Guy Lautard, 1983.

1st Makerworx printing, April 2022.

Paperback ISBN: 978-1-953439-03-1
eBook ISBN: 978-1-953439-04-8

The assistance of The Canada Council, Explorations Program, is hereby gratefully acknowledged.

Cover drawing and those of the moose and Ksan by Margaret Lautard.

THIS IS A FICTION STORY

The places described and named in this book are real, and are described in their actual settings and locations. The characters and events are fictional.

Any resemblance between any character in this story, and any person living or dead, is strictly coincidental.

There is *no such company* as Babine Copper.

There *is* a town called Granisle, on the shore of Babine Lake, in West Central British Columbia. You will find it on any up-to-date map of suitable scale. It is a company town, an "instant town", originally built to house the labour force for an open pit copper mine located on an island group about three miles away at the entrance to Hagen Arm, in Babine Lake.

Pockets of beautiful crystal and minerals are found from time to time in the Granisle orebody. I've seen them — in the bunkhouses, not in the Company's offices.

Due to economic conditions prevailing during the time period in which this story is set, the mine was shut down for a year.

None of the events comprising the story which follows ever took place.

Except . . .

Events of an historical nature are factual, to the best of my knowledge.

The two bridge disasters referred to, are, unfortunately all too real. The incident of the well placed knothole is true, but the locale has been shifted. An uncle of mine was the rancher.

Ideas credited to the following two individuals are theirs, and permission to incorporate them into this story is gratefully acknowledged:

Bill Fenton, retired master machinist, active model engineer, and Life Member of the B.C. Society of Model Engineers.

Geoff Symons, tool and die maker and model engineer, Calgary, Alberta.

Chapter 1
SEPTEMBER 7, 1982

John Kelly put down his file and wiped chalk dust from the partially finished engraving cutter with a piece of cloth. Previously he'd cross drilled the shank of the cutter with a #53 drill about half an inch from what was to be the working end, and now he slipped a ten inch length of 1/16 inch drill rod into this hole to check the alignment of the point he was filing . . . a few more strokes on the left hand side would even it up.

Mentally he patted himself on the back for the idea of the cross hole. When he went to use the completed engraving cutter, he would put the 1/16 inch drill rod through the hole, line it up over the center of the job to be graduated, and have the cutter neatly 'square' to the work in seconds — a small refinement perhaps, but handy.

He turned the cutter slightly in the vise, and commenced filing again. After a few strokes he stopped, picked up the magnifying glass and studied the angles critically. He reoriented the cutter again, and with a heavier file began to bevel its bottom face. He worked more quickly now, for this face did not matter greatly, bringing the bevel out till it reached the very tip of the cutting edge. Then, with a half round file he blended the filed areas into a clean, symmetrical and pleasing union with the untouched portion of the 1/4 inch drill rod. He worked out the last of the file marks with a piece of fine emery paper backed up by a file, and when satisfied, removed the cutter from the vise.

He was a perfectionist in such things, and although this was not a cutter he would use often, it would probably serve him for graduation-marking jobs of every description for the rest of his life, so he might as well make a decent job of it while he was at it.

He took a propane fuel cylinder from a shelf beside the bench, screwed a burner head onto it, and set it on the bench. He left the shop and returned with a soap dish and a small can full of water. He scraped the cutter across the soap cake, and with his fingers smeared the soap smoothly all over the working end of the cutter. After setting a large horseshoe magnet on the bench beside his 'quenching tank', he lit the torch.

Holding the cutter gently with a pair of pliers, he heated it slowly, watching the soap foam up, swell, and dry into a blackened skin. Then he turned up the torch, and watched as the cutter began to glow dull red. He picked up the magnet, and touched it to the glowing end of the cutter without moving the latter from the flame — when the steel would no longer attract the magnet, it would be ready to quench. He recalled how surprised Janet had been when, nine years ago, he'd shown her this phenomenon.

"A little hotter," he thought, holding the magnet close, but outside the flame. In a few seconds he touched it again to the cutter, which, for all the attraction it now exhibited for the magnet, might have been a piece of wood. He shifted the cutter slightly in the flame, laying the magnet down as he did so. Then with a movement as sudden and as quick as a striking rattlesnake, he plunged the glowing cutter into the small quench tank. There was a brief hissing, and he shook the cutter slightly under water as it cooled. When he withdrew it, the hardened area was a pale, even grey colour.

With a few strokes of the file-backed emery paper, he polished up a small area on one side of the working end of the cutter before returning it to the flame. This time he watched the steel intently, and as the first faint show of colors began to run on the shank, he withdrew it from the heat. Straw yellow was the color he wanted, and at the instant this color reached the working end of the cutter, he quenched it again.

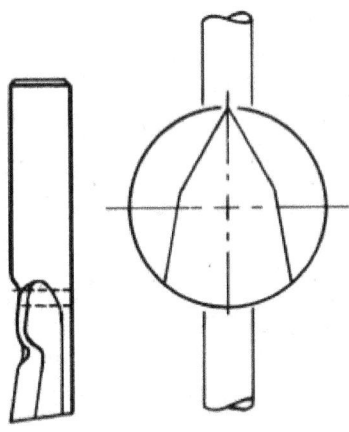

"Done!" he grunted with satisfaction, removing the lid from a bottle containing a solution of salt and vinegar, and dropping the cutter in. He replaced the lid, paused for a moment to run a hand through a head of close-cropped, prematurely grey hair, and then began putting away the tools he'd been using. He looked at his watch: it was 2:30 p.m. Now what? Lunch, then a quick trip downtown to pick up his hard-toed boots, which were in for new heels.

* * *

Coming home, he caught the West Vancouver bus, and took the last empty seat, beside a woman who was busy looking out the window. He set the heavy brown paper bag containing his work boots on the floor between his feet. From a flat, zippered briefcase, he took a pile of xeroxed pages nearly half an inch thick. Removing a spring steel paper clip from the upper left hand corner of the pile, he riffled the pages till he brought to the top the one he was looking for. Re-clipping the pile, he began to read.

After a few minutes reading, he took a pen from his pocket and made a note in the margin of the page. As he did so, he became aware that the woman was 'reading over his shoulder'. Well, let her, he thought. It wouldn't do her any harm, though on the other hand, she wouldn't make head nor tail of it either.

"Excuse me, but isn't that a MODEL ENGINEER article you're reading?"

John Kelly looked at her, surprised. She was several years younger than himself, blonde, and stunningly pretty. "Yes, it is. It's about making a dividing head. Are you familiar with MODEL ENGINEER?"

"Yes. My dad used to take it and LIVE STEAM regularly. He said they were the two best magazines in the world!" She smiled. "He said he got all kinds of ideas out of them for his work — he was a tool and die maker. Are you in the trade, or is it just a hobby with you?"

"I build models on commission, and I do some prototype and specialty work for various outfits. When I'm not busy doing that, I make tools for my shop — stuff like this," he said, indicating the papers in his lap.

"That's nice — it must be great to have your own business and do what you enjoy doing."

"It is, if you like working by yourself. For me, it's the best arrangement there is," John agreed. "And you, what do you do?"

"I'm a draftsman. Or I'm supposed to be. I just got here from Toronto yesterday, to start a new job today, and when I showed up for work this morning, I found the outfit that'd hired me had gone broke. So I'm not sure what I'm going to do next . . . "

John Kelly pushed his upper lip up with his lower lip in the universal expression which means 'That's too bad'. "And they never bothered to phone you to tell you not to come?"

"I guess they had bigger things on their minds — like their own problems," said the girl.

"Have you been looking for work today?"

She nodded. "I went to see Manpower[1], to see if they knew of any openings, but they just gave me a bunch of forms to fill out, said they'd call me if anything came up, and to keep in touch."

"Well, that's a start." He thought for a moment. "Not a good time to be looking for a job, these days. Have you got access to a private phone?"

"Yes. I'm staying with friends, and I can use their phone. Why?"

"If I were in your shoes, I'd look in the 'Yellow Pages' under every classification of business that even *might* employ draftsmen, and I'd phone every outfit I found listed. Tell 'em you're a draftsman with so many years experience with such and such a company and you're looking for work. If they're looking for somebody, tell them you'll come in and see them the next day. Be polite. Be persistent. Don't get discouraged. Don't give up. If somebody's rude to you, or whatever, just hang up and forget it, and phone the next one."

"But who'd hire you over the phone?"

"Nobody. But if they don't want to hire *anybody*, why waste your time knocking on their door when you can dispose of them in one minute by phone? And if they *are* looking for somebody, they'll be receptive to talking to you. You'll cover far more ground in a day that way than any other. And it shows you've got some initiative."

---

1   Canada Manpower, the Canadian Federal Government employment agency.

The girl nodded. "You're right. I'll give it a try, tomorrow morning. Have you ever done that yourself?"

"Twice. Got a job both times, too. Once as a night shift janitor, after high school, and once as a warehouse hand. Just a summer job, both times. That was a good many years ago, but I'd do the same thing today if I were looking for a job."

They were across Lion's Gate Bridge now, and well into West Vancouver. She looked out the window somewhat distractedly. "Whereabouts do you get off?"

"At 14th. It's my first time on the buses, and I'm not familiar with everything. I don't want to miss my stop."

John nodded. "14th is just coming up — better ring the bell . . . " She did so.

"Well, I can't do much more than wish you good luck, but I'll do that. I hope you find a job you like, and soon."

"Thanks. And thanks for the advice. I'll try it."

He stood up to let her out of the seat. "Take care of yourself," he said kindly.

"Thanks. You too. Nice talking to you." Her smile crinkled the corners of her eyes, and then she was gone.

As the bus pulled away from the stop, she glanced up at the window beside which she'd been sitting. He'd moved over to sit next to the window, but he did not look up, for he had already turned his attention back to the papers in his lap.

He sat staring at the page for a minute or two, seeing not the printed words, but the girl's sparkling brown eyes and sunny smile. "Nuts!" he told himself abruptly, stuffing the papers back into his zippered briefcase. At his stop several blocks further along, he got off and commenced the 3/4 mile climb up the hill to his house.

". . . Probably more interested in her own good looks and having a good time than anything else . . . ," he thought. Only Janet had been unlike that, and she was . . .

He fixed himself an early supper, and then returned to his basement workshop, where he fished the engraving cutter from the salt and vinegar bottle. Due to the several hours of soaking in this acid solution, he was able to rub off, with his thumb, nearly all the discoloration due to the earlier heat treatment of the cutter. This done, he examined the cutting edge under a 10X hand lens before carefully stoning it to final form. With a few more strokes he removed some small burrs raised by the pliers on the shank of the tool, and laid it on the bench.

From under the workbench he took a plywood box. Opening it, he lifted out a six inch rotary table, which he proceeded to set up on the table of his vertical milling machine. When all was in order, he dropped a #2 Morse taper shank arbor into the central hole in the rotary table, fitted a previously prepared bushing over the end of the arbor, and carefully fitted a workpiece onto the bushing. Washers, spacers and a 5/16 x 24 socket head cap screw followed, the latter clamping the workpiece from turning with respect to the rotary table.

The 'workpiece' was the table for a smaller rotary table he'd been working on in his spare time for several weeks. It followed almost exactly the "Small Rotary Table" design which had appeared in late 1976 in MODEL ENGINEER. Tonight he would graduate the rim of the table 0-360 degrees, this being the final job requiring to be done to complete the project.

When the set-up was complete, he fitted the newly-made engraving cutter into a collet in the machine's spindle nose, and with the aid of his piece of 1/16" drill rod, quickly lined it up. He could not suppress a small smile of satisfaction at the ease with which the cross-drilled hole allowed him to set up the cutter 'square-on' to the circumference of the work.

He began to cut the graduations, working methodically. Cut a graduation. Turn the graduated handwheel of the 6 inch rotary table 90 degrees, thus turning the work one degree through the 90:1 worm reduction gear. Down quill (cut another graduation). Up quill. Turn the handwheel. Down quill . . . Up . . . Turn . . . Down . . . Up . . .

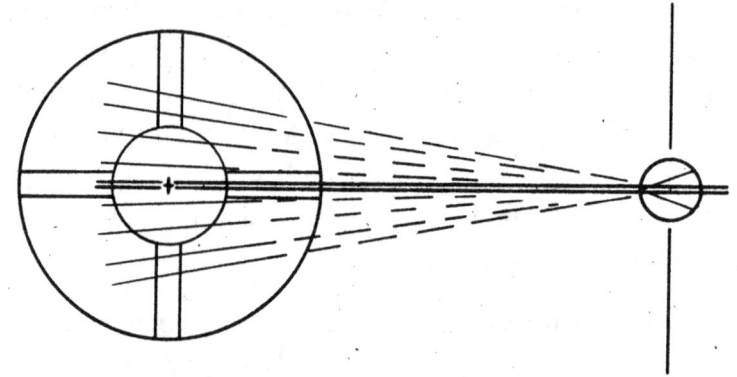

It took four trips around the job to complete the engraving, once for all the graduations, then a second and third time to lengthen the 5- and 10-degree marks, and a final trip around to both lengthen and deepen the 90 degree marks, which fell in the center of the T-slots.

By the time he was done, he was tired, but now was not the time to stop. All those little curls cut by the engraving tool must come off, and the burrs thrown up by its action must be removed. Then a good cleaning up of all the parts, and he could assemble the little rotary table, and it'd be done!

He'd just glanced at his watch — it was 9:15 — when the phone rang upstairs. He caught it on the third ring.

"Hello. Kelly here." From the background noise he knew instantly that it was long distance.

"Hello there, young fella. How's things in the Big City?"

A grin of pleasure split John's face from ear to ear. "Just fine, Bob! How are you? And how's Doris?"

"Well, I don't want to scare you, John, but in fact we're not in the best of shape . . ."

"What's happened?"

"Well, we had a bit of an accident. We got hit by another vehicle on the highway west of Smithers and wrote off my pickup truck. That don't matter, of course, but Doris got pretty thoroughly banged around, and broke her leg, and I bust my arm. Doris'll be in the hospital another week or so. Other than that, we're okay, but it's going to take us a while to get back to normal."

"Gee, I'm sorry to hear that, Bob. Is there anything I can do to help? Could you use a hand for a while?"

"That's mostly what I phoned about, John. Are you busy?"

"No. I just finished up a couple of jobs last week, and I've got nothing new in sight right now. I was going to start making myself a dividing head, but there's no rush on that."

"Well, if you'd like to come up, I could sure use you. I've got more work than I can keep up with, and I can't do much with a busted arm."

"You mean run that big lathe of yours, and that big old Garvin milling machine? Hey, my Myford is the biggest lathe I've ever run . . ."

"Makes no difference, boy. Principals are all the same, as you know as well as I do. With the kind of work you do, the stuff I'm being asked to do will be like falling off a log. Besides, I'll be able to supervise. My tongue ain't in a cast, as you can tell."

John laughed.

"How about it? I can pay you pretty well, and I'd sure like to have you here. I can't get anybody around here that I can depend on. I hired one fella who said he was a machinist, but he hardly knew where the center of the work was, even when it was turning!"

John laughed again. A visit with Bob and Doris would be like a trip home for him. "Sure, I'll come. I'll be on my way in a day or two. I'll have to pack a bunch of stuff if I'm going to stay a few weeks."

"Well, that's the best news I've heard all day. We'll probably see you Saturday, eh?"

"Should do . . . Say, how's the moose hunting situation up there this year?"

"That's the other thing I meant to mention, John. Bring along your rifle, and maybe we can drop us a moose while you're here. There's lots of them around this year."

"Fine — will do — you get one tied up, and I'll do the rest."

"Okay, John, I'll let you go. We'll sure look forward to seeing you when you get here."

"Okay. See you in three or four days."

John hung up the phone. He thought about the prospect of a stay with the Davidsons and working with Bob for a few weeks.

"Yahoo!" he roared at the top of his lungs, leaping off the floor and kicking his heels together.

This exuberant maneuver brought him into the middle of the living room. His eyes went to a portrait on the wall above the fireplace. He stood looking at it for a minute, his back to the large picture windows with their view out over English Bay and the lights of Vancouver, a city of a million people.

She had been unlike anyone else he had ever met . . .

Now what? Start thinking about what to take. What else? Phone Ailene. Next Wednesday was her birthday. Well, he'd be in Smithers then, so he'd best take her out to supper before he left, preferably tomorrow evening. What else? Clean up the house. Eat the refrigerator bare. Turn off the newspaper. Redirect the mail. And fifty other things . . . But tomorrow was soon enough to start tackling them. Tonight he'd finish the little rotary table. He wanted it done before he left for Smithers. Hey! He might even take it with him to show Bob — Bob would appreciate it.

Chapter 2
AN UNEXPECTED PASSENGER

Wednesday morning John began making preparations for the trip. He cleaned and oiled his lathe and milling machine, so that when he was done they looked as though they'd never been used. He draped them with heavy cloth covers made from old curtains. Then he went through his machinist's tool chest, removing a few tools he would not need, and adding others he wanted to take with him. After that, he put some other hand tools, wrenches, etc. in a plywood toolbox, and turned his attention to other matters. No doubt he would think of various things to add to one or both toolboxes before Friday morning, but this was a good start.

By Wednesday evening, when he went to take Ailene out for supper, he was on pretty good terms with his list of things to do. He was home again about 9:30 and heard his phone ringing as he unlocked the door to let himself in.

"Hello. Kelly here."

"John. Bob again. Didn't get you outta bed, did I?"

"No, I was just coming in the door. I've been out for supper. What's up?"

"Well, I just had a call from one of Doris' nieces. She's visiting friends in Vancouver and phoned to say hello. When I told her about the accident and all, she offered to come up to give us a hand till Doris gets back on her feet. Would you mind bringing her up with you?"

"No, I'll be glad to. What's her name, and how do I contact her?"

"Her name's Ellen MacIntyre. We haven't seen her for years. Last time I saw her she was about 15, and awkward as a stork on ice skates. Heck of a nice kid, though. She's Doris' sister's daughter. Lost her parents in an automobile crash about six months ago. Now, where did I put her phone number?" John could hear Bob rummaging around on his desk.

"Well, awkward or not, if she's your niece, she's okay with me. I'll phone her right now, if you'll just get organized and give me the phone number."

"I've got it here somewhere. You gotta have patience with us old folks, you know, John . . . ah, here it is . . ."

"Okay, got it. Nothing else?"

"That's all. See you both Saturday."

As he dialed the number Bob had given him, he noted that it was a West Vancouver prefix.

A man's voice answered.

Good evening, and could he speak to Ellen MacIntyre, please? Yes, he could, if he would wait just a minute. He would wait, thank you. Per Bob's description, he imagined her lurching and staggering to the phone, knocking over furniture as she came. What had Bob said? . . . 'a stork on ice skates.'

"Hello. Ellen speaking." The voice was pleasant, and not at all one you would associate with scattering and smashing furniture.

"Hello, Ellen. My name is John Kelly. I'm a friend of your uncle, Bob Davidson. He phoned me last night to ask if I'd come up to give him a hand in his shop for a few weeks. I just had another call from him a minute ago — he said you were coming up too, and asked if I'd mind giving you a ride. If you'd like to come with me, you'd be welcome."

"Well, that'd be very nice. It won't be an inconvenience to you, John?"

"No, it won't. But I should warn you, you won't be traveling in fancy style. Eight hundred miles in a Toyota Land Cruiser is not my idea of an enjoyable outing."

"Oh, I'm sure it'll be just fine. I appreciate the invitation, and the chance to see the scenery along the way."

"Well, we'll be going through some mighty nice country, and if you've not driven up there before, you're in for a treat. Now, can I ask you some questions?"

"Sure."

"Could you be ready to go day after tomorrow?"

"Certainly. Tomorrow, if you like."

"No. I've got a bunch of things to do myself, before I'll be ready to go. Next question: do you have much luggage to take with you?"

"I've got three suitcases, and a small trunk. I don't really need to take the trunk, but I can't leave it here either. I'm staying with friends. They have an apartment and they just don't have room to store it."

"Well, if you like, you're welcome to leave it at my place for however long you want. How would that suit you?"

"That'd be fine, thanks. You're sure it won't be a nuisance?"

"No problem at all. Next question: would it be possible for you to put the stuff you'll be taking with you, but that you won't need from now till we get to Smithers, in say two of your suitcases? That way, I could pack them while I'm packing my stuff in the truck tomorrow, rather than have to leave space for them, and try and fit them all in the morning we leave."

"Sure. I could bring them to your place in a cab in the morning. Would that be helpful?"

"Your friends live in West Van, don't they, Ellen?"

"Yes. On Clyde Avenue, about 13th."

"Well, how be if I drop by there sometime tomorrow afternoon and pick up your trunk and your two suitcases? That'd give you a chance to see the whites of my eyes before we leave, too!"

She laughed. "I'm not worried about seeing the whites of your eyes! Uncle Bob says you're alright, and that's good enough for me. Let me give you the address here, and my friends' name. It's Foxwell — Archie and Helen Foxwell. If I'm not in when you come by, Helen will be."

"Okay, that'll be fine." John wrote down the address as she gave it to him.

"And you said you'd be leaving day after tomorrow. That'd be Friday, wouldn't it?"

"That's right. I'd like to leave pretty early — say about six. Can you be up and ready to go that early?"

"Sure. Archie gets up about 6:30 to go to work, so that'll be fine. I'll be up and gone early enough so's not to be in his way. Sleepy, but not in the way!"

"Okay. We'll have breakfast an hour or two out of Vancouver, so you won't need to get up too much before six, and it'll be warm in the truck, so you can snooze to your heart's content to make up for having to get up so early."

"That'll be fine. And how long will it take us to get to Smithers?"

"Well, if we don't run into any kind of trouble — which we shouldn't — we should get there sometime Saturday afternoon."

"Okay. Would you like me to pack us a lunch for Friday?"

"That's nice of you to offer, but no, we'll stop for lunch somewhere along the way — Cache Creek, or 100 Mile House maybe — somewhere beyond the Fraser Canyon."

"All right. I'll look forward to meeting you tomorrow when you come for the trunk and suitcases, or failing that, six a.m. Friday morning."

"Okay then. Bye for now."

"Goodbye. And thanks for inviting me to go with you — I'm looking forward to the trip."

She doesn't sound like she has three heads or breathes fire and smoke, thought John as he hung up the phone.

Thursday morning he washed the truck inside and out, and then left it with all the doors open, to dry out in the sun while he mowed the lawn.

He did not meet Bob's niece when he went to the Foxwells' apartment to collect her trunk and suitcases. She was out, but Helen expected her back soon — John was earlier than they'd thought he would be. Would he like to wait a few minutes? He chose not to wait.

When he got back he began to load the truck for the trip. When he was finished, there was a space left for Ellen's one remaining suitcase, and a clear view out of the rear window over the load. His emergency gear, including tools, tarpaulin, heavy tow rope, and a triple sheaved block and tackle rigged with a hundred feet of line, could all be readily reached if needed for use during the trip without disturbing the luggage. His rifle, though not visible to even the most searching visual examination by someone outside the truck, was similarly available. "And that's just the way we like it!" John Kelly grunted to himself when he considered the matter.

The fuel tank was full, as was a 5-gallon jerry can. The spare tire was securely bolted to its carrier, which swung with the left rear door of the vehicle.

When all these preparations were complete, John brought two sheepskin seatcovers out to the truck, and fitted them to the seats. That done, he backed the truck into the garage and went inside for a late lunch. After that, he set about the job of cleaning the house up.

That night he went to bed early, with his mental alarm clock set for 5:15 a.m.

Chapter 3
A FROG STRANGLER

When he awoke, the first sound he became aware of was that of rain. He looked at his watch — 5:10. "Not bad, Kelly," he growled, rolling out of bed. Half an hour later he was ready to leave. The house was in good order for a prolonged absence. He glanced at his watch again — just about time to go. He looked out on the world beyond his windows; it was raining harder than ever now. He watched as the water hammered down outside. It was a veritable cloudburst.

He went out, opened the garage door from the inside, and after starting the truck, sat waiting for the engine to warm up. The rain seemed to be increasing in intensity even as he watched. If it got much worse you could just about drown under an umbrella! He left the truck running and went back into the house. He hadn't planned to take his rain gear, but if he had trouble on the road in this nonsense . . . better take a couple of towels, too. He got his double layered kaki "Bone Dry's" from the closet under the stairs, and pulled on first the pants, then the jacket.

He decided to call Ellen, and dialed the Foxwells' number, flinching at the thought of the noise at the other end of the line. Dear old Archie-the-Fox would not much appreciate being awakened 3/4 of an hour early. He was relieved to hear Ellen's voice almost before the end of the first ring.

"Hello?"

"Ellen. John Kelly here. Sorry to phone you so early, but with this rain, I figured I'd better."

"Do you want to delay leaving till it lets up?"

"No, no. I'm all ready to go, and the truck is warming up. What I was thinking about was this: you'll be soaked if you carry your suitcase out to to the truck in this monsoon. So when I come for you — I'll honk twice so you'll know it's me — leave your suitcase just outside the apartment building door, and make a run for the truck. I'll get your suitcase."

"But then you'll be soaked . . ."

"No I won't. I've got my rain gear on. You just get yourself into the truck as fast as you can when I pull up in front of your building."

"Okay. I won't argue. Listen: I saw an umbrella in the foyer downstairs last night. If it's still there, I'll bring it out to the truck, and you can at least use it to run back to the building. I'll leave my suitcase blocking the door so you can put the umbrella back inside."

"Okay. I hope I didn't wake your friends, phoning this early."

"No, I'm sure you didn't, but you scared me half to death! I was sitting right beside the phone with the lights off when it rang. I nearly jumped out of my skin!"

"Well, I'm sorry about that. Anyway, I'll leave now, and we'll make our formal introductions in the truck. I should be there in about ten minutes."

"Fine. I'll be downstairs waiting."

"Good. See you in a few minutes." He hung up and a minute later eased the truck out into the teeming rain. He got out long enough to close the garage door, leaped back into the truck, mopped his face with one of the towels, and headed down the driveway.

Through the downpour he could see the backlit figure of a girl in the apartment building doorway, as he brought the truck to a halt beside the curb. He blipped the horn twice. She waved, set her suitcase in the door, opened an umbrella, and ran towards the truck. As she started, John stepped out of the truck and came around to the passenger-side door, which he jerked open for her as she reached the curb. The downpour was unbelievable, and left no room for formalities. She climbed into the truck and gasped, "Thanks — here's the umbrella . . ." but it was gone from her hand, the door shut, and John was already hurrying back toward the building.

She watched him as he put the borrowed umbrella back in the stand in the foyer. He came back outside, letting the door close behind him. Through an almost solid curtain of water, she saw him heft the suitcase, then bolt from the shelter of the apartment's awninged entrance. He slowed slightly rounding the front of the truck, yanked open the door, pushed the suitcase in over the back of the driver's seat into the space left for it, leaped in and slammed the door. His head, coat, and pants looked as though he'd been attacked with a fire hose.

"Jumpin' catfish, talk about a frog strangler! Just let me dry my face, so I can see you, before I say hello," he gasped, disappearing into the towel for several seconds of vigorous rubbing and grunting. Emerging from the towel, he turned to greet his passenger.

Watching him with an amused smile was the girl he'd talked to on the bus Tuesday afternoon! John Kelly was so surprised he was at a complete loss for words for a second or two.

"Well, Mr. Kelly, you could at least say hello!"

"Hello, Ellen. John Kelly; tied tongues a specialty!" He stuck out his hand, and she shook it in a friendly manner.

"So, you're Bob Davidson's niece!"

"Yes. Didn't you recognize my voice when you talked to me on the phone Wednesday evening?"

"No, I didn't. Did you recognize mine?" he asked, as he began to struggle out of the rain-soaked jacket.

"Sure," she said, helping him with the right sleeve, "even before you said who you were or why you were calling."

"Thanks. Why didn't you say so, then?" he asked, somewhat shortly.

"You never gave me a chance. You started shooting questions at me like a machine gun," she answered, smiling again.

"Did I? I'm sorry . . ." He began to work his way out of the rain pants. "Tuck the coat down in front of your feet there, would you please, Ellen? It'll dry there in short order — the heater in this thing puts a blast furnace to shame."

"Okay, how's that? Anyway, here we are, and thanks to you I'm as dry as a bone. Thanks for bringing my suitcase out to the truck — I'd have got soaked to the skin!" She took the rain pants from him. "Shall I stick these somewhere behind us?"

"No, thanks. I'll put them under my seat here till the jacket's dry." He took them back, rolled them into a ball, and disposed of them. "Now, where's my towel gone to? I'll dry off your suitcase, and we're on our way."

John pulled the truck away from the curb, and headed for the 15th Street on-ramp to the Upper Levels Highway, which would take them through North. Vancouver and out to the Freeway.

"I should tell you, Uncle Bob told me enough about you when I talked to him on the phone Wednesday night, that I was able, with what you told me about yourself on the bus, to put two and two together and start coming up with four, so to speak. By the time you phoned I was pretty sure John Kelly and the fellow on the bus were one and the same. When I heard your voice, I was sure."

John glanced at her. Even at the low light level of the truck interior, she was exceptionally pretty. She wore a navy blue down-filled ski jacket, a white cotton blouse, a light blue scarf, and a pair of well-fitting navy blue slacks. Her hair, which he had not particularly noticed on the bus, was short and wavy, neatly done and of a gold blonde colour no one has figured out how to get into, or out of, a bottle. She was, he decided, even prettier than he'd recalled. As quickly as this thought struck him, it was pushed aside by the image of another girl, in a nurse's uniform . . . well, they had two days traveling together ahead of them, plus several weeks under the same roof at the end of the journey. He must at least make himself amenable, and treat her nicely . . . after all, his loss was no fault of hers. Besides that, she was Bob and Doris' niece, and as such needed no further recommendation at all.

He asked her what luck she'd had with her job hunting by phone after she'd talked to him. None, she told him. She'd phoned nearly a hundred possible employers, all with the same result: "We're laying people off, not hiring."

"So . . . when I phoned Uncle Bob and found out about their accident and all, I decided to take a holiday and give Auntie Doris a hand for a few weeks."

In a few minutes they were past the last set of traffic lights on the Upper Levels Highway. Within a mile they began to descend a hill. Through the rain he pointed out the lights of a bridge across the harbour below them.

"That's the Second Narrows Bridge. We came across the Lion's Gate Bridge the other day on the bus — it spans what's known as the First Narrows as you come into Vancouver Harbour, and this part of the Harbour is the 'second narrows', hence the name of the bridge. We're going to cross it in a minute or two, then we swing a little more south along Cassiar Street, and a little further on we connect up with the Freeway."

Ellen nodded. "Is that green thing another bridge beside the one we're going to cross?"

"Yes. It's a railway bridge with a rising center span. You might remember a ship smashed into a bridge here in a fog one day about two years ago, and knocked it into a cocked hat? Well, that's the one."

"Yes, I do remember seeing something on the news about that, now that you mention it."

"Now, the Second Narrows Bridge itself, it collapsed during construction back in 1957. Somebody made a miscalculation and one day the ends of two spans just fell into the water. Killed about 18 men. They say doctors bury their mistakes, lawyers put theirs in jail, and engineers erect monuments to theirs."

He paused a moment. "And us machinists? We sell our mistakes, and people are amazed that we can do such nice work!"

Ellen laughed. "From what Uncle Bob said about you, I can't imagine you selling too many mistakes! He said that as a machinist you were one of the most dedicated perfectionists he's ever known."

"Well, your Uncle Bob always gives people about 50 percent more than what's due them, so don't put too much stock in what he told you about me. As a matter of fact, he knows about ten times as much as I do about the trade. I fully intend to pick his brains naked, and to come back here knowing a lot more than I do right now. Do you know what sort of background he has?"

Ellen shook her head. "He's a machinist and has his own shop in Smithers, is all I know. Daddy always said he was a good machinist, though."

"He is — and he should be. He was trained at Aberdeen Proving Ground, Aberdeen, Maryland. His Army trade ticket reads, 'Machinist, Toolmaker, Die Sinker'. He said it himself: the Army doesn't care how long you take to do a job, so long as it's perfect when it's done. After the Second World War was over, and he got out of the Army, he got a job in a machine shop and was promptly fired 'cause he was too slow and too fussy. So he dusted himself off and went to another shop and got a job as an apprentice — said he knew how to read a micrometer, and that was about all. So he learned to work fast in his second apprenticeship.

"I've worked with him a couple of times, when I've visited him, and he's helped me in my shop when he was down in Vancouver. Working with him is a real eye opener."

"And what about you?" Ellen asked.

"I'm mostly self taught."

"My dad always said some of the best machinists he knew were the ones who'd learned on their own. He said usually they could work with less supervision, and figure out quicker how to do a particular job, than some of the journeymen machinists who'd served a full apprenticeship."

"Probably something in that — I haven't worked around other machinists enough to know, though."

In a few minutes they hit the beginning of the divided, four-lane freeway. "Highway No. 1. All the way to Nova Scotia, if you want," John announced, looking at his watch. "We should be in Hope by 8:00, about an hour and a half from now. We'll stop there for breakfast, or earlier if you get hungry."

Ellen nodded. "I had some toast and jam, and some juice, just before you phoned, so I'll be fine till we get to Hope. If you get hungry, say so; Helen let me make a bunch of cookies last night so we'd have something to eat as we drove."

"Okay, that'll be nice. Now then, there's one rule, and it applies to anybody traveling with me. If you want to stop along the way for any reason — to take a picture, pick a flower, eat something, or whatever, you just say, and we stop."

"Well, that's a nice rule, and I'll remember it. Thanks. Now, would you do something for me?"

"If I can."

"Tell me something about our route and so on. I don't have a very good mental map of British Columbia."

"Okay. First thing, nobody who lives here calls it British Columbia, except mealy-mouthed politicians and chisel-tongued travel agents. It's always called B.C., with a little accent on the 'C' — like the Yankees when they talk about Washington, D.C. — it's either 'Washington' — only they say 'Worshington' — or 'D.C.', which they pronounce more like 'De Sea'. The difference there is that we say it much faster, sorta like squirting it out of a high pressure hose, whereas the Yankees kinda say it like pouring water slowly out of a big, tall glass!"

She laughed. "Okay. 'B.C.' How's that?"

"Too slow. Leave the periods out from between the letters."
"BC."

"Perfect! Now from pronunciation we'll proceed to a geography lesson. Root around in the glove compartment there and you'll find a road map. Spread it out and you can find the places we'll be going through."

YUKON

NORTHWEST
TERRITORIES

Watson Lake

Fort Nelson

BRITISH

COLUMBIA

-N-

ALASKA

Ft.St.
John

PACIFIC

Hazelton
Babine Lake
Prince   Granisle
Rupert   Stuart Lake
        Smithers
        Telkwa   Topley   Ft.St.James
        Houston Burns   Vanderhoof
                 Lake
                        Prince
                        George

OCEAN

Quesnel

ALBERTA

Jasper
National
Park

Williams Lake

100 Mile House

Vancouver Island

Cache Creek

Banff
National
Roger's   Park
Pass

Kamloops

Hope
Vancouver

Crow's Nest
Pass

Victoria

U.S.A.

31

Chapter 4
SURPRISING TALENTS

When Ellen had the map spread out on her lap, he reached over and indicated their route with his finger, keeping his eye on the road as he did so. "We're headed east. At Hope we turn north, into the Fraser Canyon, and on through the Cariboo country: 100 Mile House, Williams Lake, Quesnel, and we swing west onto the Yellowhead Highway at Prince George, out through Vanderhoof, Burns Lake, and finally Smithers, here," he concluded, tapping the map far to the north of their starting point.

"Will we be going through Chilcotin?" She said it 'Chill-coo-tin'.

"First, it's pronounced 'chil-*coat*-in'. Second, it's not a town, it's a region, or more accurately, a river valley, I suppose. Third, to answer your question: No, the Chilcotin country is west of the highway, which goes through the Cariboo country."

Ellen studied the map for a few minutes. "Gosh, even when we get to Smithers, we're a long way from the top of the province, aren't we?"

"That's right. It's about 1300 miles from Vancouver to Watson Lake, which is just north of the 60th parallel, which divides all the major provinces from the Northern Territories. I've driven as far north as Fort St. John — here — in the Peace River country." He drew a rough circle with his finger on the map. "And I've been up here to Fort Nelson, and clear up to Inuvik, by air. B.C. is nearly four times the size of the British Isles. You could stuff Utah, Massachusetts, and Connecticut into B.C. and still have room for all of Texas, and more'n half of Rhode Island, too."

"You're kidding!"

"No, I'm not, but don't tell anybody from Texas!"

"Where's Inuvik? I've heard of it, but I've never looked it up on a map. It's in the Northwest Territories — or is it in the Yukon?"

"Northwest Territories. Just north of the Arctic Circle, just south of the delta of the Mackenzie River. Now that's enough geography for a minute. See this tree up ahead of us? See how the Freeway swings around it? The Indians hereabouts attach some significance to it, and when the Freeway was built, they made such afuss about it the Department of Highways realigned everything to miss it."

"Am I boring you with all this drivel?" asked John abruptly. "I'll shut up and let you sleep, if you want to."

"No, not at all. I was just thinking how much more interesting the trip will be than if I'd taken the bus, or the train, or flown up. You seem to know the province pretty well. I've never been very far from Toronto — except I went to Europe once on a tour."

"Did you? What sort of tour?"

John Kelly had long ago learned most people like to talk about themselves, and if you gave them an opening, and closed your mouth, you might learn something about them.

"I was in a singing group, a school choir. We went all over England, France, Holland, Belgium, Germany, Scandinavia. It was an eight week trip."

34

"Sounds great. When did you do this?"

"In high school. I was about 16. We travelled mostly by train. Of course we flew to England. Most of the kids spent their time playing cards on the train. I kept my eye glued to the train window all day. The other kids thought I was nuts, but I can remember most of what I saw. I think I got ten times more out of the trip than they did."

" 'Course you would, and more power to you. So you can sing? That's nice. I couldn't carry a tune around in a bucket with a lid on it!"

"Everybody has a different talent," said Ellen, reaching down for the towel at her feet. "I'd be a poor machinist." The towel was dry, so she began folding it up. "What's that over there?" she asked, pointing to a long row of small, black rectangles well off to their left.

"That's a unit train coming down from the coal mines in the Rockies. They make the round trip from Sparwood to the deep sea shipping terminal at Roberts Bank and back in 88 hours, and bring down 13,000 tons of coal each trip."

"And there's one train that does nothing but that all the time?"

"One? There are 14 unit trains on that run all the time. Each train is made up of 108 hopper cars plus five locomotives — three at the front, and two more in the middle of the train. The cars are equipped with rotating couplers and as each car comes to the unloading point, it's clamped in a rotating dumper and turned upside-down still coupled to the rest of the train. The train makes a big loop around the terminal, and is emptied in five hours from the time the first locomotive hits the dumper."

"Then what?"

"Then they inspect the train and in about an hour it's on its way back to Sparwood."

Ellen's eye followed the line of cars till she spotted two locos in the middle of the train, then the three at the front of the string of cars. The tail end of the train was not visible.

They rolled on through the beautifully green Fraser Valley. As yet there were few cars on the road, but they saw many freight trucks heading into Vancouver on the other side of the Freeway. John pointed out the Vedder Canal as they crossed it, and explained how low-lying areas of the Valley had at one time been a vast swamp. In the years after WWI a massive scheme had been undertaken to drain the swamp and reclaim the land for agriculture. "Today the Fraser Valley is one of the most productive agricultural areas in B.C. — dairying is the main activity, but there are poultry and pig farms, vegetable growing, small fruits, and so on," he explained.

The rain had petered out to a fine drizzle now, and the sun was showing signs of making an effort to brighten the morning. Ellen turned John's coat again, and looked about the truck cab. Her eye lit on the gearshift knob, which was partially covered with some sort of braiding. She leaned over to take a closer look at it. "What's that?" she asked.-

"I think it's the gear shift lever," John said, looking at it as if it'd just sprouted up from the floor of the truck in the last couple of seconds.

"That I know! I was referring to the braiding on the knob," she said archly, but laughing.

John cracked a grin at her. "That's a turkshead knot, done up in tarred nylon twine. I just put it there for something to do one day." He gave the knob a sharp twist, unscrewed it from the lever, and handed it to her.

She studied it for a minute or two before putting her finger on one spot. "Is that where the ends of the twine are?"

John glanced at the spot she had indicated, and nodded, surprised she would even think to ask.

"My brother was in Scouts, and he made turkshead neckerchief slides for the other boys. He would never show me how to tie them. But they were nothing compared to this! He made me learn to tie a bowline, and some other knots, but he would never teach me to do a turkshead! I even offered to make him a chocolate cake one time, if he'd show me, but he wouldn't."

John looked at her as if she'd just stepped out of a space ship in a tinfoil suit. "You know how to tie a bowline?"

She nodded.

"What's good about a bowline?"

"It never slips or jams."

"You're a genius! What other knots do you know?"

"Eye splice, back splice, Matthew Walker knot, wall knot, clove hitch, timber hitch, rolling hitch, sheet bend, Carrick bend . . ."

"Under your seat you'll find a piece of quarter inch rope about six feet long. Pull it out and tie me a Carrick bend."

"Just leave it loose, don't pull it up tight," John said, watching her out of the corner of his eye. When she finished he held out his hand. "Take the steering wheel for a minute, and keep us on the road, and I'll show you something."

She took the wheel in her left hand, and John took the knot she'd tied. He pulled the big loop up through the knot, and took the slack out of one end. Then he gave the knot a twist, like breaking a giant soda cracker, and handed it back to her. "There's your brother's turkshead, Ellen — although that wouldn't be the way he tied it."

Ellen studied the knot for a minute.

"Take the long end and run it through the knot again, starting here," John suggested. Ellen followed his instructions and soon the knot looked more like a turkshead.

"That's it!!" she exclaimed with delight.

She untied the Carrick bend-cum-turkshead, and retied it, this time running all the slack out of the knot and taking the left-over end through the knot a third time.

As she finished doing this, John drew her attention to the fact that the freeway had ended. They were now driving along beside the broad, roiling Fraser River. She put the tripled-up turkshead on the dashboard and began paying attention to the passing scenery again. The rain had let up completely, and the sun was now turning to steam the water film on the road surface.

"We'll be in Hope in a little while."

Chapter 5
THROUGH THE CANYON

They stopped for breakfast at a pancake house in Hope. Ellen ordered a waffle and a large glass of orange juice, John two eggs, two sausages, and pancakes,

"And how do like your eggs, Sir?" asked the waitress.

"Turned over and fried as hard as a rock."

Ellen wanted to pay for breakfast, but John would not hear of it. "You can make me a chocolate cake after we get to Smithers," he teased her.

When they returned to the truck, she shook out John's raincoat and folded it up neatly before putting it behind them on her suitcase. She reached across the truck and got the rain pants, which she arranged for drying in the footwell, before getting in herself.

"I sure like your seat covers," she said, when they were settled and ready to go again.

"Wool's the only thing for long trips. I learned that one time when I had to drive about 900 miles nearly nonstop in a vinyl bucket seat. Never again! Even a wool blanket folded up is pretty good. But sheepskin is the best."

"They're nice," said Ellen, digging her fingers into the thick fleece.

Now the landscape changed drastically, hemming them in closely as they headed into the lower reaches of the Fraser Canyon. Evergreens, still dripping from the morning rain, steamed on both sides of the road, and marched up the sides of the mountains to rocky bluffs far above.

Further north the vistas opened up somewhat as the Canyon widened.

From time to time as they drove north through the Canyon, they could see the railway tracks far below them, and in some1 places the highway descended to run right beside or even below the track. John explained how the C.P.R.[2] had been built through the Canyon first, and had therefore taken the preferred route all the way through,crossing the river from one side of the Canyon to the other to take advantage of whichever side offered the best construction features. When what eventually became the government-operated Canadian National Railway was built later, it had to take the worst side of the Canyon all the way, crossing the river on separate bridges wherever the C.P.R. had crossed earlier.

As they reached the north end of the Canyon, the country began to change to a drier, more sparsely wooded landscape, and eventually, to rolling, grassy hills into which the Fraser had cut its bed. This was beef and hay country, John explained. At Cache Creek, they stopped for an early lunch. Over pie and ice cream, John continued his geography lesson.

"If we were heading across Canada, we would turn east here," he explained. "The highway splits here, and the Trans-Canada heads east to Kamloops, Revelstoke, Golden, and goes over the Rockies via Roger's Pass to Edmonton, etc."

---

2   Canadian Pacific Railway

40

"Where's the Crow's Nest Pass?"

"It goes through the Rockies further south — that's the 'Southern Transprovincial' route. We'd have kept going east at Hope, on to Princeton, through the South Okanagan, Grand Forks, Fernie, etc. It's a secondary route compared to the Number 1, and it's not quite as good a road, but it's a little more scenic in places."

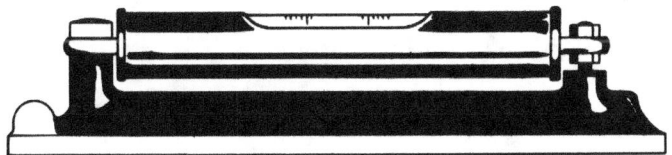

Chapter 6
FROST & JEALOUSY

After lunch, they set out again. Ellen looked at the map. "100 Mile House, Williams Lake, Quesnel, and Prince George," she read off the major towns. "Will we get to Prince George tonight?"

"We should do. We're making good time so far. If I get tired, will you drive for a while?" he asked.

"Sure, whenever you want, just say so."

After a few minutes, Ellen spoke again. "John, tell me about your business — what sort of things do you do?"

"Whatever somebody's willing to pay me to do, 'less I don't want to tackle it."

"Does that ever happen?"

"Sometimes. Job might be too big for my equipment, or they want it in titanium, or something. Fella came to me about a year ago wanting a silencer. I told him I wasn't interested unless he produced a letter from the R.C.M.P. authorizing him to have one, and me to make it. He didn't want to talk about the police at all, but he had to have a silencer, 'cause there was somebody he had to get rid of. He pulled out a roll of cash and started peeling off hundred dollar bills."

"What did you do?"

"I told him a hundred times the money he was packing wasn't enough to make me even interested in talking about it. Told him to get lost, and not come back. Told him if he had problems with somebody, he better settle them in court, not by murdering the guy. Then I shut the door in his face."

"Ugh! How creepy."

John grunted his agreement.

"What have you been doing recently?"

"Well, I just finished up a couple of jobs. One was a cut-away model of a big water pump for a pump manufacturer in California, " he took his hands from the steering wheel and enclosed a space slightly larger than a desk telephone, " . . . and the other was a couple of scaled up models of some parts of two different makes of sawmill machinery, for a patent fight."

"Really?"

He nodded. "Outfit has a patent on this particular feature on their sawmills, and a competing outfit is building pretty much the same idea into their sawmills. First outfit is suing and wants something to take into the courtroom. They came to me and asked me to make a 4X full size model of this detail."

"And you said yes?"

"No. I said 'Let's see the colour of your money.' I don't believe in doing things and not getting paid for them. People in business are usually not too bad to deal with. The absolute worst is the independent inventor types. I have a blanket iron clad rule: 'Cash Up Front. No Money, No Discussion. Like it or Lump it.'"

"You sound very hard-nosed . . . not that you shouldn't be."

"I'm in business for one reason — to make money. I'm in the business I *am* in because I like what I do, and I'm good at it. I'll never get rich, but I don't expect I'll starve, either. Or get ulcers, which I would working in an office. That just isn't my bag."

"What about while you're up in Smithers helping Uncle Bob? Won't you lose some work, if you're not there to do it when somebody tries to get hold of you to do something?"

"I might, but it's not too likely. Most times, if a model of something is wanted, it's not wanted in a terrific hurry. Also, there are relatively few people who will tackle the sort of stuff I do — which is not to say there are no model building companies in Vancouver — as a matter of fact, there are several. From time to time I do the odd thing for a couple of them. Most of my work comes from word of mouth advertising, or somebody sees something I've built and they contact me to see about having me do something for them."

"But if you're not at home, to answer your phone and your mail, then what?"

"Well, the Post Office will forward all my mail to Bob's address in Smithers till further notice. I have an "electronic secretary" gadget which answers the phone and invites the caller to leave a message. I have a friend who'll check the tape every few days and pass on any messages I need to look after, and she'll deal with the others for me."

"Well, that's handy," Ellen said more casually than necessary. John caught the note of suppressed jealousy, and decided to play innocent.

"'Tis. Ailene does lots of things like that for me. She's super."

"What did you say her name was?"

"Ailene. Ailene Larsen. She's a very special friend of mine. Really nice. You'd like her. She's about — let me see — how old are you, Ellen?"

"Twenty-eight." Frost would soon be forming on the passenger side window.

"Yes, you'd like Ailene, if you met her. She's about thirty-six . . . " John paused here for the effect of a few seconds of thoughtful consideration, " . . . no, she's thirty-seven years older than you — that's right — she'll be 65 next week."

"Oh, I thought she was your girlfriend . . ." Ellen sounded more relieved than she meant to.

"No, no. She's just a very nice lady I've known for about nine years. She's a widow. She lives just a few blocks from the Foxwells' apartment, as a matter of fact."

Just at this instant John spotted a movement in the sagebrush a few yards from the roadside. He figured his passenger could use a diversion right about now. "There's a coyote!"

"Where?" Ellen looked in the direction in which he pointed, but did not immediately spot the animal.

John slowed, and brought the truck to a halt. "There — about 20 or 30 yards away — by that big chunk of sagebrush. He's looking right at us."

"Oh! I see him! I've never seen a coyote before. Are they dangerous?"

"No, not to a human, unless it was a child, or they were really hungry, or both."

"Look," John interrupted himself. "There's another one. Just a few yards to the right of the first one."

"I see it . . . Oh, they just look like friendly dogs . . . Would they bite?"

"You'd never get near them. If you opened the truck door and got out, they'd probably take off."

46

"Can I?"

"Sure, you can do whatever you like. If they come after you, I'll try to let you get back in the truck before I take off."

Ellen looked at him and saw the twinkle in his eye. She reached over and beeped the horn. The coyotes cocked their ears towards the sound momentarily, and then went on about their business. "What're they doing?"

"Looking for lunch, probably; a mouse, or a gopher, or whatever. Like as not they'll end up eating something killed along the highway. Anyway, shall we get on our way again?"

"Okay."

John started the truck and pulled onto the road behind a tractor trailer unit which roared past their stopping place. The coyotes barely glanced up at the noise of its passage.

"Well, that was neat! I've never seen a coyote before." "You'll probably see lots more wildlife while you're up here . . . "

"I'm going to keep a list of all the animals we see."

"Okay. There's some paper in the glove compartment. Write down 'two coyotes, north of Cache Creek'. You can keep the list in the truck, if you like, and see how many different animals you can 'collect'."

A few minutes later, Ellen began to yawn.

"Sleepy?"

"A little. Do you mind if I go to sleep for a while?"

"Not at all. I'll wake you if anything happens, but otherwise, you can pound your ear as long as you want."

"There's the cookies I made last night," she said, taking a paper bag from her purse. "Have some if you get hungry."

"Okay, thanks. You be mad if they're all gone when you wake up?"

"No, I won't be mad!"

Ellen tucked her ski jacket between the seat and the window, and was soon asleep.

John drove on, wrapped in his own thoughts. How about that?! The girl on the bus was Bob Davidson's niece.

She was a nice sort, friendly, fun, and down-to-earth. Nobody could spend even five minutes with her and not like her. Funny she'd reacted to the subject of Ailene like that.

He braked the truck for a curve, gently, so as not to waken her. He could not help but draw a comparison between her and Janet. In the seven years since . . . , he'd never met another girl who even remotely interested him. Janet had been unlike anyone else.

Chapter 7
A WELL-PLACED KNOTHOLE

"Where are we now?" Ellen asked sleepily when she awoke. "We're just about into Williams Lake. You had about an hour and a half nap. How are you feeling?"

"Fine. Could we stop in Williams Lake for a few minutes?" "Sure. I've got to get some gas, and check the oil, so we'll stop at a service station. Would you like to get something to eat?"

"No, thanks. A service station will be perfect."

John looked at his watch. "Nearly 2:30. It's about 150 miles from here to Prince George. How'd you like to drive from Williams Lake? I'm starting to get a little sleepy."

"Sure. I'll be glad to. I'm not much help, dozing while you drive. I should have been helping you stay awake."

John shook his head. "You were. You snore like a buzz saw." "You're horrible!" Ellen exclaimed in mock exasperation.

"I know. I'm a beast," John said agreeably. "I ate about five of your cookies, too."

"Oh, that's good. How far are we from Williams Lake?"

"Just around the corner."

They found a service station which looked clean, and stopped for fuel, oil, and a rest. When Ellen came back from the washroom, John had moved his truck and was standing in front of it with the hood up. He was watching a scene unfold in the fueling bay he had just vacated. He drew Ellen's attention to a Cadillac, with an Airstream trailer behind and a boat on top. Beside it, a good-sized farm truck with a cattle rack was fueling from the adjacent pump island. The truck rocked with the movements of several thousand pounds of tired, nervous beef cattle. Occasionally, a hoofed foot could be heard to slam into the side of the wooden cattle rack as the animals within struggled to keep their footing on the deck of the truck, the slipperiness of which could be better imagined than described.

"The lady in the Caddy doesn't like the smell of the truck," John explained. "Her husband just asked the farmer to move his truck. Farmer told him he wasn't making the smell, and he'd move his truck when he was finished getting gas. The old girl is mad — I guess she figures she didn't spend all that money for a holiday in B.C. in her air conditioned Caddy with the intention of savouring the smells of the local economy."

Ellen laughed. The farmer was as weatherbeaten as an old stump from perhaps 50 years of outdoor work, culminated by the just-finished summer's haying season. His clothing bore the stamp of the working rancher, from his battered hat to his dusty boots.

"How's our truck?"

"Fine. Needed a quart of oil. We're about ready to go, I guess, but let's see how Mr. and Mrs. Cadillac resolve their differences with the Salt of the Earth." John continued to watch the tourist/farmer tableau over the Toyota's open hood.

The farmer had by now finished filling his truck, and was paying his bill. At this moment, one of the cattle, by coincidence perfectly aligned on a knothole in the boards of her mobile pen, was again seized by the urge to clear her bowels. An inch-diameter streak of thick, olive drab fluid emerged from the knothole and draped itself languidly across the Cadillac's front windshield. The farmer observed this sterling performance with an expression of total disinterest. Mrs. Cadillac burst out of the car and indignantly demanded, in a voice like that of a range cow on the prod[3], that the farmer clean her windshield, gesturing as she did so at the window, the knothole, the farmer and a bucket of water with a long-handled window cleaning squeegee on the pump island.

The farmer shrugged. "I didn't put it there, lady. If I was you, I'd get back in my car. Could happen again."

Having delivered this speech, probably his longest in a week, the farmer climbed into his truck, started the engine, and began to pull out. John and Ellen could see him clearly in the truck cab, grinning broadly. John made a circle with his thumb and forefinger and gave the farmer a low salute and a wink. Ellen was laughing so hard the tears were pouring down her cheeks.

John lowered the hood, latched it, and looked at Ellen, who started to laugh again. "Ready to go?"

She nodded, wiping her eyes. He handed her the keys. She went around to the driver's side and climbed in. John showed her how to adjust the seat position to her liking, then walked around to the passenger's side, as she started the truck.

"Well, that little skit was worth the price of the whole trip," chuckled John as he fastened his seatbelt. "We'll have something to tell Bob and Doris, eh?"

Ellen asked if the cattle had been fed some sort of laxative prior to being hauled.

"No. When cattle are nervous, they don't need a laxative. That cow's performance would have to be described as typical, if

---

3   "on the prod": in an ugly mood; looking for trouble.

fortuitous. Animals get nervous when they're being moved in a truck. It doesn't take much to make most cows nervous, either. If a milk cow's been mistreated in a barn — poked with a pitch fork, say — that's usually her first reaction when she comes into the barn thereafter. Usually she'll do it right after you've cleaned the barn, too, just to be mean."

Ellen began to laugh again, as she pulled the truck onto the main street of Williams Lake. John folded her ski jacket into a pillow, and leaned against the door. Glancing at his watch, he said, "Ten to three. We should be in Prince George about six. There's no hurry, though, so go along easy, and enjoy the scenery. Wake me up before we get to Prince George."

Within a half mile, he was asleep.

Ellen enjoyed a change, and the chance to do something useful as a contribution to the trip. She rolled down her window and breathed the fresh fall air, noticing signs of the onset of cool weather that had been entirely absent further south. The windshield had been scrubbed clean of splattered bugs in Williams Lake, and she noted the greatly decreased frequency with which new ones now replaced those which had accumulated in the first several hundred miles of the trip.

She looked at the sleeping figure beside her. She liked him. She noticed again as she had on the bus how grey his hair was — she wondered exactly how old he was — and reddened with remembered embarrassment at how she had reacted to his comments about Ailene Larsen. Had he been baiting her, or had he been as innocent of any such intent as he had seemed? Probably, she decided, the thought had never even entered his mind. Ellen mulled this over as she drove John Kelly's little truck north. Idly her hand fell on the gear shift lever, and the turkshead tied thereon. . . and then her thoughts turned to her brother and her parents. She missed her parents. The sight of the MODEL ENGINEER article on the bus had brought such a flood of emotions and memories of her father that it had been several minutes before she had felt sufficiently in control of herself to speak to him. She wondered if he knew about her parents' death. How would he? Uncle Bob might have said something to him on the phone . . .

John woke up once when they hit a pothole. "How you doing?"

"Just fine, thanks."

"What was that?"

"Just a little pothole," she told him quietly. He went back to sleep. It did not escape her that his first question had been for her well-being, before he'd asked her what had jolted the truck.

Thirty-five minutes later they entered Quesnel, and Ellen drove through the town as smoothly as she could, to avoid re-awakening him. An hour and a half later she reached over and touched his shoulder gently. "John, we're nearly into Prince George."

He woke immediately, and looked about them. There was a trailer park off to their left.

"We go down a hill just up ahead, past some industrial yards, then cross a bridge. About a mile further on we'll come to a big highway intersection. Peel off to the right at that intersection, and it'll take us into the downtown area."

Ellen nodded. John dozed lightly, but woke when they came to the junction, and gave her further directions by which he guided her to the Gold Cap Hotel.

They went in, and were soon in possession of keys to two second-floor rooms across the hall from one another. John returned to the truck; to get Ellen's suitcase and his own club bag. The latter had been a gift from Janet.

"How's your room?" he asked when Ellen met him by her door. She'd unlocked both rooms, had drawn the curtains and opened the window in his room to let in fresh air.

"It's fine. Yours is nice, too. Thanks for bringing my suitcase in."

"No problem. Would you like to rest for a while before we go out for supper, or would you like to get something to eat fairly soon?"

"I'm hungry, so why don't we go in say 20 minutes or so? Would that be okay?"

"Sure. Tap on my door when you're ready to go."

John eased himself onto the bed in his room, and removed his boots and heavy wool socks. He rolled up his jeans, and padded into the bathroom, where he turned on the cold water in the tub. Mercilessly he thrust one foot, then the other, under the chilling jet of water. As his feet cooled, the weariness of the long drive drained from him. It was a trick Janet had taught him.

"Two minutes of that is as good as two hours sleep," he told himself, putting on clean socks.

He was stretched out flat on his back on the bed when Ellen tapped on his door a little later.

Chapter 8
THE HUNTING MACINTYRE

"Come in. Door's not locked," he called, sitting up and beginning to put on a pair of desert boots. Ellen, coming part way into the room, watched him tie his shoes.

"Ready to go for supper?" he greeted her without looking up.

"Yes, and hungry as a bear."

John stood up then and looked at her. She had changed into a white silk blouse and a dark green tartan kilt, and carried a sweater.

"Well! Don't you look nice in the Hunting MacIntyre tartan?!" Indeed, she looked quite smashing. "You're going to create quite a stir in Prince George. This is logging and sawmilling country. The town crawls with wooly-faced, panting brutes just in from months of monk-like existence in the bush. You may start a riot," he teased.

Ellen laughed. "That I doubt."

"Well, maybe not. Anyway, I suppose it's safe enough to take you to supper. But you do look very nice."

"Thank you. But *you* are not taking *me* to supper. It's my treat tonight."

"Oh, no . . . "

"Oh, *yes*, Mr. Kelly! You bought my breakfast, and my lunch. You've provided me with not only a free, but also a very pleasant ride thus far. Whether you like it or not, supper is my treat."

John looked at her: there was a determined glint in her eye that he saw was useless to argue with. "All right, Miss MacIntyre. But you must have me home by midnight, or I shall turn myself into a pumpkin. And where do you plan to take me?" he asked, locking the door behind him as they went out into the hall.

"I don't know. You seem to know the town inside out. Where would you suggest?"

"There's a pretty good dining room in the Inn of the North, or if you fancy Chinese food, we can walk down to the Empress Gardens on Third Avenue, or . . . "

"Let's do that! I haven't had Chinese food for ages."

"Okay. We can drive down if you prefer . . ."

"Let's walk."

On the way back to the hotel after supper, she looked at him quizzically "How did you know my kilt was the Hunting MacIntyre tartan?"

"My grandmother was a MacIntyre, born under the shadow of Ben Nevis. I have a very old scarf of the same tartan."

In the hallway between their two rooms she smiled at him. "Thank you for a safe and happy day, John. Good night."

"I'm glad you enjoyed it. It was nice to have company. It's not quite 250 miles to Smithers, so if you like, we can make a later start than we did this morning."

"All right. Would it be okay to have breakfast about eight?" "Sure. We'll go over to the Inn of the North and fill up on waffles and sausages and eggs. How's that sound?"

"I'm so full of noodles and chopped chicken right now that it sounds terrible, but I'll probably change my mind by tomorrow morning!"

"Okay. Good night, Ellen. See you in the morning."

Chapter 9
PAINFUL MEMORIES

They left Prince George Saturday morning about 8:30. It was one of those clear, crisp early September mornings, beautiful beyond description. John nosed the truck back to the junction they'd hit on their way into Prince George the evening before, and swung west, onto the Yellowhead Highway. "Sixty miles of flat jackpine country between here and Vanderhoof. 450 miles to Prince Rupert," he announced, feathering the gas pedal and easing the truck into high gear without touching the clutch.

At one point they crested a hill, with the morning sun at their backs. John said, "Cousin of mine used to drive a freight truck from Smithers to Prince George and back. One morning he came over this hill with 250 gallons of diesel fuel in his tanks, and a load of kitchen appliances in his trailer. A woman was coming east in a station wagon. She was blinded by the sun, and she hit his truck head on. Hit him so hard the engine popped right out of the truck and landed 50 feet down the highway. The truck caught fire, and with all that fuel aboard, it burned so bad they had to bring a water bomber out from 'George' to put it out. The pilot missed on the first try and had to go back for another load of water. When they got the fire out, there was only 8 feet of the frame of the truck left. Destroyed the whole cargo and everything."

"What happened to your cousin? Was he killed?"

"No, but the woman in the car was. All he got was a cut on his ear. He was doubly lucky though, because he wasn't driving the truck he normally drove. His regular truck was one of those pug-nosed cab-over-engine rigs. If he'd been driving that, he told me he'd have been killed for sure. That particular day he was driving a conventional long nosed tractor like that blue Kenworth we passed a few minutes ago."

Ellen nodded.

John continued. "There was an amusing, and apparently true, sequel to that story. It seems somebody in Burns Lake had ordered a stove from a local furniture dealer there. He came in to see if it had arrived, a couple of days after the dealer'd got word of the accident. The customer asked if his stove had arrived, and the dealer said, 'What colour was it you wanted?' 'White', says the customer. 'Well, it's black now!', says the dealer. That joke was told and retold for weeks, all the way out to Smithers."

They laughed together, then fell silent, each with their own thoughts.

After a few miles, Ellen spoke. "Accidents like that are awful things. My mum and dad were killed about six months ago. A car was passing on a hill, and hit them as they came over the brow of the hill. They had just left that morning on their vacation. I was at work. My boss came to my drafting table, and asked me to come to his office. There was an Ontario Provincial Police Officer waiting there. He said, 'There's been an accident . . . your parents were killed . . . ' It was like being hit in the stomach with a baseball bat. My boss drove me home — he was a prince of a guy — about the same age as my dad. He stayed and talked to me for a while, then said to come back to work whenever I felt ready to, and he left. My brother lives in Kitchener he's a cabinet maker there — he drove to Toronto that afternoon, and stayed till after the funeral."

"When you lose somebody like that, so sudden, it makes you feel pretty numb and empty, doesn't it?" John said gently.

Ellen looked at him: there was more than sympathy in his voice.

"I know, because I've been there," he said, very quietly.

"Who . . . ?"

He shook his head, lost for a moment in his own thoughts.

"I'm sorry, I shouldn't have asked," Ellen said apologetically.

He knew he should answer her, and he had meant to do so, but he delayed too long, and then it seemed easier just to say nothing. When he finally did speak, it was many miles later, and on an entirely different and strictly conversational subject. He had no idea of how crushed with embarrassment she felt, for she gave no sign, and when he spoke, she was relieved to find the matter past. Whoever he had lost, she knew, it must have been someone who had meant a great deal to him. For his sake, she wished he had told her, for she would gladly have shared his sorrow.

Ellen, let it be said, had taken quite a liking to John Kelly the , previous day. He, on the other hand, had no interest in any such entanglement, and somehow she sensed this, for although he was nice to her, she had the impression of being regarded and treated more as a younger sister than anything else. This was due, she thought, at least in part to the age difference between them, and perhaps as much or more so, to the fact that she was the niece of a friend of his. Well, she would not wear her heart on her sleeve, but she would be friends to whatever extent he permitted.

They drove on, through an endless sea of jackpine timber interspersed with poplars; with farms, service stations, small settlements and towns spaced miles apart like scattered islands. West of Burns Lake the country became less monotonous, more settled, and more scenic.

At Topley, Ellen spotted a road which abutted the north side of the highway. "Where does that road go?"

"That goes in about 35 miles to a little mining town called Gran- isle, on Babine Lake. It's kinda pretty in there. Babine is the longest natural lake in B.C. If we get time, maybe we could drive up there some Sunday."

The highway took them through a valley of varying width, beautifully green, and well splattered with farms. At Houston they stopped for lunch at an hotel. Over steak sandwiches, John produced a short history lesson.

" 'Member when we went through Vanderhoof this morning?" Ellen nodded.

"Well, if you drive north from Vanderhoof about 40 miles, you'll come to a little place called Fort St. James, on Stewart Lake. Fort St. James was the first seat of government in B.C., which was called New Caledonia then, back in the days of the fur trade. Supplies were brought from England in tall ships all the way 'round Cape Horn, up the coast of the Americas to Prince Rupert. There, the stuff was transferred to canoes, which were paddled up the Skeena River 150 miles to Hazelton, and from there it was packed by men and horses over the Cronin-Babine Trail to the north end of Babine Lake. There they put the stuff on big log rafts with square sails, and rafted it down to the south end of Babine Lake, packed it over the height-of- land to Stewart Lake, and rafted it down Stewart Lake to Fort St. James,"

"Amazing! Wouldn't it be neat to retrace that route sometime — at least from Hazelton to Fort St. James!"

"Well, it might be. Now'd be a better time of year than in the middle of summer, because of the flies. The mosquitoes would eat you alive and the black flies and no-seeums would drive you bananas. And in October it'd be getting pretty chilly, and you might run into a moose on the trail . . ."

"What would a moose do to you?"

"Probably nothing, at any other time of year, but the rutting season begins with the first full moon in October, and during the rut, a bull moose will attack just about anything, even a train. Just a tip for you while we're on the subject: if for some reason you should happen to be driving on a back road somewhere around here in October and you come upon a bull moose on the road, *don't* honk at him! Just slow down and go by as quietly as you can. If he blocks the road, back up and get out of there."

"Oh, come on! What could a moose do to a car?"

"Okay, imagine an animal gone completely nuts, as big as a horse, with horns six feet wide, and hooves as sharp as razors. Now you tell me what he could do to a car."

"Gee, I dunno."

"Well, he could do a pretty fair job of revising the body work, and he could bust in the windows, and if it were a little car like a Volkswagen bug, I wouldn't want to bet he couldn't roll it right off its wheels!"

"Would one chase you in a car?"

"I've never heard of that happening, but it's possible. If it did, you could get away easy enough. But if you were on horseback, it'd be a different story, I'll tell you!"

"You mean a moose could keep up with a horse?"

"My dear girl, a moose can do almost 50 miles an hour in a trot — 40 easy. Your Uncle Bob and I followed one along the old Telkwa High Road one time. We went for five or six miles, and that old moose topped 40 miles an hour most of the way, and never turned a hair doing it. We finally came to a gate about seven feet high, and he sailed over the top without even breaking his stride. Went on down the road a hundred yards or so while we stopped to open the gate, and then he looked back. I guess he smelled us or something, and he took off into the bush. There isn't a horse alive that could have got away from that moose. The only thing that'd save you, if you were on horseback, would be to try to get the moose to break out of his trot — at a gallop they slow down and tire out fairly quickly — or shoot him. They can also go through the heaviest brush as quietly as so much mist, too."

Ellen gave a shiver. "I hope I never see one!"

"Well, you probably will see one, and 99 chances out of a 100, you'll have no trouble from it if you do. I'm just giving you a picture of the broad possibilities. Now then, are you all done eating?"

Ellen bobbed her head. "Yes, thanks."

"Okay. Wipe that big blob of mustard off your nose then, and let's get on our way."

Ellen's serviette flew to her nose. John laughed. "No, I was just teasing you!"

"Oh, you beast!"

From Houston to Smithers is a pleasant 3/4 of an hour drive, and the scenery is beautiful. Ahead of the traveller rise the snow-capped Telkwa Mountains, and the farms push back a forest of jackpine, spruce and poplar stretched out over a rolling landscape.

Ellen loved it, and John, though less expressive of his appreciation, enjoyed it equally.

"It's beautiful, isn't it?"

"In a week or two, when the poplars start to turn colour, it'll knock your eye out. Boy, it sure *is* nice. I'd forgotten just how beautiful it really is up here. Makes me want to move back up here, just seeing it."

"Did you live up here at one time? I guess I supposed you'd just been up on visits to Uncle Bob and so on."

"I lived up here when I was a kid. My dad worked for the Canadian National Railway on track maintenance. We were at little places like Quick — near Smithers — and Perrow, back between Topley and Houston. We moved to Smithers when I was ten and we were there till I was about 14. Then my folks moved to Vancouver, so my brother and I could go to a bigger school."

"What did your dad do then?"

"He stayed on with CN. Same kind of work, in the Yards at Vancouver, until he retired a few years ago. After that, he and my mom did a bit of traveling around the U.S. and Canada, then they settled down in Nova Scotia where my brother is. They wanted to live where they could watch their grandchildren grow up. Bro has two beastly little girls about ten and twelve years old."

She laughed. "I'll bet they're nice. Have you seen them recently?"

He shook his head. "The last time I saw them, one of them decided to use my knee as a diaper. I nearly choked the little monster!"

She laughed again. "And what does your brother, do in Nova Scotia?"

"He's a professor of mathematics at Dalhousie University. *Doctor* David Kelly! He's the educated member of the family — a Rhodes Scholar, no less!"

"Really?"

"That's right. A raving genius. Unlike myself, I might add."

"And that's how come you know so much about this part of the province? Having lived up here, I mean."

John shrugged. "Partly. I saw plenty of it while I lived up here. Some of my work before and since then has taken me around the province and elsewhere, too."

John interrupted himself, as he often did if he wanted to change the subject. "That's where the Telkwa High Road starts. It's the old road through to Moricetown, a few miles beyond Smithers. That's where Bob and I chased the moose I was telling you about."

Ellen nodded. "We're nearly at Smithers, aren't we? When will we get to Uncle Bob's place?"

" 'Bout another ten minutes. That's Hudson Bay Mountain there off our left front fender. Smithers lies right at the foot of it. When we get to Bob and Doris' place, you'll be able to look across the valley and see a big glacier on the next face of the mountain, and two waterfalls coming off the two ends of the glacier. Not surprisingly, it's called the Twin Falls Glacier."

"I wanted to ask you something, John, before we got to Uncle Bob's place."

"Shoot."

"What sort of things do you like to eat? I mean, I'm going to be doing the cooking and I just wanted to know what sort of things you like . . . besides chocolate cakes."

"Ellen, if it's food, I love it. When my dad was a little fella, his folks were so poor, they didn't eat just the carrots, they ate the tops, too. When my brother and I came along, we learned to eat anything my mom put on our plates with *no* complaints."

"Besides, I've been cooking for myself for a lot of years . . . Bachelors are easy to cook for. You just dish up whatever your Aunt Doris wants you to, and I'll tuck away my share without any complaints."

Ellen was quiet for a minute or two, then she said shyly, "I've sure enjoyed the trip with you . . ."

He nodded. "I'm glad you did. It's been nice to have your company. We turn off the highway just ahead, and work our way up behind that big knoll. That's where Bob and Doris' place is."

Chapter 10
YOU CAN'T LIVE IN THE PAST FOREVER

A few minutes later they rolled to a stop beside a large log house, surrounded on three sides by a pleasant lawn. A gravel driveway bounded the fourth side, and led to a large frame shop in the rear: "Smithers Machine Works" proclaimed a painted sign surmounted by a bird house. Later, when Ellen got a chance to look at the bird house at close range, she would find it labelled "Front Office".

A balding, powerfully-built man in his late 60's came out to greet them as the two travelers climbed out of the truck. His left arm was in a cast., "Well, what a sight for sore eyes! How are you both? Is *this* my little niece!?" Ellen was caught up in a one-armed hug that nearly knocked the wind out of her.

"Hello, Uncle Bob! Gee, it's good to see you. It's been *so* long! How's your arm? And how's Auntie Doris?"

"Arm's fine. Doris is still in the hospital, supposed to be coming home in a few days. Hey, and look at this grey-haired old man what brought you!" Bob exclaimed as John Kelly came around the rear of the truck. They shook hands, the older man and the younger, and each leaned back to look again at a much valued and respected friend.

Their grip on each other's hands tightened . . .

"Ah, you're slipping, my boy. Too much of that soft city livin'!"

"Don't kid yourself, Bob . . . "

"Well, don't stand there, come on in the house and join the mess!"

They sat and talked, about the trip, and the Davidsons' accident, and all the other news that must be savoured when friends meet again after a long absence.

After an hour or so, Bob decreed they should bring in their luggage and inspect their rooms. Ellen's was on the main floor of the picturesque log house, and commanded a view of the Twin Falls Glacier. John's, upstairs, had a window facing west. "Getting up to see the sunlight on the Telkwa Mountains is better than a king's window on all the city lights that ever burned," said John to himself as he rolled a heavy canvas duffle bag from his shoulder and straightened for another look out the window.By the time they were settled and more or less at home, it was about five o'clock. Ellen offered to get supper. Bob refused point blank. "You're not here as an indentured servant, my girl! We're going out for supper tonight. Then we will go up and visit your aunt at the hospital."

*   *   *

Sunday was a day of resting, relaxing, visiting, and getting settled in. Both of the travelers spent some time putting their respective rooms in order and getting things arranged to their liking.

Late in the afternoon, as John was driving the second of two heavy nails into one of the massive log roof stringers which exposed themselves in the sloping ceiling of his room, there was a knock on the door frame.

"Who dat?" he said over his shoulder between the strokes of the hammer.

"Hi!" said Ellen. "Would you like a visitor?"

"Who?"

"Me."

"Oh. Sure. Come into my parlour," he quipped. "I thought you'd brought somebody important to see me. Have a chair."

"Thanks. What're the nails for? Are you going to hang up your laundry in shifts to dry?"

In answer, he set the hammer on his desk and picked up his rifle from the bed. He lifted it and set it onto the two nails. "Good place for it," he pronounced.

Ellen eyed the rifle for a minute. "That looks like it's been well looked after."

"It's seen a lot of use. It belonged to my grandfather, and it saw sniper duty in Korea with one of my uncles, which explains the scope."

"What sort of rifle is it?"

"It's an American military rifle. Proper name is US Rifle, Caliber 30, M1903. Commonly known as an '03 Springfield. It was made at the Springfield Arsenal in Massachusetts. My uncle gave it to me when I finished high school. I refinished the stock and had all the metalwork re-blued about 10 years ago. There's no finer rifle made, then or now, than a 1903 Springfield." He removed it from the nails, opened the bolt, and turned the rifle muzzle-up.

"See that little star on the muzzle?" he asked, pointing at the end of the barrel as he spoke.

Ellen leaned forward and saw the tiny round-centered star stamped into the Springfield's muzzle. "What does that signify?" she asked.

"To a rifleman, it's pure magic. It means that this barrel, when measured with a device called a Star Gauge, was found to vary no more than 1/10th of a thousandth of an inch in its internal dimensions from breech to muzzle."

"What did you mean about the scope?"

"Well, most rifles like this would have iron sights only. My uncle was a sniper in the U.S. Marine Corps, and he got permission — don't ask me how — to supply his own rifle. A Marine Corps armourer put a pair of target scope bases on it for him, and he bought this scope. It's a 16 power Unertl. I keep the scope on it most of the time, but for hunting in the bush I'll take it off, and just use the iron sights. Either way it's a pretty accurate rifle."

"What'll you do with it up here?"

"I'm going to nail a moose for Bob and Doris' winter meat supply, if I can. If I can nail two, so much the better."

"What'll you do with the second one?"

"Take it home and eat it."

"I'd feel sorry for the moose."

"You did a fair job on your steak last night, and you polished off your bacon pretty slick this morning. You feel sorry for the pig, or the cow?"

"No, but that's different."

"Pig was raised for bacon. Cow was raised for beef. Moose was born to run about in the wilderness eating bushypoohs. Shoot the pig. Shoot the cow. Shoot the moose. What's the difference? 'S'all meat. Don't you like meat?"

"Yes, I do. I guess I just wouldn't like to kill an animal myself."

"Nor do I, Ellen. But I don't like to go hungry, either."

Ellen was silent — the conversation had dampened her spirits. John saw this, and grinned at her. "Let's talk about something else. You came to visit me. Anything on your mind? Got your room fixed to your liking?"

"I just came up to say hello. My room's all fixed up. It's nice. Yours is nice, too."

John nodded. "Whole house is nice. You seem kinda sad, Ellen. Is something wrong?"

"I'm not really sad. I guess it's just that I feel sort of completely out of my own element. I feel . . . well . . . not exactly lonely, but something like that."

"Well, moving 4,000 miles from home, and finding yourself out of a job when you got moved, would test anybody. Uprooting again on short notice and spending two days in a horrid little green truck driving to the back side of nowhere isn't exactly frosting on the cake."

"John, I enjoyed the last two days, driving up here with you, more than anything else I've done since my parents were killed. I really mean that."

"Well, that's nice. I'm glad you enjoyed it." He looked at her with a depth of understanding which came from she knew not what. "I know because I've been there . . . " he'd said.

"It takes a long time to get over a loss like that, Ellen. But you can't live in the past forever. I 'spect when you get busy with all the things there'll be to do around here for the next few weeks, you'll find yourself not feeling out of your element. You'll be so busy swimming you won't notice the water or the fish either, so to speak. So cheer up, and look on the bright side: you've got an opportunity to spend some time in a nice, comfortable house in a beautiful setting, with an aunt and uncle that love you and care about you, and you've got a while to decide what to do next, whether to go back to Toronto, or to stay out here in B.C. and find a job, or whatever you may choose to do."

John paused. Counseling sad young maidens was not exactly his long suit. She nodded, and feeling suddenly self-conscious, looked around the room. It was then she noticed a walnut box on the floor beside the desk.

"What's that?"

"That's this machinist's tool chest. Ailene gave it to me several years ago. Would you like to have a look at it?"

"Sure."

He too was glad of a change of subject. He lifted the chest onto the desk. Made of dark walnut throughout, with heavily nickel plated hardware, it was of a style and quality one would associate with an item made 50 years ago, but rarely seen today. He released the lid latches and hinged down the front panel, sliding it under the lowest of seven drawers, which bore a brass maker's name plate: 'H. Gerstner & Sons, Dayton, Ohio.'

"Oh, isn't that beautiful!" Ellen breathed, running her hand over the perfectly fitted joints. "And Ailene gave it to you?"

"About six years ago. Somewhere she found out about them and tracked them down, and ordered it. When it came she had me over for supper, which she does more often than I deserve, and gave it to me. I'd never heard of them, so the name on the cardboard packing boxes meant nothing to me. You could have knocked me over with a piece of lint when I pulled it out of the inner box. "

"I can imagine. It's a beautiful piece of work. Ed — that's my brother — is a cabinet maker. He'd appreciate this."

"You were saying that before. What sort of work does he do?"

"He has a little shop in Kitchener, Ontario and he does custom cabinet work for anybody who wants stuff made. Stores, people, special office furniture . . . he made me a walnut writing desk for my 21st birthday. I wish you could see it. It's every bit as nice as this."

"I bet it would be."

He paused, "Would you like to see something I just finished making before I came up here?"

"I'd love to."

John opened one of the drawers, lifted out a gleaming metal object, and handed it to her.

"Oh! A little rotary table! Isn't that neat! But . . . doesn't it have a handwheel to turn it.?"

"No. It's not a geared type. You turn it directly with a tommy bar screwed into one or another of those four holes in the rim."

"I see." She did, too. "I watched my dad do a job on a rotary table one time. He was making a fishing reel for Ed for his birthday, and he went down one Saturday to the shop where he worked, and I went with him. He put a boring head on a Bridgeport mill, and we bored concentric circles of holes all over the side plates of the reel. He'd have loved to have seen this!"

Her instant appreciation and understanding pleased him. He could not stand women who, when confronted with such an item, could do nothing more intelligent than roll their eyes heavenward and say they couldn't possibly understand what it was for. Neither did it escape him that she knew what a boring head was, nor that she remembered the type of machine her dad had used.

"I've got a really good commercial six inch geared rotary table, but for lots of things, this little guy will be handier. Your dad would have seen the article on making this one when it came out in MODEL ENGINEER back in 1976 . . . "

He pointed to the rim of the rotary table, which Ellen still held in her hand. "See the graduations? Between them and these stops, which run around the dovetail groove in the skirt of the table, you can set it to turn through whatever part of a full circle a particular job calls for. The stops come up against this block in the base, and there's a witness mark on top of it to set the graduations against."

"Oh, that is *so* slick! Have you showed it to Uncle Bob?"

"No, but I will."

She handed it back to him. "Take it downstairs when we go, and show him. It's a beautiful piece of work, John."

"Thank you." He set the rotary table back in its place in the box.

"What else have you got in there?"

"Oh, various stuff. Would you like a quick tour of the whole box?"

"Sure." From the tone of her voice, she really *was* interested.

He flicked open each drawer — micrometers, firm joint calipers, small hole gauges, taper gauges, and other measuring devices in one, tap wrenches, die stocks, pin chucks, thread pitch gauges and so on in another. In one he pointed to a knurling tool. "I made that. It's a MODEL ENGINEER design, slightly modified." From another he took a cloth-covered black box about 4 inches long and 3/4 of an inch square. The top was labelled 'Brown and Sharpe Mfg. Co., Providence, R.I., U.S.A.' in two lines of faded gold lettering. He slid the box open and pulled out a three inch straight edge: "picked that up in a funny little tool shop down near the sugar refinery in Vancouver. It's probably 50 or 60 years old, at least, but it's as good as new. Some old machinist had died and the store owner had a bunch of his tools there for sale." He put it back in the drawer and pointed to another item. . . : "and here's something else I made".

He picked up a depth gauge: ". . . that's to a design published in MODEL ENGINEER way back in 1931 by a fella called Herbert Dyer. He lived in a little place called Mousehole, way down in Lands End in England. Boy, did he ever do beautiful drawings to illustrate his articles! As a draftsman, you'd appreciate them. . . "

He opened another drawer ". . . #2 Morse taper shank for my big rotary table, made from the shank of a brand new taper shank drill what bust right up the full length of the flutes . . . and here's something you won't see very often . . . " He pulled four strips of blued steel from the drawer. "A set of Starrett #249 screw slotting blades. Handier than a monkey's tail. When I ordered these from the Starrett dealer in Vancouver, I ended up talking to the Starrett rep, and he said to me, 'You know, next week I'll have been with Starrett 25 years, and this is the first time I've ever had a call for a set of those blades!' "

"What do you use them for?"

"Anywhere I might use a slitting saw. Just stick them in a hacksaw frame, and get on with it. They won't replace a slitting saw entirely, but I've slotted screw heads, and split collets, and cut a slot in a cast iron part where I had a boss bored out to fit over a shaft, and wanted to split it for a locking bolt . . . "

"Do they do a nice job?"

"If you're careful. Once you get them started, they cut real nice — just like a milling machine. Heck of a lot faster than setting up a slitting saw on an arbor in the mill just to put a slot in a screw head, I'll tell you!"

He opened the bottom drawer. "That's an old, old Starrett vernier protractor. It belonged to an old machinist who lived near my place in West Vancouver, It must be 75, 80 years old. Like the little straight edge, it's as good as new."

"And how'd you come to have it?"

"He died. I'd known him for a number of years, and his wife gave it to me as a kind of memento of him, which I thought was kinda nice."

"There's a funny little idea: it's called a Jennings cube." He handed her a square steel block with a brass plate screwed to one face. The brass plate was thinly coated with solder. Slots crossed the four adjacent faces at right angles. "You can solder small, awkward-shaped parts to the brass plate, screw it onto the block, and then clamp the block to a faceplate, or stick it in the 4-jaw chuck, or in the milling machine vise, or whatever, and do any machining operation on it as easily as you might on a larger or more easily chucked workpiece."

"Why is it called a Jennings Cube?"

"Fella by the name of Jennings mentioned it in an article he wrote in MODEL ENGINEER back in the late '30's. He made a model of an artillery piece of some sort, and he came up with this idea to cope with some of the parts of the breech mechanism, which were pretty small."

"Have you ever used this one?"

"Sure. Half a dozen times. It can sure get your tail out of a crack when you need it, too!" John set the Jennings Cube back in its place, and slid the drawer shut again.

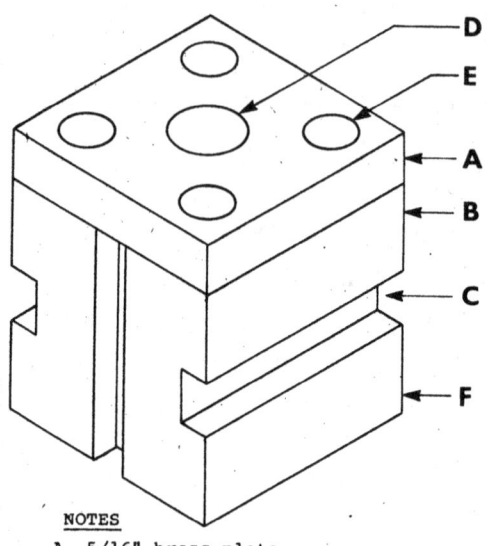

NOTES

A 5/16" brass plate.
B 1-3/8" steel cube, square all over.
C Clamping slots, width & depth 5/16".
D 3/8"Ø hole right through, bore & ream
   truly central.
E 4 holes: (Locate 1/4" in from edges)
   —in cube, drill #21, tap 10-32 x 1/2";
   —in plate, drill #5, counterbore 0.200" deep
   for 10-32 socket head cap screws.
F Make one cube as shown for use on faceplates
   and T-slotted tables. Make another cube
   without slots for use in 4-jaw chuck. Make
   brass plate common to both cubes, or make
   another plate, without center hole, and
   interchangeable between both cubes.

"And what's in the top?"

He lifted the lid of the chest. Like the drawers, the entire interior of this part of the chest was lined with hard green felt. "Some more stuff: Machinery's Handbook, toolmaker's surface gauge, an old Brown & Sharpe six inch vernier caliper, and a new Mitutoyo dial caliper, and an eight inch precision level —." It also had been a gift from Janet.

"What's the little sign say?" she asked, pointing to a piece of paper attached to the inside of the lid.

"Read it," he invited.

Ellen leaned closer, and read half aloud.

> " 'The Secret of the Old Master: The
> secret . . . lies in knowing what nice work is,
> and in being willing to take the pains to do it
> that way.'

"You and my dad would have got along famously!"

Just then the mantle clock downstairs struck five o'clock.

"I'd better get busy making the supper."

"Okay. I'll peel the spuds for you, if you like . . . "

"We're having chicken with rice tonight. But thanks for the offer; I may take you up on it another time."

As she went downstairs, John Kelly sat down on his bed and looked out toward the Telkwa Mountains. His own words came back to echo in his ears: "You can't live in the past forever . . . "

Chapter 11
GETTING DOWN TO WORK

"Well, sir, do you think you can drag your broken old bones out to the shop and show me what you want done?" John asked the following morning, as Bob drained the last of his coffee. They had agreed the night before to deduct an allowance for overhead from the weekly 'take' of the shop, and split the rest down the middle. There was plenty of work to be done, and with Bob unable to work for the last several days, there was a backlog to catch up on.

"You figured out how to get the dent out of that hydraulic cylinder yet?" Bob asked as they walked out to the shop.

"No. I've been puzzling over it half the night, too! You must have some trick up your sleeve, or you wouldn't sound so chipper about doing it."

"Well, let's get the old girl fired up, and then we'll have a look- see."

The 'old girl' was a seven horsepower open crank horizontal oil engine with twin 28-inch cast iron flywheels. A truck tire and wheel was attached to the outboard side of one of the flywheels, and provided a simple friction drive for a system of overhead line shafting for the shop. Additional rubber tired automobile wheels were mounted at various points along the main line shafts. Long, heavy multiple V-belts came down to drive the various machines, and wall mounted levers connected and disconnected the drive to each.

On the other flywheel of the power plant was the ring gear from a truck flywheel. A starter motor had been bolted to a steel plate welded to the engine base. Cables ran from the starter to a battery beside the engine. Bob showed John how to start the engine, running it first on gasoline while it warmed up, then switching it over to stove oil.

"We'll leave it to tick over like that for a few minutes while we take a look at that hydraulic cylinder, but we'll start the water injection before we get the lathe going."

"Water injection?"

"Yup. We put a drip of water into the intake manifold, right here," said Bob, "and she turns to steam in the cylinder, and cushions the stroke — otherwise the old girl will knock like a cement mixer on every stroke when the lathe is running.""Well, I hope it quiets down when it warms up. Sounds like a whole herd of pigs right now."

"She'll quiet down all right. Let's have a look at the job."

The 'job' was a four foot long three inch i.d. hydraulic cylinder from a back-hoe. A section of I-beam had fallen against it on a construction job, denting the cylinder wall in about half an inch. The owner of the machine needed it ASAP, having brought it to Bob Saturday morning.

"Any ideas?" Bob asked with a twinkle in his eye.

"Yeah. A replacement from the dealer."

"Cost three hundred dollars or more, and could take six weeks. We charge him 75 dollars and we'll have it ready to put back on his machine before noon today."

"We will?"

84

"We will. I want you to turn up a plug about four inches long, and exactly the same diameter as the piston that runs in this cylinder. Put a little taper on the chuck side and drill a 5/8 inch hole two inches deep in the exposed end before you part off the plug."

Bob produced a piece of material, while John miked the piston, which was leaning against the far wall of the shop.

The lathe would swing 24 inches and take ten feet between centers. It carried an 18 inch diameter three-jaw chuck, and the chuck key had a cross bar 12 inches long. However, the approach was no different than with his Myford, and John was soon ready to take his first cut. Bob speeded up the power plant, adjusted the water drip, and came back to the lathe. "You flip this lever and you've got power on the headstock, John. When you want to stop, you lift the lever back again, and I defy any man to pick up the chuck key — which you hang here — before the chuck stops turning. She's crude, but she works! Now, go to it."

Bob left John to work and busied himself with other preparations.

John familiarized himself with the various controls on the lathe, before starting on the plug at hand. The gibs on the cross slide and top slide were tighter than he would have liked them, but he realized he would have to take much heavier cuts here than he'd become accustomed to in his own shop. He took a skimming cut the length of the plug he wanted, and measured the resulting O.D., then took another cut ten thou deep. When he measured the diameter this time, it was 0.020 inches smaller than on the previous measurement. Fair enough: the old lathe was as honest as his Myford. He fed in the tool to take a good, heavy roughing cut, with enough left for a couple of finishing passes, and dropped the lever for automatic carriage feed. He recalled the rule he'd learned from Bob several years ago, when Bob and Doris had been in Vancouver and stayed with him. They'd been working in the shop and he'd asked Bob how heavy a cut he would take on a particular job: "Only the man who tightens the chuck knows that, Johnny, but the basic rule is this: run as fast as the tool will stand without burning up, and take a cut as heavy as the machine will give you without slipping the belts. Your chips will tell you long before you burn the tool that you're doing it right."

In due course, the plug was ready, and parted off. "Now what?"

"Bring it around here to the milling machine, and put a flat on it about that wide," Bob said, indicating the desired dimension with his thumb and forefinger. With his one good arm, Bob had been getting the milling machine set up, and John had only to complete a couple of adjustments which could not be done one-handed, before clamping his plug in the vise, and going to work on it.

The big old Garvin carved out the flat to Bob's satisfaction in about three passes.

"Compared to my milling machine, the table on this thing looks like the deck of an aircraft carrier!" said John as he removed the plug from the vise. Bob had by now got out a length of three-quarter inch black iron bar, and was setting it up in the lathe. When he began to feed it through the spindle, John decided to have a look at the size of the latter; 9/16 inch was about the maximum the Super 7 would take. Bob's lathe could take nearly four inches down the spindle bore!

"Part us off about 18 inches of that for a handle, John, and then turn down the end sticking out of the chuck, to let it enter the hole in that plug of yours. Then part that off at about three and a half feet long."

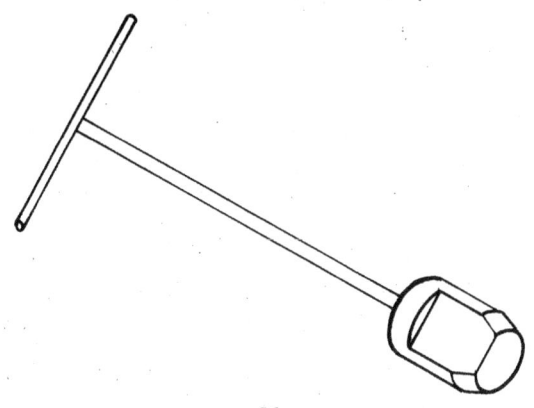

When these parts were ready, Bob switched on his electric welding outfit and, unhampered by his broken arm, soon had the sparks flying. John remained utterly mystified as to the ultimate application of the tool under construction. Bob had told him to set the damaged cylinder up horizontally in the big six-inch bench vise, which he did. "Okay, boy, cool these welds off with the hose, and I'll show you how to amaze your friends and mystify the customer!"

John brought the dripping tool back to the bench where Bob waited.

"Slide that plug down the bore, John, with the flat lined up on the dent. Don't force it — just come up till you feel resistance." As John did so, he began to tap the cylinder wall in the area of the dent.

"Now, ease that plug around with your tee handle, boy, as I tap 'er, and we'll just iron that dent right out of there." It worked exactly as Bob described it, and took about twenty minutes. The plug then slid smoothly past the damaged area as easily as in any other portion of the cylinder.

"You know, Bob, you're like me — you're not as dumb as you look!"

"Not a bad hour and a half's work, eh boy?" Bob said, digging John sharply in the ribs as he came back from placing the repaired cylinder outside. "I'll call the owner and give him the good news."

"The next thing we gotta do is about eight sets of brake drums. You ever seen a brake drum turning fixture, John?"

John shook his head.

Bob indicated a fixture under the bench. "Hoist that up and chuck the stub end in the three jaw chuck, John, and we'll make us some real easy money!"

They put in twelve hours that day, with stops for lunch and supper.

The next day was much the same. John enjoyed the variety, and the opportunity to work with Bob. Sometimes Bob left him to his own devices, other times he made a suggestion. The first couple of suggestions as to methods of running the lathe were made somewhat cautiously. At the second one John got the picture, and flipped the lever to stop the lathe.

"Bob, something you want to understand, if I'm going to work with you for the next couple of months, and get it straight from right now: if you want to tell me how to do the job, tell me. Don't be polite, don't mince words, don't beat around the bush. You've been at this trade a lot longer than I have, and I'm gonna strip your brains naked while I'm here. The only way you're gonna make me mad is if you make it difficult by holding back on the advice. You couldn't offend me if you set out to. Now, do we understand each other?"

"We do."

By Friday evening Bob and John had worked their way through the backlog of jobs and the new work that came in was being taken in hand with satisfactory dispatch. Also, by the end of the week, the two men were working together like a well oiled machine. Neither had enjoyed a period of time so much as they had the past several days. There was mutual respect for each other's abilities, each learned something from the other daily, and the banter, teasing and good natured criticism rarely let up for an hour at a time.

Ellen, for her part, was soon forced to revise her ideas of how much to cook for the two of them. The quantities went up for three days in a row, before she felt she was keeping up with their capacity to eat.

Tuesday morning she'd served pancakes. Bob and John were sitting at their places with expectant looks on their faces, and licking their chops after the last of the batter had been transformed into a 5/16th inch thick golden brown disc six inches in diameter. She'd thought they'd come to blows over who would have it. Bob had tactfully suggested she might make some more, so she'd whipped up a second batch, which still did not suffice. Finally, as she set about making a third batch, John had leaned back in his chair and, patting his stomach fondly, had said, "You make pretty good pancakes, Ellen. I'd say, as a rough guide, you ought to figure on about fourteen for me. Bob's had nine so far, and I think he's beginning to falter."

"I don't have a bowl big enough to make that much batter at one time."

"Get us a drawing of what you need, and we'll turn you up a really nice one," teased Bob. "You can feed us just like Paul Bunyan and Babe the Blue Ox."

"Yeah, 'cept in that case, the ox wasn't the boss," said John, with a wink at Ellen.

Chapter 12
A VOICE AS CLEAR AS CRYSTAL

Late Friday afternoon when John went to his room to clean up for supper, he found his laundry all done, ironed, folded and laid out neatly on his bed. He washed, and went down to the kitchen, where Ellen was mashing a bowl of potatoes.

"Thanks for doing my laundry Ellen, but I sure don't expect you to do that again . . . "

"Why on earth not? You're part of the family here just as much as I am. If I weren't here, and Auntie Doris didn't have a broken leg, she'd have done it, and you wouldn't get to first base arguing with her about it. I don't mind doing it, any more than I mind seeing you sitting there at the table eating what I cook. Having you do your own laundry would be like having you cook your own meals up in your room and eat them by yourself! Besides," she said, smiling, "I don't have to take them down to the creek and beat them on a rock, you know. There's an automatic washer and dryer behind that door, in case you hadn't noticed. Now here, put this bowl on the table, please."

John did as instructed, and came back. "Well, it was real nice to find everything all nice and clean when I went up to my room. I was going to take a bunch of stuff into town to the laundromat tomorrow. Maybe I could spend that time doing something for you instead . . . "

She smiled at him. "You don't have to . . . "

"I know I don't *have* to. Anyway, think about what you might like to do tomorrow afternoon."

"I think we'll be pretty busy getting Auntie D. home and settled in and all. But if we even had time to go for a walk, it'd be nice."

After supper Bob and John returned to the shop, where they finished off a set of 16 beam hangers bent up from 3/16 inch steel plate, for a contractor putting up a small concrete block building in Telkwa.

That evening John found himself far more tired than he would willingly have admitted, and when they came in at 8:30, he lay down and was soon fast asleep.

Ellen had been shopping earlier in the day, and had been busy in the kitchen while the two men worked in the shop after supper. She came upstairs a little after nine, and knocked on John's partially open door. "Can I come in?"

John woke with a start. "Oh! Man, you scared me, Ellen! Sure. Come on in. I musta dozed off."

"Oh, John, I'm sorry; I didn't mean to scare you. I didn't know you were sleeping. Are you feeling okay?"

"I've got a bit of a headache — doesn't matter — what's on your mind?"

"Uncle Bob's gone to the hospital to see Auntie D. I made us a treat. Will you come downstairs and try it?"

"Sure."

Ellen put two bowls on the table, and poured a quantity of crisp brown mixed cereals into each.

"Do you like pears?"

He nodded. She took a jar of home canned pears from the refrigerator, and dished out several pieces into each bowl, along with a quantity of pear juice.

"I found a dairy farm near here, and we'll be getting fresh whole milk from them from now on. This is some cream the farmer's wife gave me today. Look — a spoon will just about stand up in it!" She poured a generous amount into each bowl, and handed John a spoon. "There now. You try that."

'That' was enough to make John's eyes roll in their sockets. It was delicious. "What's the brown stuff?"

"Granola."

"What?"

"Granola. Haven't you ever heard of granola?"

"Never. What's in it?"

"Well, it's just a mixture[4] of wheat flakes, and sunflower seeds and sesame seeds, and honey, and so on. Do you like it?"

"Never had anything like it in my life. It's good. Sounds healthy, too."

Ellen nodded. She was making short work of her own bowl. The combination of fruit, fruit juice, thick cream, and crisp cereals was truly delightful. John cleaned up his bowl and grinned at her. "You know, I just might put you in a duffle bag and take you back to Vancouver with me!" he teased. Ellen blushed, and stood up, whisking the two empty bowls off the table as she did so.

---

4   See Appendix.

"You musn't eat too much of it at one time. It's like eating sandpaper, and it'll rasp your tongue as raw as a carrot if you overdo it. Anyway, how's your head now?"

"Same as before. It's not bad."

"Would it bother you if I played Auntie D's piano?"

"Not in the slightest. It'd be nice. Do you mind if I stretch out on the couch and listen?"

"No. Come on."

Ellen sat down at the piano and began to play softly. After a while the tune changed, and then changed again. Finally, she began to sing.

She had a beautiful voice, rich and warm, and clear as crystal. The tunes varied from old folk songs to popular and sacred, all without the aid of written music. It was a performance which would have delighted any audience, but John, though he might not let on, was more than an ordinarily attentive listener. Reluctant though he might be to admit it, even to himself, everything he saw about this girl impressed him: her manners and general behaviour, her industrious and thorough approach to the housework, her thoughtfulness, and her cheerful good nature.

When Ellen tired of singing, she turned around on the piano bench to face him. "How's the headache now? Have I made it worse?"

John thought a minute, mentally 'feeling' his head to see if it still hurt. "It's gone, completely! You have a lovely voice, Ellen. I enjoyed that more than I can tell you. Thank you, that was really nice."

"Thank you."

John looked at his watch. "I was supposed to phone Ailene tonight. I should do it now." He got up, went to the phone, and dialed. After a wait of some seconds it was answered at the other end. The trip had been fine, and they had arrived without incident. Bob was well, and Doris would be home from the hospital tomorrow. Ellen was liking it, and had enjoyed the trip up. How was everything going for Ailene? Any messages he should know about? Had she taken the castings out of the deep freeze? Wonderful. He said goodnight, promising to phone again in a week or two.

"How is she?"

"She's fine. She asked how you were enjoying it up here. There's nothing in the way of messages at my place, which suits me fine for now."

"What were you asking her about taking some castings out of the deep freeze?"

"Do you remember that MODEL ENGINEER article I was reading on the bus — the one about the dividing head?"

"Yes."

"Well, I'm going to start making one when I go back home. I ordered the castings in 1979 and I've been cycling them in and out of the deep freeze for a week at a time ever since."

"What for?"

"It's supposed to be a kind of accelerated seasoning process, to get rid of any stresses in the castings, so they don't warp when they're machined. Probably three or four months is plenty. I've just never gotten around to starting on that project, so I kept on taking them in and out of the deep freeze right along. I got the idea from an old tool and die maker in Calgary, fella by the name of Geoff Symons."

They heard Bob's car come into the driveway just then, and Ellen went to switch on the porch light for him. As she did so, they heard Bob honk the car's horn three times in quick succession.

John moved to the door ahead of Ellen, and opened it.

"Is Ellen still awake?" Bob's voice came out of the darkness beside the car.

"She's right here. What's the matter?"

"Nothin'. The two of you ought to come out here and take a look at the sky. Turn off the porch light before you come out.'"

John led the way toward the car, in the darkness, Ellen pulling a sweater around her shoulders with one hand, and holding John's elbow with the other as her eyes adjusted to the darkness. Their breath turned to steam in the sharp night air.

"Take a look at that!" Bob said, his arm encompassing the black dome above them.

The stars glinted like diamonds on black velvet. Bob pointed out half a dozen constellations and then said, "And there's the Milky Way."

"Where?" Ellen asked, trying to follow his direction.

John, standing on her opposite side, now pointed to a vast and majestic band of stars which spanned the sky. "That's our Galaxy — the thousand million stars of the Milky Way. You'll never see it like that in a big city, because of the dirty air, and the glow of the city lights. Can you see it now?"

She did. The beauty of it took her breath away.

Chapter 13
THE FLYING FARMER

Saturday morning Bob and Ellen drove into Smithers to bring Doris home from the hospital. John was left to turn three sets of brake drums, and turn out a small part for an obsolete outboard motor. The latter job required a 1/4-20 thread, but John was unable to locate a die for this size among the selection in Bob's rat's nest of taps and dies.

"Well, Bob says he can make a 6-48 screw on this brute if he has to. Let's see can old John Kelly screwcut a 1/4-20 thread on it."

The disproportion of the job versus the machine was ridiculous, but it worked out quite all right, and John left the job in the lathe for Bob to see when he got back. With nothing else to do, he decided to fix the 'rat's nest of taps and dies' once and for all.

He hunted up a couple of sound, dry blocks of 4" x 4" fir, and turned out the box of threading tackle. In a few minutes he had everything sorted out and laid out in order.

Using the drill press, he drilled rows of holes to take the taps. He had learned in his own shop that the way to have such tool racks end up looking half decent was to drill the holes *just* big enough to let the taps enter easily — say 10 to 15 thou oversize. If the holes were too large, the taps leaned at haphazard and drunken angles, and the result was a mess. Evenly spaced holes of uniform depth in straight lines was the only other requirement to make a decent job of it. Nails driven into the front face of the block would take the various dies.

John had the two racks completed, and had given them both a light sanding, and a squirt of oil in each hole to combat rust, and was just driving the last of the nails into the front face of the second rack when he heard Bob's car coming into the driveway. He stuffed the taps into their holes and hung the dies on their nails before leaving the shop.

Although he had gone to see Doris in the hospital, it was good to see her back in her own home. She was still learning to manage her crutches, but was reasonably mobile without help. She tired easily, and could not stand for long periods.

Lunch that day took much longer than normal.

"Did you get that gizzer made for Andy Pratt's outboard?" Bob eventually asked, when the conversation lagged.

John nodded. "Couldn't find your 1/4-20 die though, so I had to screwcut the thread. If you need any screws made up for your watch, I'm the boy to see, for sure."

Bob started to grin. "Where'd you look for the die?"

"Where you keep all your ill-treated threading equipment," John shot back in their standard form of banter-by-contempt.

"Well, I knew you'd be needing it, and I dug it out for you. Guess I musta got careless and tucked it into my pocket before I left for town." He dug into his shirt pocket with such directness that John knew he'd taken it with him deliberately. Well, he would think of something to top that trick in his own good time.

"I got finished early, so I made up a couple of racks to hold all the taps and dies you've got — at least all the ones I could find. It was either get them organized or start squirting oil in my hair and saluting the neighbour's cat."

"Speaking of squirting things," said Ellen, "did John tell you what we saw in Williams Lake?"

Bob shook his head. John nodded at Ellen to go ahead, but she would not. "You tell it. I'll just start to laugh if I try."

So John proceeded to describe the saga of the tourist and the well-placed knothole, with a deadpan style that only added to the story. By the time he had finished, his listeners were holding their stomachs from laughter.

Lunch over, John and Bob went out to the shop to inspect the new tap racks and the outboard motor part still chucked in the lathe. Although he did not let on, Bob was pleased with both the racks and with John's 'well, let's get it done' attitude when he had been unable to find the appropriate die. John parted off the job and began to clean up the lathe.

"I told you we'd take the rest of the day off, John," Bob said, seating himself on his stool.

"I know, but this won't take long to do. Besides, Ellen's probably still busy with the lunch dishes. I was thinking we might go for a walk, or take a drive through the Telkwa High Road and up to the fossil beds at Driftwood Creek. I think she ought to have a break from time to time. She shouldn't just be cooped up in there cooking and cleaning seven days a week."

Bob nodded. "I know. She's a hard worker, but she's not here as a hired servant." He considered his next words carefully before he spoke. "Do you like Ellen, John?"

John paused in his wiping down of the lathe ways. "Sure I like her. She's a nice person." He resumed his wiping.

"Good. I ran into a farmer this morning in town. He wants us to build him a rig to mount on the back of a tractor, to carry an aircraft propeller, which he wants to run off the tractor's power take-off shaft. It should be easy enough to do. I told him to bring the tractor up here tomorrow afternoon and we'd go to work on it."

"What's he want with a prop on the back of his tractor? Is he going to start a Flying Farmer service?"

"No, he's been clearing land for the last couple of years and he's got quite a few big piles of brush, logs, stumps and so on, that he wants to burn. He's going to back the tractor up to each pile once he gets a fire going, and pour the air to it. He figures it'll cut his burning time in half."

"At least. Probably more than that. Heck of a good idea."

When John was finished cleaning the lathe to his satisfaction, he went in to see what Ellen was doing. She was in the kitchen washing up some bowls and dishes. He washed his hands and came back to the kitchen to dry the dishes for her. "Do you want to go for a walk when you're done in here?"

"I'd like to, but I've got to go into town again to get some things. I'm out of flour and . . . "

"Okay. How about we drive into town, get what stuff you want, and come home by way of Driftwood Creek and the Telkwa High Road?"

"Isn't Driftwood Creek where that fossil place is? That'd be fun."

"Fine. As soon as you're ready, we'll go."

"I just put some baking in the oven. It'll be done in about half an hour . . . "

"Okay. Off you go and get ready, and I'll dry up the last of these things."

Chapter 14
THE WEASLE ON THE KNOLL

Located within a few minutes drive of Smithers, the Driftwood Creek fossil beds are an ancient deposit of sedimentary materials in which the public can hunt for the fossilized remains of plants on a 'finders-keepers' basis. Ellen found a beautiful fossil fern. Not all who visit the site are so lucky.

Leaving the fossil beds, they drove west on the highway a few miles to Moricetown Canyon, and crossed the Bulkley River on an old wooden bridge at the western end of the Telkwa High Road. At one point they parked the truck and climbed to the top of a grassy knoll above the road, from which vantage point they could see Hudson's Bay Mountain, the town of Smithers, and several miles both ways along the valley of the Bulkley River.

They sat down on a log and drank in the view for a few minutes in silence. Finally, John spoke.

"How are you liking things up here, now you've been here a week?"

"It's beautiful. In some ways, I wish I could stay here forever. The town is nice, the people are nice, and the setting has to be one of the most beautiful anywhere."

"I was thinking more in connection with what we talked about last Sunday. Now that you're busy, do you still feel 'out of your element'?"

"No. I've been so busy I haven't had time to worry about that at all. I guess I'm happiest when I'm busy doing something for somebody else."

"Well, you sure have been busy, and if you keep on cookin' like you've been doing, you're going to spoil us all absolutely rotten. Just don't work *too* hard, and wear yourself out."

"Don't worry. I'm in no danger of 'wearing out'!" Ellen laughed. They were both quiet for a minute, then John spoke again.

"Bob's lined us up a job to make a tractor-mounted fan rig for a farmer near here. He wants it for fanning fires in brush piles on land he's been clearing. Bob says there's nowhere in Smithers to get the bearings we need, but we can get them, and the V-belts and V-pulleys, and everything else, in Terrace. We'll have the job far enough along by Monday night to know exactly what to buy. Bob wants me to drive to Terrace on Tuesday to get everything, while he does the welding on the main frame. Would you like to come with me?"

"Sure, I'd like to, but I'll need to stay to look after everything at the house . . . "

John shook his head. "Bob suggested you go along. He doesn't expect you to work seven days a week without a break."

"In that case, I'd love to come. What sort of place is Terrace?"

"Nice town. Bigger than Smithers. Most of its economy is based on logging and sawmilling, and tourism in the summer. It's a nice drive down there from here, too — about 130 miles each way. We'll leave early, and be back by mid-afternoon."

They sat talking a while longer, before deciding it was time to leave. Just as they were about to, John spotted a movement beside a stump a few yards away, He put his hand on Ellen's arm, and pointed. "Do you see it?"

"No. Where? What is it?"

"It's a weasel, just to the right of the stump. See his head beside the dandelion?"

The weasel made a movement and Ellen saw it. "Oh, isn't he beautiful! Look at his funny little ears! And his little eyes — they're just like black marbles! Will he bite?"

"He sure would if you tried to pick him up, but he won't attack us, if that's what you mean," John said. "Can't say I'd want to be sitting here like this if I were a rabbit, though!"

They stood up and began to walk towards the brow of the little knoll.

"Look! He's following us!" Ellen exclaimed. The weasel disappeared over a log, and a moment later reappeared at the other end, standing with both front feet on a knot, its head raised, looking at them with a consuming curiosity. As they passed, the weasel dove into a pathway known only to such creatures as itself and its prey. From behind a rock a little further ahead, its head and shoulders popped up, like a furry brown snake, for another look.

They walked slowly back to the truck, watching, and watched by, the weasel all the way. Its fluid grace and delicate appearance belied the ferocity with which it extracted its livelihood from the other small creatures of the knoll.

Chapter 15
SHROUDING

After supper that evening John went up to his room to write some letters. He had completed one, and was just starting another when there was a gentle knock on the open door.

"Can I come in and visit you?"

"Sure, come on in and have a chair. Just writing a couple of letters. What've you been doing?"

"I was writing to my brother. And I drew this for you." She handed him a cartoon depicting an airborne farm tractor driven by a farmer in bib overalls, battered cowboy hat, and goggles, with a silk scarf streaming behind.

John chuckled. "That's good! If I could have drawn my mental picture of the Flying Farmer, when Bob started talking about what the fella wanted, that's about what I'd have drawn. Have you shown it to Bob yet?"

Ellen shook her head. "He's busy right now. I was thinking it'd be fun to paint something like this on the shrouds for the fan. What do you think?"

"How do you mean, 'shrouds'?"

"Well, you can't very well build a fan unit like you were talking about and give it to the farmer, without incorporating some sort of guards to keep people from getting their hands and heads chopped off in it, can you?"

"You know, I never thought of that! Neither did Bob, so far as I know. But you're absolutely right — we can't. What made you think of it?"

"I'm a draftsman, remember? That's one of the draftsman's jobs, to flesh out the engineers' designs. Some of them get pretty annoyed when you point out shortcomings in their ideas: they think they are on a pinnacle far above a mere draftsman. And a girl at that!" she concluded with an expressive snort.

"I know exactly what you mean. Anyway, it's a good thing you thought of it. By all means, if you could paint that on the shrouding, I'm sure Bob will be tickled pink. Let's take it down and show him."

"Okay."

John patted his stomach. "Is there any granola left, or did you take it off to your room and eat it all?"

"There's lots left. Would you like some right now?"

"Yes. Let's go have a snack and give Bob a bad time about the shrouds he never thought of for the Flying Farmer!"

Chapter 16
DISTURBING ALLEGATIONS

Sunday afternoon, the Flying Farmer delivered his tractor into the hands of the owner of the Smithers Machine Works, who, with his helper, was soon busy with the work of adding a prop drive unit to it. By Monday night, the trip to Terrace for pulleys and bearings was definitely 'on' for the following morning.

They made good time on the trip to Terrace, and were on their way back well before noon. Ellen had packed a picnic lunch and John suggested they stop for lunch at Ksan Indian Village.

"Where's that?"

"At Hazelton," John replied. "There's an unusual situation here. There are actually three towns, all within three or four miles of each other, which is unusual in such a sparsely populated area. The first town, Old Hazelton, developed at the head of navigation for stern wheel boats on the Skeena River. Later, when the railway came through, South Hazelton developed adjacent to the right of way. Finally, when the highway came along, New Hazelton sprang up. Old Hazelton remained as a service center for the local people of the area while the other two towns are more tourist and travel oriented."

"But you still haven't told me about Ksan Indian Village."

"I'm coming to that. Ksan is a sort of an Indian museum, at Old Hazelton. It's housed in several cedar plank Indian buildings, with totem poles at the doors, and artifacts of the Skeena Indian culture. It's an interesting place for a half hour visit. We can eat our lunch there and then get on our way again."

John looked at his watch as they pulled back onto the highway at New Hazelton after lunch.

"One o'clock. We should be home in an hour."

When they arrived home, Bob and Doris were waiting for them, and one look at their faces told them something was drastically wrong.

Bob wasted no words. There had been a phone call from the mine on Babine Lake. One of their 85 ton ore trucks had had a brake failure and had thundered off a haul road at 50 miles per hour into Babine Lake. Divers would have to be brought up from Vancouver to handle the underwater work connected with the salvage of the truck. No diver could be on site sooner than a week from now.

"Well, that's tough luck for Babine Copper, but what's it got to do with us?" John wanted to know.

"Everything. I did a small repair for them on a part of the brake system for one of those ore trucks just about three days before Doris and I had our accident. Apparently, it was that truck that went into the lake. The mining company claims that my repair was faulty, and they are going to sue me for the costs of salvaging and repairing the truck."

"Well, I don't even need to ask if the repair was done right or not! It *was*, or you'd never have let it out of the shop. It may have *failed*, but I'm willing to bet any amount of money it wasn't faulty!" said John.

"I appreciate your confidence, John. Even if it was faulty — and I am sure it wasn't — it doesn't matter. I carry enough liability insurance to buy them a brand new truck if it came to that. The thing that upsets me is that the driver was drowned. They can't get the body out of the truck till they can get a team of divers up from Vancouver. The financial side of the whole thing couldn't matter less. The insurance company will pay, if my work *did* turn out to be the cause of the accident. But if that truck driver drowned because of a fault in my work, there's no amount of insurance can undo his death."

The seriousness of the matter hit home with Bob's last words. They discussed the situation from various angles. Finally, John asked if the insurance company had been notified yet.

"No, I haven't got that far along in my thinking."

"Well, the first thing we better do is phone the insurance company. They may want an adjuster on hand during the salvage operation, and to oversee the tear-down of the part you repaired. They'll need proof that your part failed. Wait a minute! Why did you have to do the repair? Babine Copper has its own machinists and complete machine shop facilities! Why didn't they do it at the mine?"

"Normally they would have, but they'd had a major breakdown in the crusher, and both machinists were fully committed to that at the time. They phoned me and asked if I'd do it. I said sure, bring it out and I'd drop everything and do it right away, so the guy could take it back with him. Sort of a good-will thing, you know?"

John nodded. Ellen had been quiet during most of the discussion, but now spoke to John.

"It's a pity I didn't get you to bring my trunk up with us when we came up from Vancouver . . . "

"Why do you say that?"

"I'm a scuba diver. I brought my scuba gear out from Toronto, because I was looking forward to doing some diving in the Gulf of Georgia and Howe Sound and so on. If I had my gear up here, I could go down and at least recover the driver's body for them."

"Babine is a pretty cold lake, at the best of times. You couldn't spend very long down there . . . " Doris said.

"I've got a 'wetsuit'. I'd be as warm as I am right now, even if there was a foot of ice on the lake."

"If we could get your scuba gear up here by say, tomorrow, would you be ready and able to go out to Granisle right away?" asked John.

"No, my scuba tanks are empty. They have to be empty for air travel. They'd have to be filled once they got up here, and I don't imagine there'd be an air filling station in Smithers."

"Probably not. Look, why don't we phone the insurance company for starters? While Bob's doing that, let's think about the diving angle. Maybe you could phone the mine manager and see if they'd be interested in having you at least get the body out of the truck. Could you go down alone, or would you need another diver to accompany you?"

"As a rule, at least two people should dive, but I'd be willing to risk it. If I encountered anything that looked bad, I'd scrub the dive right away."

They talked further while Bob went to the phone in the other room to call the insurance company. In a few minutes he came back. "They'll send an adjuster up tomorrow. They didn't seem to be too excited at first. I guess they thought I was talking about a pickup truck. I finally had to tell them the truck is worth almost a million dollars, new. They began to wake up pretty fast after that!"

"Okay. Ellen's going to phone the mine manager, and see if they'd be interested in having her recover the body. If they are, we can get the tanks up here, and get them filled somewhere. What about at the hospital? Would they have equipment from which your tanks could be filled?"

Ellen shook her head.

"Okay: there'd be diving service facilities in Prince Rupert. We could have your gear flown there. I'll meet the plane, get the tanks filled, and bring everything up from Rupert in my truck."

"But how can you drive to Prince Rupert and back? You've already driven nearly 300 miles today. You said the round trip from Smithers to Rupert and back is about 450 miles. You can't do that on top of what you've already driven today," Ellen protested.

"If necessary, I can. Why don't you get on the phone to the mine, and see if they're interested?"

"All right, but I don't want you to . . . "

"Don't worry about me. Let's do first things first."

He turned to Bob. "Has this whole thing been on the news yet?"

Bob nodded. "We heard it on the news about half an hour after they called me. There was no mention of me, but the accident, and the fact that divers couldn't be on the lake till next week and the driver's name — Jimmy Fredrickson — was all mentioned."

"Good. Ellen should just play it that she heard it on the news, for now. She doesn't need to tell Babine Copper she's your niece, does she?"

"That's the last thing to tell them!" said Doris.

Ellen had been busy looking up the phone number for Babine Copper, and now began to dial.

"Good afternoon. Babine Copper."

"Hello. Could I speak to the mine manager, please?"

"Yes. May I tell him who's calling?"

"My name is Ellen MacIntyre."

There was a click and a pause, then a man's voice, with an English accent, on the line. "Hello. Thatcher here."

"Mr. Thatcher, my name is Ellen MacIntyre. I understand from the news on the radio that you've just lost a truck today, and can't get divers up from Vancouver to recover the driver's body for at least a week. I'm a scuba diver and I'm right here in Smithers. I'd like to offer to bring the body up if that'd be helpful to the driver's family, or whatever . . . "

"Well, young lady, we appreciate your offer, but I don't think we'd want to let an amateur diver go down. If anything happened, it would be . . . well, most awkward for us . . . I'm sure you understand."

"I'm not an amateur, Mr. Thatcher, nor am I a 'young lady'. I'm twenty-eight. I've been a qualified diver since I was fourteen. I've been a certified diving instructor for the past ten years, and I'm a founding member of the Great Lakes Emergency Volunteer Rescue Service."

"Well, I see. That puts quite a different light on the matter. I think we'd be most grateful if you could recover Jimmy Fredrickson's body for us, Miss MacIntyre."

"Fine. I'll charge you $300 for my services, and I'll expect you to cover all my expenses, including the cost of getting my scuba gear up from Vancouver. That could run pretty high, because it'll probably have to be flown to Prince Rupert for the tanks to be filled, and a friend of mine may have to drive down to Rupert to arrange for filling the air tanks and to bring the equipment back to Smithers. I'm just up here on holiday for a few weeks."

"I understand. Don't worry about the expenses: we'll be glad to cover them in full, and whatever's reasonable for your friend's assistance, of course. When can you come out to the mine?"

"I'll try to get my diving gear up here overnight, and if I can do that, I'll be out to Granisle tomorrow afternoon. I'll give you a call to confirm as soon as I know for sure. Can you have some sort of a boat available?"

"We'll have the Babine Mistress waiting for you when you get here. She's a 25-foot inboard cruiser. We've used her as a diving tender before."

"That sounds fine. I'll call you some time tomorrow morning, Mr. Thatcher."

"All right, and thank you very much for your call, Miss MacIntyre."

"Ahhgg!!" exclaimed Ellen as she hung up the receiver. "If he hadn't called me an amateur, I'd have done it for nothing."

John laughed. "Your voice got so cold, I thought you'd freeze his ear solid when you started nailing your qualifications down all over him! Very impressive, I might add, 'young lady'!"

Ellen shot him a sour look. "Okay, Joker. How do we get one only locked trunk of scuba gear out of a locked empty house in West Vancouver and onto a plane, up to Prince Rupert, my scuba tanks filled, and then to Smithers in less than 18 hours?"

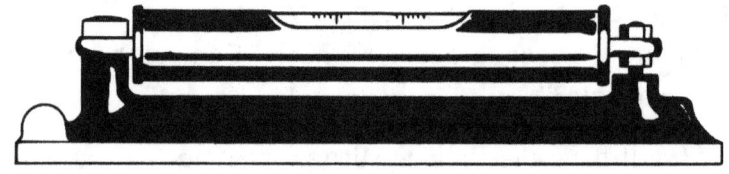

Chapter 17
A PIECE OF THE WEB

"Very simply. I have friends I haven't used yet. Let me think for a minute." John buried his head in his hands. After a second or two, one eye appeared between two spread fingers, and focussed on Ellen. "Will you need more than one filling of your tanks?"

"Probably. Certainly, if I help them get the truck up as well. What we really need is my gear plus a portable compressor. Usually air filling stations have compressors which can be rented out."

"Could you handle the tank filling operation if you had a compressor?" Bob asked.

"Sure. Routine."

"Now we're getting somewhere! It's time to call out the troops. We're going to get Ellen's stuff on the PWA[5] plane to Smithers tomorrow morning, along with a portable compressor, which we'll rent from Vancouver. I know a guy in the Club who's got a brother who's a diver . . . "

"What Club?" Ellen asked.

"The B.C. Society of Model Engineers." John began to dial.

"Hello?"

---

5   PWA --- Pacific Western Airlines

"Ailene. It's John. How're you?"

"Fine. What's on your mind today? You weren't going to call till the end of the week."

"I know, but we need some help, Ailene. There's a grey trunk at my place. It's in the spare bedroom downstairs. It's Ellen's, and it's full of scuba gear. We need it up here in a hurry. Can you go up to my place and dig out the BCSME membership list from my desk downstairs? It's in the upper right hand drawer, right at the front. It's on two sheets of legal size blue paper. I need a name and phone number off it. When you've found the list, would you phone me from my place at Bob's number? You'll find it in my telephone index under 'B' for Bob Davidson."

"Okay. I'll go up right away. I'll call you in a few minutes."

"Great. You're a jewel beyond compare, Ailene."

"I know. But who's going to get the trunk out to my car? It'll be too heavy for me to carry . . . "

"The neighbour will help you, or somebody else will. We'll look after that by remote control in a while."

"Okay, John. I'll call you from your place."

"Now what?" asked Ellen.

"Now, we hook into a small piece of the invisible global web of model engineers Nevil Shute described in his book, TRUSTEE FROM THE TOOLROOM. We get Jake-what's-iz-name's phone number, and we phone him. His brother will fix him up with a rental compressor, which he'll bring to Ailene's house tonight. In the meantime, Ailene gets your trunk into her car, and takes it home, and later she takes everything out to the Air Cargo building at the airport and consigns it to you, freight collect. Poof, nuthin' to it."

Ellen laughed. "Well, I don't know if it's going to be poof-nuthin'-to-it or not, but I better start poofing together some supper for us. How does fish cakes and hash browns sound?"

The first fish cake hit the pan with a hiss just as the phone rang. Bob nodded for John to answer it.

"Hello. Smithers Machine Works. Kelly here."

"John. I'm at your place, and I've found the Club list. Who do you want off it?"

"Fella by the name of Jake. Last name starts with a 'W', I think. Lives in North Vancouver."

"How about J.E. Williams on Grand Boulevard? Would that be the one?"

"That's him! Jake Williams. What's his phone number, please Ailene? . . . Okay, got it. Now, while I phone him, you call one of my three neighbours — the names are Austin, Tait, and Webb. You'll find them all in the telephone index under 'N' for neighbours. Ron Tait's your best bet. Tell him who you are, and ask him to put Ellen's trunk in your car for you. If he balks, or thinks you're swiping it, just get him over to my house and have him phone me, and I'll give him the word. Okay?"

"Okay, John. And what do you want me to do when I've got Ellen's trunk in my car?"

"Lock up my place again, and go home. I'll be in touch with you later, or Jake Williams or his brother will. They're going to find us a portable rental air compressor, and it's going to come up to Smithers with the trunk. Clever, huh?"

"You're a genius, John, and I can see it's bothering you today," Ailene teased. "I'll press the neighbour into service, and hear from you later, Son."

John hung up', and after a wait of about six seconds to let the phone get over that call, he began to dial Jake Williams' number. "Hello?" A woman's voice answered.

"Hello, Mrs. Williams. John Kelly here. I'm a member of the Club. Is Jake around right now?"

"No, he's not home from work yet, but he should be here any minute. Can I have him call you? . . . No, wait, I hear him at the front door now. Hang on and he'll be in to speak to you in a minute . . ."

"Okay . . ."

"He's just coming in from work. He's a pharmacist," John explained to the others.

"Hello. Jake here."

"Hello, Jake. John Kelly. Got a little problem, and you're just the boy to solve it for me."

"Well, what can I do for you?"

"I'm up in Smithers right now, Jake, working with a friend who's had a car accident. He's got a little machine shop up here . . ." John outlined the situation in as few words as possible. Jake agreed to call his brother and make arrangements for a rental compressor. John gave him Ailene's address and phone number.

"Call me if you run into any problems, Jake. I'll square up with you for your help when I get back to Vancouver."

"You forgotten those pieces of cast red bronze you gave me this spring when I was overhauling my 'Heilan Lassie', and needed to make new axleboxes and that new throttle body which you also gave me the drawings for? I think maybe tonight we'll start to get squared up again — which we ain't been since April, Johnny."

"Well, I don't keep a running account of stuff like that, Jake, but that's fine. If you can do the leg work to arrange for a compressor for us, and set it in Ailene's car, I'll consider us square, with things a little bit my side of top dead center!"

"Okay Johnny. Say, while I've got you on the phone, can I ask you a couple of questions?"

"Sure."

"How can I get rid of the black scale on hot rolled steel? I hate turning black iron and getting the scale dust all over my lathe . . . "

"Easiest way I know of, although it isn't real fast, is to stick the piece of material in a plastic bucket with some salt and ordinary brown or white vinegar."

"Any special proportions?"

"Nope. Just enough vinegar to cover your material and a little extra, and maybe a couple of tablespoons of salt per cup of vinegar, or, say as much as will dissolve in the vinegar — I dunno — it's not critical."

"And what'll it do?"

"Well, if you leave it in that stuff for a day or two, you'll usually find you can rub off most of the black scale with your hands, and what's left you can get off easy with a wire brush. Sometimes it takes a few extra days. It'll also take off rust just as slick as you please — same treatment. You'll end up with a nice, dull grey chunk of steel with no scale on it. Give it a good wash with soap and water to get rid of any remaining vinegar before you machine it. I generally do the whole thing outside, because I don't like the smell of vinegar, but I keep a little bottle, with a lid on it, on the bench in the shop. I think I showed you that one time when you were at my place, didn't I?"

"Yes. That's how you get all your cutters to look so nice after you heat treat them, isn't it?"

"Well, I dunno about how nice some of them look, but it does take off the heat treating colours. Anyway, what's your next question?"

"Do you know what a Keats-type Vee angle plate is?"

"Yeah."

"Do you know where I can buy one?"

"Not locally. I think you'd have to send to England for that. Have you got an ordinary unhardened V-block that's big enough to hold your job?"

"Yes, but I have no way of bolting it to a faceplate . . . "

"Well, drill and tap four holes in one end of the V-block. Make 'em say 1/4-28, or 5/16-24 if there's room for that big a hole. If it's a cast iron V-block, you might be better to use a coarse thread. Don't forget to counterbore them about 1/64th over your screw size say about one thread deep before you tap the holes, so you don't get a burr at the surface. . . Then get yourself a scrap piece of 3/8 or 1/2 inch steel plate, square it up and slot it on four sides just like the real McCoy, and face it off nice and flat both sides if it isn't real flat to start with, then drill and counterbore it for four socket head cap screws. Then just bolt the V-block to the plate with four Allen head cap screws — say an inch long. Your V-block's not harmed by it, and you've doubled what you can do with it. You'll probably need to make a heavier clamp of some sort to hold your work with — the usual horseshoe clamp with one screw coming straight down into the Vee might not be man enough for a machining operation in the lathe. Might foul the bed or something, too. Anyway, you can sort that out for yourself."

"Okay. I'll have my V-angle plate fixture in a couple of evenings!"

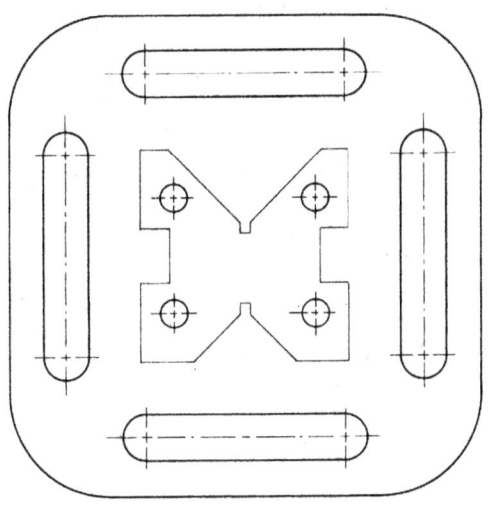

"Good — and I'll give you a tip about milling those slots in the plate without wasting any time. You've got a vertical mill, haven't you?"

"Yes."

"Okay. Drill a row of holes down the centerline of each slot. Just mash 'em through quick, never mind starting each one with a center drill. Make 'em about 1/64th under your nominal slot width. Space 'em out so they don't quite touch each other. Then switch over to an end mill holder and an end mill, and put it straight down between the drilled holes. Ninety-five percent of the metal in the slot'll be gone when you've done that, and you can clean it out full length, then take a couple of clean-up cuts on each side of the slot so you end up with a slot about 1/32nd of an inch over your nominal bolt size. The trick is to drill those holes first. A drill is a much more efficient tool for ripping out metal in a hurry than an end mill."

"I follow you. Now, one last question for you, Johnny?"

"Shoot."

121

"You showed me something you rigged up on your Super 7 that let you index your headstock spindle around with the bull gear, but I've forgotten how you did it."

"Jake, I oughta hang up the phone on you!" John laughed. "I told you when I showed you that, that if you didn't go home and fix your Super 7 up the same way, I'd never talk to you again."

"I know. That's the only part I remember, Johnny, but I've been looking at my lathe for about a week, racking my brains to try to remember how you did that."

"Very simple. On the Super 7 headstock casting, when you lift up the belt guard, you'll see a couple of little black rubber buttons. One of them is above the 'M' in the word Myford, what is cast on the front face of the headstock casting, and the other is above the 'D', more or less. You follow me?"

"Yeah."

"Okay. Now in the corner just to the right of the little rubber button above the 'D', you'll see there is a little triangular web in the casting. You might call it a lip or a gusset or whatever. Anyway, there it is. Take a file and flatten off the surface of that web just enough to clean off the paint and filler material underneath right down to the cast iron. It's not real critical, but get it as flat and as parallel as you can to the lathe bed. After you've done that, drill and tap a 1/4-20 hole in that web, drilling straight down toward the floor. The web is maybe 5/16" thick, so there's lots of metal there; you can feel around underneath with your finger to kinda size up the situation.

"Now, you gotta make a detent, to work in the bull gear. Get yourself a little piece of metal, say 1/8 by 5/8 and about 2-1/2 long. Probably best to make a cardboard mock-up first, maybe even before you drill the hole in the casting, but after you've decided where you think you're going to put the hole. Now the detent comes out from the web towards the bull gear at an angle, sorta diagonally across the headstock casting . . . You still with me?"

"Yeah."

"Good. Now clip your cardboard detent mock-up off at an angle so the end is parallel with the lathe axis and the face of the bull gear. Now hacksaw off the end of your little piece of 1/8 by 5/8 metal so it's the same, and bevel the top and bottom faces so the end fits right in between two teeth in the bull gear just real nice. Then mill a slot along the length of the detent, so it'll clear a 1/4" bolt. Turn up an 1/4" i.d. washer, and stick the detent onto your lathe with a 1/4-20 socket head cap screw. You can leave it in place all the time if you like. I keep mine in my toolbox, but suit yourself. Anyway, that's all there is to it. The whole job should take you less than an hour from start to finish."

"Well, that's the simplest detent idea I've ever heard of! And now that you've told me about it again, I can remember yours. How'd you think that up, anyway?"

"I didn't. Bill Fenton's the boy what thought it up. But it sure works slick. 'Course, it isn't for precision dividing, but with that 60-tooth bull gear, it'll do more tricks than a heifer on ten feet of rope." John winked at Ellen. The latter was one of Bob's favourite expressions.

"Okay, Johnny. Hats off to Bill Fenton, and yourself. I'm gonna get to work on that right after supper!"

"What about my portable air compressor?" John said in mock alarm.

"Oh! I forgot about that! Okay, right after I fix you up with an air compressor."

John laughed. "Good enough. I'll let you go for now. And I sure appreciate your help, Jake."

"No problem at all, Johnny. Thanks for the advice. Give me a buzz when you get back here, or if there's anything else we can do for you while you're up there."

"Okay, Jake. Thanks a lot. Bye for now."

John hung up. "One only air compressor, probably, comin' up. I hate to think what the air freight charges on this stuff is gonna be . . . "

Later that evening, Ailene got a phone call, and half an hour later a pickup truck backed into her driveway, and Jake Williams lifted a portable air compressor into the trunk of her car.

An hour later, a PWA employee wheeled the trunk and the compressor from Ailene's car into the Air Cargo building at Vancouver International Airport for weighing and documentation. When PWA's Boeing 737 lifted off for the flight to Smithers the next morning, Ellen's gear was aboard. So was Mike Cliffmont, senior insurance adjuster.

Chapter 18
ANOTHER FATALITY

Over a fast lunch which Ellen had waiting when John returned from the Smithers airport, with Mike Cliffmont in tow, they discussed the entire situation. It was decided that for the time being Bob would not go out to Granisle, nor would Ellen yet reveal the fact that she was his niece. John would drive her out to Granisle, and the insurance adjuster would arrive in a separate, rented car about the same time. He would not let on that he had already met Ellen and John.

*   *   *

Just after he swung his truck off the Yellowhead Highway onto the Granisle Road at Topley, John reached into his shirt pocket and withdrew some papers which he handed to Ellen.

"How'd you like to be paying that out of your own pocket, 'young lady'?" They were the bills for the air freight on the compressor and the trunk full of diving gear.

Ellen looked at the bills momentarily. "They can reimburse me double this amount, because it'll all have to go back to Vancouver, too. Plus an allowance for all those long distance calls."

"Boy, you're a regular cut-throat when it comes to Babine Copper, aren't you?" laughed John.

"No, I'm not. First, a team of three commercial divers plus gear, which is what they'd normally have to hire for a salvage job, would cost them about $1500 per day. Second, they're trying to blame Uncle Bob for the loss of that truck without any evidence that the repairs he did were either faulty or even the cause of the accident."

"True."

"Besides, if I help them salvage the truck, I'm going to soak them another $200 — *if* we can do it this afternoon. If we have to wait and do it tomorrow, it'll be another $500."

About 20 minutes later they topped a rise and the blue waters of Babine Lake sprang into view below and ahead of them. "About 10 to 12 miles from here to Granisle. Man, I can't get over this road being paved! I worked at Granisle a couple of summers just about the time they were getting the mine started, and in those days, this was just a rough dirt road full of potholes and 'washboard'."

A few miles further on they came to a series of regular artificial channels full of flowing water beside the road.

"What on earth is that for?!" Ellen asked.

"That's the Fulton River spawning beds. It was the largest artificial salmon spawning channel in the world when it was put in about 1969/70. May still be, for all I know. People came from all over the world to see it. Even the Russians came over to have a look at it, apparently."

"Isn't that neat! Where do the salmon come from?"

"Up the Skeena River, up the Babine River and into the north end of Babine Lake, down the Lake, and up the Fulton River, which flows into Babine. They dammed the Fulton just upstream a little ways from here, to provide a reliable source of water for the project. When the salmon come up to spawn, you'll see them in the river and in the channels by the thousands, all red and battered, at the end of their life cycle. The eagles have a field day, feasting on the carcasses. They perch in those big cottonwood trees alongside the river and the spawning beds, watching for a likely looking prospect, or eating one.

"When do the salmon come up to spawn? " Ellen asked, looking back over her shoulder at the site, which was now disappearing behind them.

"This month. We've probably missed the main part of the run. Would you like to come out here some Sunday to have a good look at the whole place?"

"Yes, that'd be fun."

"Well, let's do that, then. Maybe we'll be lucky, and get a moose, too. You can help butcher it if we do!" He grinned at her.

As they came in sight of Granisle, Ellen spoke. "When I talked to Thatcher this morning, he said when we got here to go down to the barge landing and have the barge operator call him on the mobile radio. ."

John nodded. "Where will you change into your wetsuit?"

"Thatcher said I could change at the hotel in town."

John drove down to the lakeshore and pulled up at the barge landing. The barge, with two pickup trucks and an empty flat deck freight truck aboard, was just easing in to the landing slip.

When it was fully into the slip, a man got out of one of the pickup trucks, unhooked a safety chain across the bow of the barge, stepped ashore and dropped a shore-anchored cable eye over a bollard on the barge. He waited on the landing while the freight truck drove off the barge, and got back into the first pickup which followed the freight truck off.

John and Ellen got out of the Land Cruiser and went aboard the barge. A small tug boat was cabled to its stern to provide a means of propulsion, and John led the way to the tug's diminutive wheelhouse. They entered, and after introductions, the barge operator, a huge, bearded, sleepy-looking individual, picked up the radio phone.

After a wait of some seconds, the radio broke forth with a crackle of static and a woman's voice with a strong New Zealand accent came on. "Mr. Thatcher will be on the radio in a moment."

"Okay."

After a further brief wait, the radio crackled again.

"Roger Thatcher here."

"Roger, I'm over on the townside barge landing. There's a lady frogman — better make that a frogperson — here by the name of Ellen MacIntyre."

"Good. Tell her I'll be over in the Babine Mistress in 15 minutes."

"Will do."

"That'll give me time to change into my wetsuit. Will you run me up to the hotel, please John?"

"Sure. Let's go."

The hotel manager gave Ellen the use of a staff dressing room, and John was sent off to find a couple of gunny sacks. He got several at the company-operated general store, which had not changed at all since his days at Granisle. He was waiting in the truck back at the hotel when Ellen emerged a few minutes later. She was covered from neck to feet in a form-fitting navy blue wetsuit. John could not suppress a smile when she climbed into the truck. "Hello, Frogperson!"

Adopting a flat metallic monotone, Ellen quipped, "Take me to your leader, Earthling!"

"We need to get some rocks, John. I saw lots on the slope above the barge landing. Will you help me collect some in those sacks, please? I'd like about 25 pounds in each sack."

They drove down to the barge landing, parked the truck, and soon collected a quantity of rocks. Ellen produced two short lengths of rope from the trunk, and tied the necks of the sacks shut with them, leaving a free end of rope about three feet long beyond the knot on each.

"What's this for?" asked John.

"Disposable weights. When I get down there, and get the driver out of the cab of the truck, I just cut loose my sack full of rocks, and up we come."

"Clever. But why two sacks?"

"In case I have to go down twice, for any reason. Look — there comes Mr. Cliffmont." She indicated a white Pontiac coming down the hill toward the barge landing.

"Good. He's right on time, too. There's the Babine Mistress coming. Boy, she really moves, eh?"

John and Ellen watched the cruiser slow as she neared the floating dock beside the barge slip, and come neatly into position alongside. A man emerged from the cabin, stepped onto the dock, and proceeded to tie up the boat.

John started the truck and drove over to the gangway leading out to the dock. The man from the cruiser came forward to introduce himself. He had black hair, greying at the temples, brown eyes, a double chin and a stomach to match. "Roger Thatcher. Miss MacIntyre?"

"Yes. Ellen MacIntyre. Pleased to meet you, Roger. This is my friend, John Kelly. He brought me out from Smithers. He'll come out on the lake with us." It was not said as a question, but rather as a statement of fact.

"Fine. Are you ready to go?"

"Not quite. I've got to fill my scuba tanks." She turned to John. "Can you bring the compressor onto the dock, please, John? I'll fill the tanks right here, and we needn't take the compressor with us."

"Care to give me a hand?" John asked of Roger Thatcher as he turned to go to the rear of the truck. The two of them carried the compressor to the dock. Ellen busied herself connecting the air tanks to the compressor, and then lowered the tanks into the lake and suspended them about two feet below the surface with a rope. She started the compressor quickly: it was obvious she knew exactly what she was doing.

When the compressor was operating, she stood up and, indicating the submerged tanks, explained, "If a tank should burst in filling, it'll expend its energy throwing water out of the lake, rather than in throwing shrapnel around in the air. It'll take a few minutes . . . Oh, who's this coming?"

They turned in the direction of Ellen's gaze, to see a tall, greyhaired man in his late 50's step onto the dock.

"Are you Roger Thatcher, by any chance?"

"Yes, I am. What can I do for you, Sir?"

"I'm Mike Cliffmont, senior insurance adjuster for Bob Davidson's insurance company. I'd like to be present when the body is recovered, and during any salvage operations."

"That's fine. It's good to find you people so keen to settle this matter. We don't much appreciate the loss of production this accident has cost us, to say nothing of the loss of a man's life."

"Mr. Thatcher, I'm not here to *settle* anything. I'm here to act as a representative for our client. Until the truck is brought up on dry land, and the actual cause of the accident determined, the matter of settlement isn't even under consideration. I am simply here to find out *if* Mr. Davidson's repairs are the cause of the accident. *If* they are, then we will discuss the matter of settlement. Is that clearly understood?"

"Yes, . . . ah . . . yes, Mr. Cliffmont. That does seem like a reasonable course of action."

"Fine. Then we understand each other. I take it this is the diver who is going to go down to recover the body?"

"Yes, Mr. Cliffmont. Miss Ellen MacIntyre, and her friend, John Kelly."

John and Ellen shook hands with Cliffmont with the utmost solemnity.

After a brief, general conversation, John said, "I'll put your trunk with the rest of your gear aboard the boat, Ellen."

"Okay, thanks. These tanks are just about full — another couple of minutes."

By the time John had made a second trip to the boat with the two sacks of rocks, Ellen had turned off and disconnected the compressor, which Thatcher helped him carry back to the truck.

"Park anywhere over there," Thatcher said, indicating a parking area on the other side of the barge landing.

*   *   *

The ride across the lake was cool and pleasant, for the day was sunny, clear and windless. As they sped across the water, Ellen spoke to the mine manager, who was at the controls of the powerful cruiser.

133

"You came alongside the dock back there beautifully, Roger. Where did you learn to handle a boat like that?"

"I was in the Royal Navy for eight years."

"Were you? What did you do in the Navy?" She sounded impressed.

"I was a chopper pilot on the Ark Royal . . . "

"Well, they certainly must have taught you something besides flying!" said Ellen.

"Yes. They teach you to be a seaman first."

Thatcher set an arrow-straight course across the lake towards the island group on which the mine was located. At the entrance to Hagan Arm, the Babine Mistress heeled into a right turn which took them around the rear of Starrett Island. At a point which John knew would be somewhere south of the open pit mine proper, Thatcher slowed the engine to a burbling idle, and they drifted to a stop.

"The truck lost its brakes and ran away, coming down that road, with 85 tons of waste rock in its box," the mine manager explained, pointing as he spoke. "It went over the bank where those trees are smashed, and went into the lake there. You can't see it, of course, the water is about 60 to 70 feet deep here, but we know pretty well where it has to be."

"Let's get on the line the truck would have taken going into the lake, and I'll go down and see what I can find," said Ellen. "If you've got something to use for a float, and a line, I'll attach a marker buoy for you when I locate the truck."

Thatcher rummaged around in a locker and produced three odd lengths and sizes of rope. "What could we use for a buoy?" he wondered out loud.

"How about a chunk of wood from shore?" Mike suggested.

"Right." Thatcher eased the Babine Mistress shoreward, and John stepped from the bow to a rock on the island, where he quickly found a piece of tree trunk about five feet long. He knocked off the worst of the knots on the rock, and stepped back aboard again, where he secured the line to the log float, and tossed it overboard, as Ellen instructed.

She tied the other end of the makeshift buoy anchor line to her wrist, and having donned the remainder of her gear while John was ashore, now eased herself over the side into the water and adjusted her mask, tanks, and breathing hose.

"Hand me one of those sacks of rocks, please John."

He lowered it to her by its rope.

"I'll be back up within 20 minutes."

"Be careful down there, Ellen . . . "

She gave him a thumbs-up signal and sank into the water, streaming bubbles at intervals as she descended, disappearing rapidly from sight.

The rocks pulled her down quickly, and her eyes scanned the murky depths. Fifty feet down she spotted the truck, slightly to her left, its Caterpillar-yellow paint job making it more visible than it might have otherwise been. "Talk about luck!" she thought. "Right on the button!"

As she descended further, she could see that the truck had fetched up on the muddy bottom on its right side, the load of waste rock long gone. She swam along the length of the truck toward the cab. As she approached the cab she could see the driver's door was open, the left front window was smashed out, and . . . the cab was empty! The number '65' was neatly painted on the door in figures 18 inches high.

A closer examination showed there was no mistake: there was quite simply no body to recover. She tied the buoy line to the catwalk railing, and dropping the sack of rocks, filled her lungs with air, and began to ascend, exhaling as the air in her lungs expanded under the decreasing pressure.

She surfaced not far from the Babine Mistress, and swam towards it. Strong arms reached down over the stern and with one powerful heave lifted her aboard.

"No body?! What do you mean 'there's no body'?" asked Thatcher in surprise.

"Exactly what I said. The truck is empty. The door is open and the windshield is shattered." She went on to describe the truck's situation.

After a few minutes discussion, Roger Thatcher raised the matter of recovering the truck. "Do you think you could attach a cable to the truck, such that we could hook onto it with a couple of loaded ore trucks and pull it out of the lake?"

"I don't know. I'm willing to try. It's going to take quite a pull to move it, though. It's muddy where the truck is now, and . . . well, you can see for yourself how sharply the bottom drops away at the shore. Is there a towing point on the truck somewhere?"

"There'll be towing pins at each end. Let's give it a try!" He picked up the radio phone handpiece.

"Calling the Pit Shifter."

There was a crackle. "Pit Shifter here."

"Is that Alex Phillips?"

"Yes."

"Alex, this is Thatcher speaking. I'm on the Babine Mistress. The diver from Smithers has just been down to try to recover Jimmy

Fredrickson's body from Number 65, but he's not in the truck. He must have got out of the cab and drowned. Anyway, there's no sense speculating about that right now. The body will turn up somewhere on the Lake, soon enough. Can you arrange for one of the trucks on waste rock haul duty to bring some cable up from the boneyard in a little while? We may be able to get a cable onto 65 and pull it out of the lake this afternoon."

"Sure. Just let me know when the cable's ready. You talked to anybody about that, yet?"

"No. That's all for now, thanks Phillips."

"Okay."

"Calling the Mechanical Superintendent."

"Johnson here, Roger. You want some cable from the boneyard, right?" The voice had a slow Nebraska drawl.

"Right."

"Okay. I'll go see what there is down there. We'll have to put an eye on whatever we use. I guess a clamped eye, with about half a dozen cable clamps, would do, wouldn't it?"

"Yes. Get on it right away, will you? We'll cruise along the shore of the Island and see if we can spot the driver's body in the meantime. Call me as soon as you're ready with that cable." Thatcher started the Babine Mistress's engine.

They had made three slow passes along the south shoreline when the radio crackled into life.

"Calling the Mine Manager."

"Thatcher here."

"Dave Johnson here, Roger. We've been looking around the boneyard and there's lots of cable here, but it's not in very good condition . . ."

"Don't worry about that, Dave. Stick a half a dozen cable clamps on whatever's easiest to get at, and get the little mobile crane down there. Drop the spool into a cradle and put the whole lot in an ore truck and get it out to where 65 went in. We'd better have a couple or three hundred feet of half inch nylon line too — we'll need it to pull the cable out from the shore to somewhere near the truck, so the diver can get it onto the tow pin."

Just as he hung up the radio handpiece, Mike Cliffmont spoke. "Hold it, Roger. There's something by that tree trunk leaning into the water . . . "

In a minute, Ellen went over the side to recover a green and black plaid flannel workshirt, badly torn. "It's probably his," said Thatcher, "though half the men on the Property wear a shirt like that to work — the other half wear *red* and black plaid shirts. You'd think it was a uniform!"

It was fairly late in the afternoon before all preparations were ready. The cable was indeed in poor shape, and Ellen flatly refused to handle it without some form of protection: short broken wires protruded viciously in the vicinity of the eye and all along the cable. In due course a pair of coveralls were brought, cut up, and wrapped around the cable just back of the clamped eye.

When all was in readiness, the Babine Mistress, with the half inch nylon rope attached to her stern, dragged the jury-rigged cable into the water in line with the buoy and over the sunken truck. Ellen went down, and with considerable effort got the rear towing pin free, worked the cable eye into place and replaced the pin. Someone had had the foresight, before sending it into the water, to beat the cable eye into a shape which would readily enter the tow pin opening in the frame of an identical truck.

When she surfaced, and again described the muddy bottom, Roger Thatcher pooh-poohed its significance.

"You come back aboard, and we'll have that truck on dry land in short order." He reached for the radio phone again as he spoke.

"Pit Shifter, come in please."

"Phillips."

"Alex, can you send down three loaded ore trucks? Give me your three best drivers, and tell Paget to put lots of rock in those trucks. We've got a bit of a pull coming up."

"Comin' at ya, fast as we can fill 'em up, Sir."

Three loaded ore trucks lumbered into view on the 'runaway' route about ten minutes later. They were soon connected in line astern, with additional cable, and the cable from the sunken truck hooked to the rearmost of the three loaded giants.

Roger stood the Babine Mistress well off to one side, and told the Pit Shifter to start the pull whenever he was ready.

From the boat they could see the drivers getting into their vehicles. A moment later they heard them rev the huge diesel engines and saw the trucks begin to move slowly ahead. The cable in the lake came taut and the trucks jockeyed to tighten the cables between themselves. At an arm signal from the pit shifter, the drivers gradually put a strain on the cable, with no result. The shifter waved his arm for them to increase the pull. Across the water the four on the cabin cruiser could hear the engines speed up like an orchestra responding to a conductor's baton. Dirt and rocks began to churn from behind twelve 8-1/2 foot diameter rubber wheels almost simultaneously.

"I don't think your truck is going to come out of the mud all that easy," Ellen said.

"Those trucks put out 870 horsepower each from V-12 Cat diesel engines. You watch, they've hardly got the cable . . . "

Whatever he was about to say was drowned by an appalling snap and roar. In the blink of an eye, the cable parted deep under water, and came snaking out of the lake like a giant whip. They saw the figure of the pit shifter sliced down by the cable as though by a scimitar, and a moment later his scream, mercifully short, and a blast louder than a dozen shotguns, reached the observers from across the water.

"Will you look at that!" exclaimed John. "That cable took the back tire off that last truck like a knife."

"Oh, that poor man!" cried Ellen simultaneously.

Cliffmont said nothing.

Mechanically, Thatcher reached for the radio phone, but he was so shaken he could not function properly. John took the handpiece from him.

"Calling the Kiwi at the mine office, please."

The New Zealand girl's voice came on the air with a crackle: "Who's calling me a Kiwi?"

"John Kelly on the Babine Mistress. We've just had an accident out here trying to pull that ore truck out of the lake. Get an ambulance and a first aid man up there as fast as possible. It looks like you've just had another fatality."

Chapter 19
A CONFESSION AND A PROPOSITION

Two days passed before Babine Copper was ready to make another attempt at retrieving the sunken vehicle. They had called Ellen the previous afternoon and asked if she could come out again the next morning. Ellen had agreed, after asking about the preparations which had been made this time.

"I'll have nothing to do with another slapdash try like Wednesday's," she'd told Thatcher icily over the phone.

Satisfied with Thatcher's assurances that they would be using nearly new cable this time, with spliced eyes, and of a heavier size, Ellen promised to be on hand by ten o'clock, and offered to tell Mike Cliffmont, who was staying in Smithers, that another attempt was to be made to recover the truck.

Everything was in readiness, and the Babine Mistress was at the townside dock when Ellen and John arrived. They were soon on the way across the lake and Ellen went overboard just before 10:30 to connect the new cable to the truck. As she did so, the first of four fully-loaded 85 ton trucks rolled into position on the shore. A D9 Cat had been improving the site for several hours, and was now to be connected up with the trucks to attempt to pull #65 back onto dry land.

The cable held this time, but no amount of pulling would budge #65.

"Let's knock it off till after lunch," Thatcher finally radioed to the men on shore.

Over lunch at the hotel's restaurant John Kelly said almost nothing until he'd finished eating. As he ate, however, he did several two- and three-digit arithmetic calculations on a table napkin. Eventually the latter disappeared into his shirt pocket, and at a lull in the conversation, he spoke.

"I'd like to make you a proposition, Roger, and a confession."

Thatcher's fork stopped half way to his mouth. "A confession?"

"I'm a long-time friend of Bob Davidson's, and Ellen is his niece. I don't buy your allegation that Bob's repairs were faulty, or the cause of the loss of your truck. I'll salvage the truck for Babine Copper on the following basis: *if* Bob's work is the cause of the accident, it won't cost you a penny. Bob's insurance company can make whatever settlement it pleases with Babine Copper, and also pay me for salvaging the truck." He paused, then went on.

"However, if Bob's work is *not* the cause of the accident, Babine Copper pays me for salvaging the truck, at say one quarter of its net book value as of one day before the date of the accident, or $20,000, whichever is greater, up to a maximum of $40,000. Plus all expenses, of course."

"What makes you think we can't get #65 back on the Island ourselves?"

"I didn't say you couldn't. But you haven't. If you can't, I can."

"And how would you go about doing it?"

John smiled, and his easy tone underscored the irritation evident in Roger's voice.

"For $39,500, I'll be happy to explain it to you in any degree of detail you want."

"If we can't get it out of the lake, we'll write it off and leave it there before we'll pay you $40,000 to do it for us."

"Please yourself. I'm sure Mike Cliffmont's people would be quite happy with that decision, too."

"What makes you say that?" Roger snapped.

"Well, until it's back on dry land, the cause of the accident can't be determined, so you aren't going to get a nickel from Bob's insurance company. And as long as you claim his work was faulty, why should your own insurance company cough up any money for it? Besides that, so long as it's in 70 feet of water, it's not hauling ore, and that's going to cut into your operation's productivity. You're going to have to get #65 back on the job, or shell out the best part of a million dollars to replace it. Right?"

Roger Thatcher's reply was to down his coffee in one savage gulp. John Kelly's eyes never wavered.

"Right?" he repeated.

"Yes, we'll have to get #65 back on the job, or replace it."

"And if you can't get it out of the lake, you can't prove where the blame for the accident lies. Right?"

Thatcher raised his empty cup. half way to his lips, and then banged it down in anger, realizing it had nothing left to offer him.

"Point made. No answer required. So you can't collect insurance from anybody, unless you drop your allegation that Bob's work is the cause of the accident. Right?"

"Possibly."

"And your bosses are going to wonder just what sort of a job their mine manager is doing if he has to spend a million bucks to replace a truck he can't get out of the lake. Right?"

Roger's pupils narrowed, and a muscle in his right cheek began to tick rapidly.

"And there's a man dead because you said the condition of the cable didn't matter, just to grab whatever was easiest to get at in the boneyard. Mike, Ellen, and myself heard you say that, plus as many of your own people as were within earshot of a radio phone. Right?" Thatcher's left eyelid began to tick in counterpoint to the opposite cheek.

"You could face a charge of criminal negligence, Roger, along with manslaughter. You of all people should have known better than to use a cable in poor condition."

"What makes you say 'me of all people'?"

"Eight years in the Royal Navy, and 'taught to be a seaman first', to quote your own boast to Ellen. With that background, you should have known better than to use a cable that's in such bad condition it has to have a pair of coveralls wrapped around it before it can be handled." John paused, and turned to Ellen. "Ellen, you said that cable was about one inch in diameter, didn't you?"

"Yes, that's what I'd guess."

"Well, I looked up the capacity of a one inch cable in Machinery's Handbook last night. A cable that size, in good condition, has a breaking strength of around 40 tons. I wouldn't presume to guess what sort of a tractive effort three loaded 85 ton trucks can produce, but I'd be willing to bet it'd be enough to snap a *brand new* one inch cable, never mind one in splinters."

There was silence at the table for a moment before John spoke again. "However, skip the Royal Navy, if you like. You wear the Iron Ring[6]. As a Professional Engineer, you're supposed to know the fundamentals of your particular field of engineering. Steel cable, and all aspects of its use, would be pretty clearly within the province of a mining engineer, would it not? I'd say you are wide open for charges of gross negligence and failure to apply proper professional judgement."

Mike Cliffmont now spoke. "You wanted to get that truck out of the water. You had a diver on hand, and it looked like a good opportunity to do it. You threw caution and what John has correctly described as your professional judgement to the wind, and a man died because of it."

The colour had drained from Thatcher's face in the last minute or two, and he now sat, ashen, with the full implications of his impetuous actions laid bare.

"I've made you a proposition, Roger. I'll raise the truck and put it on dry land for you. All I'll ask is such of your crew as I may need for some simple construction, and the aid of that D9 Cat when I'm ready for it. How about it?"

"I . . . I . . . I'll think about it."

"You do that. I'm going back to Smithers. You can call me at Bob Davidson's place."

Ellen rose from the table with him. "I'll send you a bill for the freight costs and related expenses, plus $1,000 for my diving services Wednesday and today, as agreed. We'll expect you at Uncle Bob's for supper tonight, Mike."

As they backed out of their parking space in front of the restaurant, another dark green Toyota Land Cruiser, identical to

---

6   Professional Engineers in Canada wear an iron ring on the little finger of their writing hand. This symbol of the Professional Engineer was first made from material taken from a bridge in Quebec which collapsed during construction, and reminds the wearer of his obligations to himself, to his profession and to the public.

John's, pulled into the space beside them, and a man about John's age got out, and went into the restaurant. He was of medium build, with a much receded hairline, and wore a red and black checkered shirt.

"Now, there's a man with good taste in vehicles," John quipped, as he put his own truck into gear and eased out the clutch.

Ellen smiled, and then returned to the matter at hand.

"Boy! Did you ever go after Thatcher!" she exclaimed.

"That's right. I did. No sense in fooling around with him. If you want something, you've got to strike while the iron is hot." John said grimly.

"Well, I don't blame you for going after him the way you did, but how can you raise that truck, John?"

"Piece of cake."

"But how?"

"Nuthin' to it."

"But how?"

"Float it out."

"Well, that's an interesting concept."

"Hmmm. Just so long as Thatcher and his people don't tumble to the same idea.

"You're serious?"

"Deadly serious. If he takes me up on my proposition, I'm going to attach a cable, or cables, to the towing pin on the front of that truck, and hook the other end of the cable to a frame of steel I-beams lashed to timbers for flotation, and I'm going to connect a bunch of big rubber fuel bladders to the timbers. I sink the frame, hook onto the truck with the cable, and inflate the fuel bladders. I'll pull that truck up off the bottom like a drowned mouse being pulled out of a bucket by his tail. When I get it off the bottom, I tow it to a suitable take-out point and they can pull it up onto dry ground with their D9 Cat. Poof! Nuthin' to it!"

"Of course, 'poof, nuthin' to it'. Where are you going to get all the stuff you'll need to do all this? We're not exactly in the middle of downtown Toronto, you know."

"Anything Babine Copper can't supply, we can bring in on a freight truck from wherever."

"You know something?"

"What? That I'm not as dumb as I look?"

"No, 'though that's true, too. I was going to say, you're going to need a diver to help you if Thatcher takes you up on your proposition."

"Bah — divers can be hired very cheaply. I'll get a couple of big husky girls, mit vhiskers. You're too skinny!"

"Phooey on you. I was going to offer to teach you to use scuba gear, so you could be some use to yourself."

John Kelly's bantering tone disappeared abruptly. "That's the best idea I've heard all day!" he exclaimed, thumping the steering wheel. "Will you?"

"Sure."

*   *   *

Mike Cliffmont arrived about the time John and Ellen finished telling Bob and Doris about the second attempt to recover the truck, and John's proposition to Roger Thatcher. Mike had stayed to talk to the mine manager for a few minutes after John and Ellen had left.

"By the time I left, I think he was beginning to see the light. You may hear from him next week."

"If you do end up doing the salvage, and if it should prove to be Bob's fault, we'd be the ones who'd pay you for the salvage. What would you figure would be a fair payment?"

"About the same as I'd expect to make per day working at home in my own shop." John named a figure, and Cliffmont nodded.

"That's a long way down from the level you offered to do the job for Babine Copper . . . "

"They've tried to stick the blame for the accident on Bob, and without any basis for it. I'm prepared to bet they are dead wrong, and when I bet on what I figure is a sure thing, I make the bet big enough to make it really pay off."

"If you gentlemen pirates will clear out of the kitchen, I'll start getting dinner ready," Ellen offered.

"Good idea," Bob said. "Mike, why don't you come out to the shop and see the Smithers Machine Works answer to Boeing Aircraft Corporation?"

Chapter 20
AN OLD BRITISH NAVY RECIPE

Ellen straightened up from the stool on which she'd been sitting and looked critically at her efforts. "What do you think, you two?" she called over her shoulder to where Bob and John were finishing the assembly of the major parts of the 'Flying Farmer'.

Bob twisted round to look at the portion of the shroud on which Ellen had been painting the caricature and its caption. "Looks good. Soon as John gets his foot out of the belts, and figures out which way to turn the last two nuts to tighten them, we'll put everything together and try it out."

"Be careful, Bob, or I'll drop a pipe wrench on your stomach the next time I have to step over you. I'll never get used to working with a guy who lies down beside the job, with his head on a pillow, no less, and criticizes every move the other poor sod makes. You sure you wouldn't like to have a spoonful of this here monkey dung to chew on?"

"You two are terrible! What on earth is this 'monkey dung' stuff? That's all I've heard out of you both for the past half hour: 'Gimme some monkey dung.' 'Put some monkey dung in here.' 'Smear some monkey dung on that piece' . . . "

"We've taken up scatology," said John, winking at Bob as he stood up. "Hey, that does look good, Ellen!"

"Thanks. And what, pray tell, is scatology?"

"The systematic study of animal feces."

"Oh! You two should be kept in a pit with a bear!"

John laughed. "Should we tell her what monkey dung is, Bob?"

"Sure."

"Monkey dung is a mixture of one third oil, one third thick greath, and one third white lead. It'th an old British Navy rethipe for threaded jointh and athemblieth expothed to the vithithitudeth of the elementh at thea. No rutht, no theithing, no problemth if you ever have to take it apart. Wonderful thtuff for preth fits, too."

"Where'd you hear about it? And stop that horrid lithp . . . I mean *lisp*ing!"

"One of the old guys in the Club, Bill Fenton — he's about 72, with 70 years in the trade, so to speak, and probably forgotten more stuff than Bob and I'll ever know. He's the boy that put me onto the stuff, and out of deference to your goodself, we two gentlemen have disciplined ourselves to refer to it as we have while your shining presence graces our humble workplace."

"Well, it probably works well enough, since neither of you thought it up, but I hope the novelty of talking about it wears off soon! I almost painted another line on the caption. I was thinking of making it read:

'The Flying Farmer,

Fortified with Monkey Dung'."

"Not nice," said John, shaking his head.

"Horrible girl," added Bob.

Eventually, in spite of the bickering, baiting, and banter, the fan attachment was fully assembled and pronounced 'ready to fly'. John started the tractor and backed it out of the shop. In the yard, he positioned it so the blast from the fan was directed down the driveway. Easing the PTO into gear, he let out the clutch. The belts took hold, and they could hear the engine slow slightly as it took the load of the stubby, steep pitched propeller. They let it run at idle speed for a few minutes before shutting it off for a quick checkover.

"Now let's run 'er up to operating speed, and see what sort of a monster we've created," said Bob.

John restarted the tractor and slowly increased the engine speed to 2200 rpm. Leaving the throttle set at this speed, he climbed down, and stuck his hand into the air blast.

"Just like a hurricane!" he grinned across the blast at Bob and Ellen. The machine ran smoothly and without vibration. John came around to the other side of the tractor and stood beside them.

"Runs nice, doesn't it?" she said.

"Yeah. If the tractor doesn't take off, the brush piles will. Man! Can't you just imagine that thing backed up to a pile of burning stumps and brush 20 feet high, flogging the air into it! That's something I'd like to see."

They left the fan running for ten minutes, before shutting it off. The bearings were cool, and Bob pronounced it good: "Looks like we done it a-purpose!" He went off to phone the farmer.

Chapter 21
AN AGREEMENT IN WRITING

The following morning, which was Tuesday, John had just started to set up a job in the lathe when Ellen came out to the shop and spoke to him. "Thatcher's on the phone. He wants to talk to you, John."

"Okay. Tell Bob I'll be back out in a few minutes."

Five minutes later he was back in the shop, where he motioned to Bob and Ellen to come outside where they could talk without competition from the one-lunged 'Old Girl'.

"That was Thatcher, all right. They tried twice more to pull the truck out of the lake. No luck. In fact, they finally snapped the second cable Ellen put on for them. Nobody got hurt, but they wrote off the differential housing on the tail end truck: the cable came up and hit it so hard it cracked the cast iron into about a dozen pieces. Thatcher says the replacement assembly will cost them nearly $50,000."

"He's had enough. He's willing to retain me to salvage the truck. They'll supply, or get, anything I ask for in the way of supplies and equipment. One stipulation: they want the truck on dry land in four weeks."

"What did you tell him?"

"I told him I'd do it, providing they get me what I need in a timely fashion, and providing they give me $5,000 up front to demonstrate 'good faith', and put $35,000 in the hands of an independent third party, for disbursement upon completion, according to a simple, written agreement which I'll write."

"What did he say to that?"

"He doesn't have much choice, so he's agreeable. I said I'd come out there tomorrow with the agreement for discussion and signing. I told him I'd start, and so would the period in which the job is to be done, when they lay on the $5,000 front money and the 'third party' takes receipt of the other $35,000."

"Who's going to be the third party?" Ellen asked.

"I don't know — either a credit union or a trust company with offices here and in Vancouver, I guess."

"Well, boy, I sure hope this pays off, and I've got a hunch it will."

"So have I, or I wouldn't be doing it. Now let's get back to work. I gotta think about my 'agreement'."

Two hours later, John went into the house and up to his room. After a while Ellen brought up a plate of cookies and a glass of cold milk for him. The end of the pen with which he was drafting up the terms of his 'agreement' was almost smoking. He paused only long enough to thank her, and resumed his work, printing in block capitals at a furious pace.

When Ellen called him for lunch, he was done.

After eating, he read out his agreement for their opinion. When he finished, Doris was the first to speak.

"Well, that's plain English if I ever heard any!"

"Nobody could sidestep or misunderstand that. Auntie D is right — it's in plain English."

"What do you think, Bob?"

"I want to get to know a man pretty well before I'll turn my back on him. You take a guy like Thatcher, backed up by a busload of lawyers like their parent company probably has, and if they decide to, they'll sign that agreement one minute, and turn around with more tricks than a heifer on ten feet of rope the next. If I were you, I'd go into Smithers and let Gary Meetersev have a look at it. He's about the sharpest lawyer this town's had in a long while, and he's honest. It'll be money well spent . . . "

"Okay. He'd also have a secretary there who could type out the final form of the agreement for me, wouldn't he?"

Bob nodded.

*   *   *

"Gary Meetersev is pretty sharp, like you said. He picked out half a dozen holes in my agreement, and patched them up. And he added one clause that alone could be worth the $75 he charged me," said John later, when he came back from town.

"What was that about?"

"If Babine Copper takes over the salvage operation at *any* time before completion, the whole $40,000 becomes immediately due and payable to me, regardless of the cause of the accident."

"I'd say that's worth 75 bucks quite a few times over."

John nodded. "Will you give me part of tomorrow off so I can take it out to Granisle for discussion and signing?"

"Oh, I suppose," said Bob, with feigned resignation. "It's hard to get good, reliable help these days. Ya gotta take what comes along. I'll take it off your paycheck, though!"

John was half way through starting to say, "You do that," when the knuckle of Bob's forefinger went up the length of his rib cage. "Oh, you miserable old . . . " said John, rubbing his side.

When Bob's back was turned, John screwed his stool down another half turn, as he'd been doing daily since the day they'd brought Doris home from the hospital and Bob had taken the 1/4-20 die to town in his shirt pocket. Ellen had a bet on with him that it'd take him less than two weeks to notice the shrinking height of his stool. Three more days and she'd owe him a chocolate cheesecake.

Chapter 22
FROGSKINS AND FIGURING

"They signed it, and gave me a cheque for $5,000, and the $35,000 to pass on to the Smithers Credit Union," John said as he climbed out of his truck the following afternoon.

"Great!" said Ellen, who, when she heard the Land Cruiser come into the yard, had come hurrying out of the house to hear how the meeting with Thatcher had gone.

"I phoned Finning[7] in Vancouver for full information on the truck, weight, etc. That'll be in the mail tonight. Also, after I left the mine, I made a couple of calls about fuel bladders, and so on. By the weekend we should have all the information we need, and next week we'll start ordering stuff. What will it take for you to turn me into a frog? One kiss?"

"Oh! You are horrible! "

"Of course. But if I kissed you, you wouldn't turn into a frog, would you?"

Ellen looked at him with a mischievous twinkle in her eye. "I don't know. You've never tried to."

John blushed slightly. "What will we need in the way of diving gear?"

---

7   Finning Tractor & Equipment Co. Ltd. --- the Caterpillar dealer for B.C.

"You'll need a wetsuit and tanks, mask, flippers, and a weight belt. You said there'd be a diver's service facility in Prince Rupert. Why don't we get on the phone and see if they've got what you'd need in stock?"

"Okay. You know what we need, so you phone and see what's what. If we could get everything, maybe Bob would loan you to me for a trip to Rupert to help me pick out a set of frogskins."

"I'm sure he would. He's just gone into town to get some stuff he needed, and pick up a couple of small jobs that want doing. Auntie D is sleeping."

When Bob came home, they told him of the most recent developments, and he readily agreed that they should go to Rupert the following day. They would make a very early start, and be back the same evening. Bob agreed to deliver the $35,000 cheque to the local credit union manager's office first thing in the morning.

The trip to Prince Rupert was successful but uneventful. They left at 6 a.m. Ellen slept most of the way to Terrace, where they stopped for a late breakfast. She drove the remaining 90 miles to Rupert, while John slept. For much of this distance, the highway follows the right bank of the Skeena River closely, and the drive is particularly pleasant. Their shopping took about two hours, and John added two battery-powered divers' lamps to Ellen's list. Before they left, John suggested they take in the museum. Across the street from the museum was a small steam road roller, which they had a look at. It was a Watrous #2, largely complete, and heavily painted to protect it from the torrential rain and salt air which characterize the local climate.

"There's guys in the Club who'd swoon if they saw this thing," said John.

"Really?"

"Oh yes, some of them are completely buggy about such stuff. They can tell you at a glance whether it's a Fowler or an Aveling & Porter, or a Burrell, or whatever. Worse'n a bunch of car-crazy teenagers!"

During the drive home, Ellen gave John a lecture on the fundamentals of freshwater scuba diving. Thus he was fairly well prepared for the practical instruction which followed in the next few days at Round Lake, an appropriately-named small body of water just east of Smithers. An apt and interested pupil, due to the job at hand, John quickly gained confidence in the other-worldly underwater environment, and after three lessons, Ellen pronounced him sufficiently trained for the salvage operation.

Friday's mail brought the information about the fuel bladders and the Cat 777 truck. John spent most of that evening in his room and was just finishing the last of some calculations when Ellen knocked on the door.

"Hi, Ellen. Come on in."

"Hi. What're you doing?"

"I've been figuring out what it's going to take to get that truck off the bottom of the lake. How'd you like to let me run it all past you, so you can see if I've missed anything?"

"Okay. Would you like a snack first? That chocolate cheesecake[8] I owe you is ready."

"Let's run through this stuff first, and then have it, okay?"

"All right."

"Okay. Here goes: The truck is a Cat 777, with an all-up operating weight of 129,150 pounds, no load. Call it 130,000 pounds. So, to pick that up with a submersible, inflatable float, we

---

8   See Appendix

have to displace at least 130,000 lbs. of water, plus some more for whatever the lifting frame itself weighs. You follow me?"

"Yes."

"The frame might weigh two or three tons, so call it five tons, or 10,000 lbs. So, 130,000 4- 10,000 = 140,000. To be on the safe side, we make the displacement capacity 180,000 lbs. Now, water weighs 62.4 lbs. per cubic foot. Soo . . .

"180,000 lbs. divided by 62.4 lbs./ft^3 = 2885 ft^3. Call that 3000 ft^3, which would be 3000 x 62.4 = 187,200 lbs."

"But when the truck is under water, it'll weigh less than it will on dry land, by the amount of water it displaces," said Ellen.

"True. But that just gives us a little extra margin on our lifting capacity."

"How much would it amount to?"

"Well, suppose the truck was made entirely of steel, which it ain't: there's copper, and rubber, and aluminum, and plastic, and so on. But say it's 130,000 lbs. of steel. That much steel would have a volume of . . . let me see: the density of steel is about 0.283 lbs. per cubic inch, so say 0.283 lbs./in^3 x 1728 in^3/ft^3 is about 490 lbs./ ft^3 = 7.85 times as heavy as water."

"Wait a minute. How'd you do that last one . . . ?"

"490 lbs/ft^3 divided by 62.4 lbs/ft^3 = 7.85 and no units — it's a pure number. The specific gravity of steel is about 7.85 times that of water. You follow that?"

"Okay."

"Good. Then 130,000 lbs. of steel at 490 lbs/ft^3 = 265 ft^3 of steel. So the truck displaces say 265 ft^3 of water, which would be 62.4 x 265 = 16,536 lbs., say eight tons. So we've got a built-in eight tons of extra capacity. Brutally speaking, about 10%, or a bit less.

Not enough to make much difference either way, but it's on our side, anyway."

John shuffled the sheaf of papers and brought up a drawing. "We sink the whole thing down till it's just above the truck. We hook onto the tow pin, and pour on the air, from a big air compressor up above. When we get enough air in the bladders, that is, when they displace something like 140,000 lbs. of water, the whole thing'll start coming up . . . "

"At which point you better have some means of spilling air," said Ellen.

"Right! Same as you showed me about coming up from depth with a lung full of air."

Ellen nodded.

"We'll have a manifold on the frame, with air supply and dump valves to control the volume of air in the bladders."

"What are those blobs hanging from the lower I-beam? The 'mill liners'?"

"That's for ballast, so when we want to sink the frame, we spill some air from the bladders and down she goes."

"What are mill liners?"

"They're cast steel wear plates bolted to the inside of the rod mills and ball mills where they grind the ore from its fine crushed size — say 3/4 inch minus, or about as big as the end of your thumb — down till it's like fine sand. The liners wear out, and have to be replaced. They weigh maybe 200 lbs. each, and they've got holes in them for the bolts which anchor them to the shells of the mills. The holes'll be handy for tying them to the I-beams with rope.

"I've got all the details worked out, all the materials required, cables and I-beam sizes, everything."

"How'd you figure it all out?" asked Ellen.

"Mostly from information in Machinery's Handbook."

"But, a. . . how could you. . . I mean. . . "

"Oh, I get it! You're wondering how does a poor, dumb boob like me — a machinist — ever find out how to use all those formulas . . . "

"Formulae," Ellen corrected him.

"Quite so, my dear . . . all those formulas for the mechanics of a beam under various conditions of load and so on?"

"Yes."

"You remember I told you I worked a couple of summers at Granisle when the mine was being started up?"

Ellen nodded.

"Well, that was about 1967/68. I'm 36 now, so that'd make me 21/22 when I was up there, wouldn't it?"

She nodded again.

"What do you suppose I was doing having summer jobs at that age?"

"I don't know."

"Well, I was earning a degree in civil engineering. When I graduated, I got a job with a firm of consulting civil engineers. One day I discovered MODEL ENGINEER Magazine in the public library and decided then and there to adopt that as my hobby. Eventually I made it my business, too."

"You're an engineer, too? That's neat, having two strings to your bow, so to speak."

"Well, it's not a bad thing. The kind of training I got you don't forget. I don't normally wear my Iron Ring, but I've kept up my registration as a professional engineer. But I can do better for myself, and have more fun doing it, as a 'model engineer' than as a civil engineer. The odd time I've taken on some small consulting projects for one outfit or another, but mostly I keep myself busy in my own funny little shop."

"Well, that does explain what I was wondering about, I'll have to admit. It looks to me as though you've thought this salvage job out pretty thoroughly," Ellen said.

"Sure. I figure it's an easy year or two's wages in about a month. I've been thinking about it every day and every night since I put my proposition to Thatcher. And speaking of wages, how about your wages? I take it you are prepared to help me with the underwater work?"

"Well sure, but I'm not expecting you to pay me . . . "

"Why the heck not?! You're a capable diver, and I'll have to have somebody. If you don't help me, I'll have to have, and pay, somebody else. How about the same $500 per day you charged them before?"

"Well, I guess that'd be okay . . . but it seems like an awful lot, if it has to come out of your pocket."

"It doesn't come out of my pocket, either way. It's 'expenses', and it just gets tacked on to the end of my bill to whoever ends up paying for the salvage. Now let's quit blithering about it, okay?"

"All right then. When are you going out to Granisle again?"

"Monday. And Bob's got a bunch of little jobs we've got to get finished up tomorrow . . . Say, I just about forgot, this weekend is the first full moon in October. Time to start hunting for moose, when the mooses start hunting for each other. I think I'll take my rifle along with me in the truck from now on. And I had another idea. There's a place further north on Babine Lake called Smithers

Landing — it's more or less a deserted logging camp. I think a few Fisheries people are stationed there in the summer. How'd you like to take a drive out there on Sunday? I've never been up there, and it might be interesting."

"Sure. That'd be fun. I'll pack a lunch for us."

He had had a letter that day from his brother, and with it a colour photo of his brother's two daughters. This he had temporarily tucked into the gap between the bolt and extractor of his Springfield. When he mentioned taking the rifle in the truck, Ellen's eyes had gone momentarily to where it hung on its nails on the roof stringer. She had noticed the photo, and now asked if she might have a closer look at it. When he nodded, she reached up and took it from its place.

"They look like nice little girls," she said, studying it, and then turning it over. There was a handwritten message on the back. She turned it over again immediately, saying, "May I?"

He would have preferred that she not read it, but he shrugged — "sure, if you wish."

She turned the photo over again and read the laboriously printed message. The style of printing changed half way through; they had each written part of it:

"Dear Uncle John: This is us on our new bikes you sent us the money for this Spring. Daddy helped us picked them out. He said we had to lern to be good horse traders, or you woun't like us so he showed us how. Daddy made the bike store man throw in the baskets and safety flags you said to get so we didn't get hurt and reflecters for our seats. Thank you very much you are the best uncle in the. world. We love you. Karen Kelly and Diane Kelly."

Ellen replaced the print. "Obviously monsters, both of them. No wonder you don't like them."

164

He grinned at her sheepishly. "I guess they're improving as I get older. Now how about that chocolate cheesecake? And I shall leave it to you to explain to your Uncle how it came to be made!"

Chapter 23
ELLEN'S MOOSE

In the course of the day's jaunt to Smithers Landing, Ellen added a bobcat and a black bear to her list of animals, and was first to see the moose which John shot.

They had rounded a bend in the road in the early afternoon on their way home. Ellen had seen it just as it disappeared over the bank beside the road. John rolled to a stop, digging cartridges from his shirt pocket as he did so. He was out of the truck in an instant, rifle in hand. He stripped five shells into the magazine and quietly closed the bolt on a round as he went to the edge of the road. He spotted the animal and paused to size it up.

It was a yearling male, in nice condition, its fur glistening black brown, rippling as it shifted its weight from one foot to the other. As John watched, it headed back towards the road somewhat ahead of his position. He decided to take it, and waited — "if it gets up on the road, it'll be that much less work to do . . . " He was glad he had removed the scope and left it in his room at Bob's that morning.

Sure enough, the yearling bull ambled up the bank and onto the road perhaps 50 yards ahead of where John stood. It crossed the road and started up the bank on the opposite side.

John raised the old Springfield and sent a bullet into the moose's brain which, though it is a small target, provides the most merciful of deaths, being totally instantaneous. At the rifle's crash, the moose's legs collapsed and it went down as though a rug had been jerked out from under it. John approached the downed animal with caution, and touched the muzzle of his loaded rifle directly to its fast-glazing eyeball. If it had so much as twitched, he would have fired instantly, but no second shot was needed. John cut its throat and motioned to Ellen to bring the truck up to where the moose lay, blood pumping from the gaping throat. Ellen parked the truck well off to the side of the road, and climbed out to have a close-up look at her first moose, as he unloaded his rifle, and put it back in the truck.

One leg twitched spasmodically, drawing up under the belly, and slowly straightening, then twitching again two or three times in quick succession, before stilling forever. ,

"Oh, isn't he big? And his legs! They're so long and awkward looking!" She ran her hand over the thick, shining fur. "He's beautiful. . . " she said sadly.

John Kelly looked down at her. "That he is, Ellen," he said kindly, "but he's also several hundred pounds of prime moose meat for Bob and Doris for this winter. Now comes the messy part. If you want to help, you can. If you don't want to, you don't need to even watch."

"What do we have to do?"

"We take off his head, and his legs below the knees. We gut him, and quarter the carcass with the hide on. We load the quarters in the truck, and take him home, where we hang him up and skin him. When he's cool, we let him hang for a week or so, and then we cut and wrap the meat."

"Sounds like you've done this before."

"Many times — more often with beef cattle than wild game, but they all come apart the same way . . . " said John, as, bending the left front leg sharply backward at the knee, he split the skin with his hunting knife, and separated the joint. With a twist and a bend in the opposite direction and a quick trip around the back side of the leg with the knife, it was detached. The right front leg was similarly dealt with.

"Moose is like a cow, walks on his toes. His 'knee' is actually the same joint as your wrist, and up here where his front leg separates itself from the body, is his elbow. On his back leg . . . " John proceeded to remove one of the latter as he spoke . . . "what appears to be the knee is called the 'hock', and is actually the same as your ankle — though it's a bit hairier than yours are, I must say!"

With the legs off, he returned to the head and continued the cut in the throat around the entire neck. "This takes a bit of fishing for . . . " he explained, as he worked the knife to find the joint between two vertebrae. By the time the head was off, John's arms were bloody half way to the elbows.

"Now, let's split him open down his centerline. How'd you like to stand there, and hold the stump of that leg about like that?" he asked.

Ellen took hold of the leg gingerly, and it promptly slipped out of her grip. John pulled it back where he wanted it. "This time don't try to hold it by the longest hair you can find. Wrap your hand around here, like so . . . " he demonstrated, grinning at her, "and pull. And, to answer your favourite question when we see a new animal, no, he won't bite."

"Well . . . okay, is that all right?" She smiled at his teasing.

"That's perfect. You made a skin diver out of me in three lessons; I'll make a moose skinner out of you in one. We start here, at his belly button, and we unzip his pyjamas both ways, full length."

John kept up a running commentary as he worked, pointing out various organs and structures as the gutting operation proceeded.

The quartering was done with a small axe from the truck. He split the ribs away from one side of the spine carefully, and separated the front and rear quarters with a knife cut between two ribs right up to the spine, and with two strokes with the axe, split the latter.

"That's a crude way to do it, but it's a lot faster than sawing all the way down through six or seven feet of vertebra bones."

"Could you saw him in half?"

"Sure. By hand. It's routine if you've got the carcass hung up by the back legs high enough to get the neck clear of the ground. But when it's all flat smack down on the ground, like our friend here, it's the devil's own work with a saw. Nice to have a crossbar between two big trees, and a pulley on the crossbar and a tractor to hook onto the cable. That's the set-up you'd find on most ranches.

"Farmer shoots the cow when it's facing in just the direction he wants, drags it out to his butchering hoist with a tractor, and everything else, including pails of hot water, is equally handy. But out here in the bush, you gotta make do with what ya got, which is pretty good here. Better'n butchering him in two or three feet of water, as we might have had to do if we'd shot him beside some little lake . . . Now then, how'd you like to turn the truck around, and back it up so I can chuck the remains of our friend inside?"

She did so, and then opened the rear doors of the truck wide. John lifted a front quarter, and hipped it in as far as it would go, hair side down. The second one followed, and the rear quarters went in on top, hair side up.

"What do we do with the head and legs and the insides?"

"We'll put the head and legs over the bank, and the coyotes and other critters will clean up every scrap within a couple of days. I guess you've noticed we've seen only three other vehicles on the road today? Leaving the guts there isn't going to offend anyone."

"And the coyotes will clean it all up?"

"Everything. Between them and the crows and ravens, owls, mice, maybe a bear, and who knows what all else, if you came back here a week from now, you'd be lucky if you could find one leg bone. Do you want to take the nose?"

"The nose? What do you mean?" asked Ellen in surprise.

"The moose's nose. To eat. The Indians regard the nose as the best part of the moose. Can't say I've ever tried it myself."

"Let's skip it, thanks!" said Ellen.

"Okay. Now you've managed to keep yourself all nice and pink and clean, how'd you like to drive and we'll stop at the first place we find some water so I can wash up, and then we'll go home and hang up our friend and finish taking his pyjamas off."

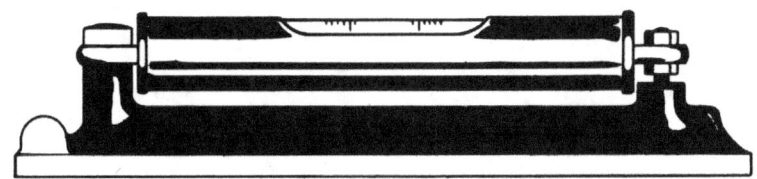

Chapter 24
FAST TRIP TO FRISCO

John spent Monday and Tuesday of the following week at Granisle, staying overnight at the hotel.

The Goodyear people had earlier suggested he come down to their plant in San Francisco to discuss details regarding the proposed application of their fuel bladders as a means of raising the truck, and methods of securing the bladders within the lifting frame. As he drove from Granisle to Smithers late Tuesday afternoon, he decided to go to Frisco the following day, if it could be arranged.

When he arrived at Bob's, he was promptly collared and dragged off to the shop to work on a repair job which had come in, and it was nearly midnight when they finished it. When Ellen brought out a snack for them, about an hour after he'd arrived, he asked her if she would make the necessary arrangements for the trip. Much later, when he went to his room, he found a note on his desk:

"All is arranged. I will pick up your Air Tickets early Wednesday morning. Ellen." Attached was a succinct itinerary: flights, hotels, rental car reservations, dates, places, and times.

He read the note agin. There was not one wasted word in it. She was no dummy, he reflected.

Bob kept him busy much of Wednesday morning, and after a fast shower and change of clothes he was ready to go. Ellen produced a ham, lettuce and cheese sandwich two inches thick, and drove him to the airport. She waited with him till the flight departure was announced. At the last minute she gave him three envelopes to mail " . . . job applications — they'll go faster from Vancouver . . . "

Nodding, he thrust them into an inner pocket of his jacket.

"I think you're a lucky dog, getting to flit off to San Francisco like this. I wish I were going with you."

John Kelly picked up his club bag, and grinned at her, shaking his head: "That would never do. Your Uncle would peel my hide off in strips and nail it to the wall of his shop. Besides, I'd never be able to pass you off as carry-on luggage — you don't match my club bag at all."

She smiled wryly. "Thanks! Off you go, and have a safe trip. Wait a minute — your collar is all crooked!" She reached up with both hands, grasped his jacket collar firmly, and as he leaned forward to let her fix it, she suddenly planted a very solid kiss on his cheek.

He could still feel it an hour and 20 minutes later when the Boeing 737 jet banked into a descending turn several miles out over the Gulf of Georgia, and roared in from the seaward approach to a grease- smooth landing at Vancouver International Airport.

He had a two and a half hour wait for the connecting flight to Frisco. After mailing Ellen's letters, he called Ailene, then passed the time mentally reviewing a number of matters with which he could deal on this trip. It was not entirely the Goodyear invitation which had sparked the decision to make the trip, though that was the main factor.

Eventually he decided to go see the U.S. Customs boys, so as to avoid a rush at the last minute before the Vancouver/San Francisco flight was called.

Friday night he stepped off the plane in Vancouver at 9:30. It was a clear, cool evening when he emerged from the terminal building. He caught an airport bus into town, and flagged a cab on Burrard Street between the Hotel Vancouver and the Public Library. The cabby, a man in his early twenties, was at the end of a twelve hour shift. He was sleepy, and said so.

"What do you do with your time off?" John asked him.

"I'm building a boat . . . "

"How about that! What sort of boat?"

"Sailboat. A 21 footer."

They talked about the boat all the way to John's place. When he paid the fare, the driver thanked him and said, "You know, I was dead tired when I picked you up, but I'm wide awake now."

"That's why we talked about your boat, chum. Thanks for the lift, and good luck with the boat." He shot the cabbie a grin and was gone into the night, down his own driveway.

He let himself in by the kitchen door and flipped on a light. Taped to the refrigerator door was a note:

"There's a pint of fresh milk in here for your Shreddies for breakfast, but come for lunch and dinner. A."

He grinned. Ailene knew him well. For the sake of simplicity in a thing which mattered naught to him, he ate 'shredded wheat' for breakfast about 362 days a year.

Dumping his club bag in the bedroom, he returned to the living room, and sat down on the couch. It was good to be home. He looked up at the wall above the fireplace, where a large, well-lit photograph hung, framed in black and gold. The girl in the: photo looked back at him. She wore the white starched uniform of a nurse, and held a sheaf of red roses. It was a graduation photograph, taken a year before he'd met her.

"You can't live in the past forever . . . " His own words came back to him. He sat quietly for a time, recalling how he'd met her. The thin, white scar which ran across his right hand would forever remind him of both his own carelessness that Christmas morning in 1973, and her quick friendliness . . .

It had happened in a split second: a large piece of sheet metal he'd been cutting had slipped from the bench, and slit his hand open from the crotch between thumb and forefinger across the heel of his hand and clear up into the wrist. Never had he imagined one person could have, or lose, so much blood. He'd wrapped it in a towel and driven himself to Lions Gate Hospital in North Vancouver.

She had been on duty in the Emergency Ward that day, and had helped sew it. up. She was quiet, efficient, and gentle, with a ready smile and a serene manner. Due to the amount of blood he'd lost, they'd kept him in Emergency for several hours and finally he'd asked for something to eat. She'd brought him a sandwich and said, "There's Christmas dinner for you, then, Mr. Kelly."

"*John* Kelly. Thanks for the sandwich — it's as good a Christmas dinner as I'd have had at home. What's the 'J' for?" he'd asked abruptly, indicating her name pin.

"Janet. " She sat down on the edge of his bed. "Don't you have any family to spend Christmas with?"

"Not this year. They're down in Nova Scotia visiting my brother and his family."

"That's no fun, being all alone Christmas Day. I don't blame you for hacking yourself half to bits as an excuse to come in here and see a few new faces!"

He shot a wry grin at her. "I didn't do it on purpose. This'll set me back a week. Anyway — what about you? You're working today."

"Somebody has to. Mum and I are having our Christmas tomorrow. Look, you'll be out of here tonight. Why don't you come and have Christmas dinner with us?"

"That's a nice invitation, but I wouldn't want to barge in on your family's plans."

"You wouldn't be. There's just the two of us. It'd cheer us both up, if you'd come. My father passed away about three months ago, so it's our first Christmas without him. Will you come?"

He'd held out his stitched and bandaged hand. "Twist it." She smiled.

He'd been so nervous the next day he'd thought he would be sick on their doorstep. He took several deep breaths and expelled them slowly before he rang the doorbell. But the moment she'd opened the door, she'd welcomed him, taken him warmly by the arm, and brought him into their home to meet her Mum.

"Never marry a girl unless you like her mother," was a piece of advice his father had often dispensed to John and his brother when they were boys. John Kelly had liked Ailene Larsen from the instant he'd first seen her. About two years later, he and Janet were engaged. On that fateful day, just after they'd left Birk's, the jewelry store at Granville and Georgia in downtown Vancouver, she'd stepped off the curb too quickly when the pedestrian signal turned to 'walk'. A boozed up kid in a stolen car had run the light and hit her, killing her instantly.

" . . . I know, because I've been there."

He recalled how Ellen had apologized when she'd asked 'Who?' and he had not answered her. It had been rude of him — she did not deserve to have been embarrassed in such a manner, for he had invited the question, had he not?

He thought of her, and all that he'd seen of her since the day she'd spoken to him on the bus. In every way, she was as fine a person, and as much a lady, as Janet Larsen had been. He had recently begun to realize that he liked Ellen a great deal. And that kiss in the airport Wednesday . . . that was no act of impulse. It had been premeditated, without a doubt. And look at the way she'd pitched in and helped dress out that moose last Sunday — no feigned squeamishness or anything . . . Yes, she was quite a girl.

The wall above the fireplace would look oddly empty for a time, he knew, "but this whole house has been empty too long . . . " He got up, took down the portrait, and went downstairs to the shop.

Taking a key from a concealed spot, he opened a heavy oak trunk under the workbench. He lifted out a 30cc V-twin engine he'd built several years previously. The cylinders and head and valve gear were almost straight off ETW's 'Kittiwake', but the crankcase and cam arrangements were his own design. He'd since built 12 more, in batches of four, for sale, and they had proven popular with engine collectors, for they ran well and looked 'right' somehow. He put the engine on the bench, and reaching into the trunk again, brought out a Colt M1911A1 Government Model .45 automatic. He handled it by the rosewood grips, checking the exterior over thoroughly for rust. The Colt factory's blue job was faultless, and the gun had never rusted, though it might remain untouched in the trunk for two or three years at a stretch. He set the heavy slab-sided pistol on the bench beside the V-twin Kittiwake. From a far bottom corner of the trunk he took a small blue box. It disappeared, unopened, into his shirt pocket.

Shifting a few other items in the trunk, he made room for the framed photograph, then replaced the .45 Auto and the engine. Then he closed the trunk and locked it.

Chapter 25
THE WOODCHOPPER'S BELLE

With about 30 other passengers, he stepped off the jet in Smithers shortly before noon Sunday, into minus five degree temperatures and the first snow of the season. As he approached the terminal building, his eyes scanned the windows for a head of short, wavy, gold blonde hair. Inside, he was still looking for her so intently that Bob had to grab his elbow to get his attention. "Hey! Quit looking for pretty girls!"

"Oh! Hi Bob! Man, you scared me! I wasn't expecting you . . . I mean, I thought Ellen would come to pick me up."

"Well, you'll just have to swallow your disappointment and put up with my chauffeuring instead. Have you got any other luggage?" he asked, indicating John's club bag.

"No, that's all."

"Come on, let's get outta here, then," said Bob, shouldering his way through the crowded terminal building. In the car he shot John a grin as he started the engine. "The girls are up to their elbows in flour and lard and apples — that Ellen never stops. And wait'll you hear what she did while you were away!"

"What did she do?"

"Well, you'll have to wait till we get home to hear about it. How was your trip?"

"Well, you'll have to wait till we get home to hear about that too!" said John, lapsing into momentary silence. "What have you been doing while I've been away?"

When they arrived at the house, the second of two apple pies was just disappearing into the oven, and the table was set for lunch. Over the latter, John allowed them to pry out of him most of the results of his trip.

The Goodyear people had advised the use of bands of nylon webbing at close intervals along the entire frame, down each side to the lower I-beam to retain the bladders. The bladders would be supplied with modified filler-caps incorporating a connection for the air supply line. " . . . and we just run a length of flexible rubber hose from the manifold to each air bladder," he concluded.

Then, before the pies emerged from the oven, he produced a large package which he gave to Doris to open. From the counter, where she was whipping half a pint of thick, fresh cream, Ellen watched Doris open the gift.

By the time the cream was whipped, a 'coffee table' book had been extracted from its wrappings, and exclaimed over. It was filled with beautiful colour photographs of the varied California landscape — wild, agricultural, urban, coastal and mountain. Both Bob and Doris were pleased.

The pie was served, with an extra 'spluck' of whipped cream on John's piece, and when Ellen went to sit down, she found a slim, flat, gift-wrapped package on her chair. Her face lit up with surprise, pleasure and appreciation. Her pie forgotten, she slowly unwrapped the package, as the others ate and watched. At length, a beautiful silk scarf emerged, hand painted with the golden poppy[9] and scenes of

---

9   California's state flower.

several San Francisco landmarks. She was, to say the least, delighted. John tilted his chair back on two legs, and regarded her. Her eyes spoke her thanks across the table.

"Bob tells me you pulled off some sort of one-man coup while I was away. What's the story on that?" he asked as she began to eat her pie.

"Oh, I wouldn't exactly call it a one-man coup!" laughed Ellen.

"Actually, it was more of a two-man coup," put in Doris with a wink.

"Smartest girl I've ever seen," said Bob. "Do you know what she's done, John?"

John shot him a pained look. "I asked you that 45 minutes ago in the airport parking lot."

"Ellen," said Bob, "has lined us up a sequel to the Flying Farmer."

"After she took you to the airport Thursday, she went to see if there was any mail for us at the Post Office. She overheard a couple of guys there talking about all the firewood they could sell if they could cut it fast enough. So like a good salesman she introduced herself and suggested they come up and see me. She told 'em I could build them a firewood mill for about any volume of production they'd like to see."

"Good enough! And did they come up?"

"They did. Right then and there. And they want a firewood mill built. The only snag is they haven't got much money, and the banks told them Friday they won't back them because they figure they'd be undersecured if the boys go belly up. I don't know whether to let them pay us out of future production, or what." Bob shrugged his shoulders.

"Do they really have a market for a lot of wood?" John asked.

"They say they've got orders for 300 cords and they've quit taking orders, 'cause it'll take them three or four months to produce that much. With a mill like I have in mind, which they could tow behind their pickup truck, and set up in five minutes in about a ten foot square, they could do 300 cords in about two weeks."

Doris, as she often was, had been quite quiet: now she spoke. "If they're willing to work hard, why not build it, and *rent* it to them, and get a continuous income from it?"

Bob's head swung sharply left to his wife. His fist came down on the table like a steam hammer. *"That's* the best idea I've heard from anybody in a week! Doris, you are a genius! If you weren't already married, I'd run off with you just to steal an idea like that!"

John winked at Ellen. "I can see the headlines already: 'SMITHERS MACHINE WORKS SOLD. Local fatcat retires, fortune made by wife's perspicacity, niece's salesmanship.'"

They all laughed.

"Have you got this Woodchopper's Belle built yet, or even designed, or does Ellen have to do that, too?"

"Well, I been doing some figuring and made some sketches. If you can walk after all the flying and eating you've been doing, why don't you come into the living room and I'll show you what I have in mind."

John gave a groan of mock dismay. "You mean I've got to spoil a beautiful lunch like this, looking at your so-called working drawings? I may become violently ill."

"Never mind, John. Just remember he's old and shaky in both hand and eye," teased Ellen. "Here, I'll give you the last of the whipped cream with another chunk of pie, to strengthen you for the ordeal." As she handed it to him, she said, in a more serious tone, "Thank you so much for the scarf, John, it's beautiful."

"Nobody nicer to give it to than you, Ellen."

Bob rounded on him suddenly: "Say! Did I tell you about the Flying Farmer?"

"No, you didn't."

"Well, he came up here last night to see us. Seems he likes his new rig pretty good. He started a couple of big brush piles on fire about a week ago. He parked his big fan up close to one of them and the whole pile burned up in about half a day. He just had to move the tractor a few times. He figured it cut his burning time to less than 30 percent of what it'd be without the fan. He says he's got six weeks of rental work lined up for the Flying Farmer all over the Bulkley Valley and as far east as Burns Lake."

"Good. We'll probably end up building about half a dozen more of them," said John.

"More'n likely. In the meantime, you've got about two more weeks to get that truck up on dry land for Babine Copper. How do you see that shaping up?"

"So far, so good. I'm going out to see how things are progressing out there tomorrow, and to order the fuel bladders, nylon webbing, cable slings and so on. They'll take about a week to get here. Everything else is on schedule; we'll have it up on the Island the middle of the week after that."

Chapter 26
A CALL FROM ST. JOE

The following day John was up early and headed for Granisle. He got across the lake to the mine with his truck about 9:30 and found work on the lifting frame well along. He spent part of the morning inspecting the work and noted few shortcomings. He spent an hour writing further instructions and a brief progress report, and then went to the mine office where he requested these items be typed, while he met with Roger Thatcher.

"The next part of the salvage operation is going to require the ordering of some fairly expensive stuff, Roger, and I just thought I'd let you know what you're in for before you get the bills."

"What do you need?"

"Three big rubber fuel bladders."

"That's fine — go ahead. But would you mind telling me what you need them for?"

John told him.

Thatcher sat looking at John Kelly for a few seconds. "Why, we could have done that ourselves. We don't need you."

"Maybe. Maybe not. If you want to take over the job as of right now, it's okay by me, but don't forget our agreement."

"What about the agreement?"

"I get the whole $40,000 as of today if you want to take over the job, regardless of the cause of the accident."

"Oh, I'd forgotten that. No, that's fine — carry on. I'll authorize the purchase order for the fuel bladders today, and if there are any other big items, you might as well let me know about them now, too."

"Well, we need some nylon web strapping and . . . " he named some other items, and went on to explain that he'd need a large air compressor and the barge, or some suitable substitute, to make the lift.

"No problem. We'll give you the compressor off the Airtrack drill. We have a smaller work barge and another little push boat, tied up near the main pumphouse below the concentrator. You can use that."

An hour later, John was headed for Smithers. The mine would call him as soon as the fuel bladders left San Francisco, and that'd give him enough time to check out the lifting frame and make sure it was ready for the bladders before they arrived.

Full darkness had fallen by the time he pulled into Bob's yard. Ellen waved to him from the kitchen window. When he came in, she said, "There was a phone call for you this morning from a man in St. Joseph, Missouri. He asked me to have you call him as soon as you got in. He said any time up to midnight his time'd be okay with him."

"Okay. Any idea what it's about?"

"No, he didn't say. Just left his name and phone number, and said to call 'collect'."

"Okay. How long till supper?"

"I can have it on in about 20 minutes. Uncle Bob and Auntie Doris were asked out for supper by some friends. How'd things go out at Granisle?"

"*First* class. Lifting frame's nearly done. Thatcher okay'd the orders for the fuel bladders and nylon webbing, and I gave him a progress report and some more instructions."

"How'd he react when you told him about the bladders?"

"Well, it was kinda funny. He just sort of sat there for a second or two, like he was stunned, then said he didn't need me in that case. I reminded him about the 'take-over' clause in the agreement, and he said, 'Oh, I forgot about that — carry on!' "

"You should have let him take it over, and you'd have collected the $40,000 tomorrow," said Ellen.

"Oh, that's no fun! I want to see the job through myself. It's interesting. They do all the bull work, and put up all the money, and I get paid for it. Not a bad deal, eh what, what? Say! How come you didn't go out with Bob and Doris? Weren't you invited?"

"Yes, and they said to come, but I knew you'd be hungry when you got home, so I decided to stay, and have your supper ready."

"Ah, you should have gone with them, Ellen! I could have found myself something to eat . . . You spoil us . . . you truly do spoil us . . . I better phone that guy — what's his name?"

"It's on a piece of paper on the counter. Bellemeau, I think." She pronounced it "*Bell*-a-moe'."

John scooped up the paper, and adopting a thick French-Canadian accent, burst out in a deep voice:

"Oh, mais oui, Monsieur Bellemeau,

(Dat mysterious man from St. Joe,)

I'll call you collec'

Since dat's what you 'spec',

And we'll ver' soon see

Jus' what you want from John-ee!"

Ellen laughed. "Where'd you get that?"

"I just made it up. I'm a veritable Henry Drummond when I get going."

He went to the phone and dialed the number. The operator came on and he asked her to put the call through 'collect'. He heard a woman's voice answer: "Hello?"

"I have a collect call from a Mr. John Kelly. Will you accept the charges?"

There was a very brief pause at the other end. "Oh, yes, operator, I will . . . "

"Go ahead, sir."

"Mrs. Bellemeau?"

"Yes."

"Mrs. Bellemeau, this is John Kelly calling. Your husband left word for me to call him. Is he there, please?"

"No he's not, Mr. Kelly. About an hour after he phoned you, he got a call from one of his men out in New Mexico and he had to fly out there right away. He asked me to give you his apologies for not being able to be here when you called. He said to tell you he'd call you as soon as he gets back."

"Okay. Can you give me an idea what he wanted to talk to me about?"

"He wants you to build him a model — an engine. You do that sort of work, don't you?"

"Yes, I do."

"Well, you can expect to hear from him soon. I know he's very keen to talk to you. He was up in Ottawa a few days ago, and he saw that model of a steam operated deck windlass . . . "

"Oh, yes. I built that two or three years ago."

"Well, David came home from Ottawa on cloud 9 after seeing it. He said he'd finally found somebody who could build him the model he wanted, and nothing would do but he must talk to you direct! He made some enquiries and finally phoned your home in West Vancouver and left a message on your tape machine Sunday afternoon. We had a call from your friend Mrs. Larsen this morning, and David phoned you right away. He was certainly disappointed when he had to leave for New Mexico, but he'll be in touch with you in a few days, I should think. He was absolutely transported by that windlass model!"

"Well, I'm pleased to hear somebody liked it. I'll be happy to hear from your husband when he can call me, Mrs. Bellemeau." "All right, Mr. Kelly, and thank you for calling."

"You're welcome, and thank you."

John hung up the phone and explained the call to Ellen, who was just putting the plates on the table.

"What sort of an engine does he want you to build?"

"Don't know. He must be some sort of a big shot. One week he's in Ottawa, then he phones me and now . . . poof . . . he's off to New Mexico at the drop of a hat."

"Well, I hope it's something interesting he wants done."

"It'll be interesting. I've built several engines and I kinda like doing them."

"Now then, seeing as how you've passed up a dinner invitation and stayed home to have my supper ready, is there anything you'd like to do this evening? Go out to a movie? Watch TV? Send me off to my room so you can read a book in peace and quiet?

"Why don't we make some 'peanut brittle' candy after supper?"

"Now whatever gave you a notion like that?" asked John in surprise, noting also that she had not taken up his suggestion about going out to a movie.

"Well, I ran across Auntie D's candy thermometer this afternoon when I was cleaning out some of the cupboards. And the other day I noticed a book in the bookcase in the living room that my dad used to have a copy of, and it has a recipe we used for peanut brittle at home. And . . . I like peanut brittle," she concluded, smiling, as she served helpings of spare ribs, pineapple, and rice onto the plates.

"The book wouldn't be GUNSMITH KINKS[10], would it, by any chance?"

"That's the one! Do you know it?"

"Sure. I've got a copy at home. Heck of a good book. I don't think I've ever picked it up without getting some useful idea from it. I've noticed that recipe in it too, and that was the first thing that crossed my mind when you mentioned peanut brittle."

After the dishes were done, Ellen went to the living room and came back with a grey, hard cover book. She looked in the index and turned to page 408.

---

10 Highly recommended: GUNSMITH KINKS, Edited by Bob Brownell.
Available from Brownell's Inc., Route 2, Box 1, Montezuma, Iowa 50171.
(About $13.00 in 1983.) The extract contained herein is used with permission.

"Old fashioned Peanut Brittle. . . Hmm . . . Let's see where he gets down to business . . . Okay, now listen to this, and be prepared to make yourself useful, John."

". . . 'Smear some butter on your wife's cookie sheet about the same as you would were you smearing grease on a gun for storage . . . not so much as to make it gobby — but enough to cover real good.

On this, sprinkle about l/4th teaspoon of table salt.

Now, in an aluminum stew pan dump 3/4 cup of white sugar, 1/4 cup of white Karo and 1/4 cup of drinking water. Stir a bit and then put on the stove and turn on the heat. Stick in a candy thermometer . . . and let the mess boil until the temperature reaches exactly 238 degrees F. (Do not stir once it starts to boil.)

When it reaches 238 F. add 1/2 pound of shelled, raw peanuts, and let it keep on boiling for four or five minutes — or until you hear the first peanuts start to go 'pop' or things start to smell a bit like well roasted peanuts — a bit of smoke starts at the same time.

Now, whip it off the stove and add 1 teaspoon full of baking soda. This makes the gunk fizz — stir it thoroughly while it is doing this and as fast as you can, dump it out on the cookie sheet and spread it out thin with your spoon.

Makes the best dingnabbed peanut brittle you ever sunk your teeth into and doesn't take, from start to finish, more than about 15 minutes' . . . "

It took somewhat longer than 15 minutes, but the results were all that the recipe promised.

As they were cleaning up the pots and spoons, John said, "How about some music? I haven't forgotten that evening you sang and fixed my headache . . . "

"Oh, you just want me to sing because you know I can't sing and eat peanut brittle at the same time. You'll eat it all while I'm singing, you horrid schemer!"

"No, I won't. We'll divide the whole batch scientifically into two equal portions, and you can eat your half in your room, all by yourself. Greedy beastie."

Ellen took a swipe at John's ear with a long-handled wooden spoon.

"Now, you cut that out, or I'll have your uncle spank you when he comes home!"

She became suddenly serious. "How come you always think of me in terms of Uncle Bob?"

"What makes you think I do?"

"Things like what you just said — 'I'll have *your uncle* spank you . . . ', and when you were going off to San Francisco, and I said I wished I were going with you, you said, '*your uncle* wouldn't stand for it' . . . "

"Well, fair enough, maybe it does sound that way, though I don't *only* think of you as Bob's niece. He wouldn't either," he added.

"I suppose he wouldn't. I didn't mean what I said in that context, anyway."

"I know that, Ellen," he said quietly. "At any rate, you *are* Bob's niece, and that's a fact."

"Yes, I am. But I am also *me*."

He set the dish towel down on the counter and caught both her hands in his, and leaned back from her slightly, her weight balancing his own. "That you are, Ellen, and you are a very nice, and a very attractive girl, too."

She blushed.

"And a good kisser."

She blushed deeper, and smiled, but said nothing.

"Don't underrate the value of being Bob's niece, either."

"What do you mean?" She made no move to withdraw her hands.

"If you weren't his niece, I'd never have met you, at least not to find out who you were, and to have had the chance to get to know you. Nor would we be standing here like this, holding hands in the middle of dear old Uncle Bob's kitchen." He looked up at the kitchen clock, still not releasing her hands.

"Now then, considering the fact that you passed up a dinner invitation in order to put my supper on the table, would you let me take you out to a movie this evening?"

"Sure, I'd like that. What's the movie?"

"It's 'Fiddler on the Roof'. Have you seen it?"

"Yes. Oh, I'd love to see it again! Let's go! I'll be ready in no time. What would you like me to wear?"

"Whatever you please. You'll be the prettiest girl within a hundred miles no matter what you wear."

She hurried off to her room. In five minutes she was back, hair combed, lipstick on, wearing her white silk blouse and a straight navy blue skirt with a crisp box pleat down the front, and knotting the San Francisco scarf around her neck as she came.

John Kelly was waiting by the kitchen door with her coat in his hand. He let out a soft whistle. "My, my, my, you look like a millionaire's daughter in that skirt!"

"Do you like it?" she asked, turning around to let him help her with her coat.

"Looks very nice on you." Indeed, she filled it in a singularly satisfactory manner.

"Thank you. We should leave a note for Auntie D and Uncle Bob."

"I did. It's on the table there. Let's go."

As he started the truck she said, "I made this skirt myself just before I left Toronto. Do you really think it looks okay?"

"Oh, come on! That came right out of the most expensive store in Toronto!" he exclaimed.

"No it didn't. I saw one in a store — and it was *very* expensive! — so I bought some material and made one just like it."

"Well, if you say you made it, then you did, and you are a very talented lady, which I knew already." He backed the truck around and off they went.

Chapter 27
MOMENT OF PANIC

The following Monday Babine Copper phoned to say the fuel bladders and nylon webbing would arrive Thursday. John spent the next two days at Granisle. They launched the lifting frame, rigged the lower I-beam to it, and attached the sling cables. John spent most of the second day in the water. When they had finished the work to be done, John decided to dive down for a first hand look at the truck.

Following the buoy line down, he reached the truck and swam around it several times. He noted the remains of the second broken cable hanging from the rear tow pin and swam to the front of the truck to check the ease or otherwise of removing and replacing the front towing pin: it was fine.

Next, he swam up to the cab, and looked in through the smashed out front windshield. The beam from his diving lamp illuminated the interior eerily. He swam up and over the cab and opened the door. Twisting himself onto his back, he jack-knifed into the open door for a look around from inside. Perhaps . . . John's train of thought was interrupted abruptly by the sound of his air tank bumping the steering wheel, and when he tried to move, he found himself trapped — the regulators had slipped inside the rim of the steering wheel.

Fighting the panic which sought a toe-hold in his mind, he took a deep breath, then another. Now what? Carefully, he worked his position down till he could feel the regulators hook onto the rim of the steering wheel. He forced his back towards the wheel, trying to visualize as he did so the relationship between it and the regulators. When it seemed they should be free, he pushed himself carefully sideways — downwards if the truck had been sitting on its wheels — and in a moment he was free. Easing himself out of the cab, he let the door close of its own weight, and decided the surface was where he wanted to be. On the way up, three freshwater sturgeon arrowed by him, swimming nose to tail, and disappeared from sight into the tea-brown depths.

At the surface, he caught his bearings, and swam toward the lifting frame which was moored to a tree at the shore. He emerged from the water and began to remove his gear, assisted by the mine employee who'd been assigned to help him. The man was a local Indian, quiet to the point of almost utter silence as a general rule. With John, he had opened up somewhat, speaking with the slightly blurred and softened tones characteristic of his people.

"What you fin' down there?"

"Not much; saw three sturgeons."

"Good eating. Hard to catch."

They loaded John's gear and the tools they'd been using into a battered yellow pickup truck and headed for the mine office.

"If that truck gets here tomorrow with the fuel bladders and the webbing, we'll be busy getting that stuff in place on the frame."

The Indian nodded almost imperceptibly, but said nothing.

He would rather have one helper like Danny Mathias than the four talkative, slipshod whites they'd given him yesterday. They'd done three hours useful work among the lot of them, and he'd gone into Thatcher's office with a tight rein on his temper in the late afternoon.

"Give me men who'll work, and do a day's work in a day, or we'll extend the time limit on the salvage job in proportion to the time those guys take to do what's got to be done," he'd told Thatcher.

"What do you want? "

"I want one man, who knows how to put his back into a job and get it done, and who doesn't take five minutes to get a pipe wrench from a truck parked 40 feet away."

"I'll talk to the surface crew boss tonight, and we'll see what we can do for you."

"Do that."

He'd left Thatcher's office without another word, and this morning they'd given him Danny. Within ten minutes John wouldn't have traded him for the entire bunch of the previous day.

The freight truck arrived on schedule Thursday morning, in the midst of a mild snow flurry, and they had it onto the Island, down to the shore by the lifting frame, unloaded, its tarps folded, and on its way by 10:30. They tackled the webbing first, John working underwater, attaching each strap to the lower I-beam, and passing them up to Danny, who gave each piece two turns around the outer log of the 'deck', and spiked down the end. It was Danny's idea to leave all the straps on one side of the lifting frame attached only to the lower I- beam "so we kin shove the bladders in from the side, then hook up the straps. Tuck 'em in good that way."

When they were done, it looked like a wooden ship, deck awash, planking gone, and half its ribs turned to hanging, flapping cartilage.

That afternoon they began the work of getting the bladders into the lifting frame. They used ropes to pull the slightly inflated bladders sideways into position, and tied each of them in place temporarily. When all three were in place, they began fastening the remaining webbing straps to the other side of the frame. That done, they removed the temporary ropes. Connecting the air supply manifold finished the job, except for the installation of the mill liners for ballast.

"Quitting time, Danny. Tomorrow we should get this thing finished. We'll have another diver to help us. We'll attach those mill liners and then tow the whole mess out into the lake a little ways and sink it, to see if it works."

"More better not sink it till you know it does."

Chapter 28
RIDING THE TROJAN HORSE

John drove to Smithers and early the next morning (Friday) he returned with Ellen. They worked most of the morning in the water, stopping only long enough to recharge their scuba tanks as necessary. By noon they had three tons of mill liners hanging from the lower I- beam, and all else ready. They had arranged earlier that Danny would bring the work barge around to the site right after lunch, with an air compressor aboard. By 2:30 they were ready for the 'sea trials' of the Trojan Horse, as Ellen had nicknamed the lifting frame.

"What's a Trojan Horse?" Danny Mathias had finally asked. Ellen had explained, and after that Danny never referred to the lifting frame by any other name.

They towed the Trojan Horse out to a point near the marker buoy, and first inflated the bladders to full capacity. As John had expected, it turned on its side slowly as the bladders filled. "With 130,000 lbs. extra ballast, she won't be so frisky," John observed.

"Let's see how she likes scuba diving." He opened the air vent valve and air whooshed out. Slowly the ballast brought the deflating Trojan Horse to an even keel, and as more and more air spilled, the lifting frame sank lower and lower in the water. Finally, its deck of logs was completely awash. John closed the valve and motioned to Danny to untie the tow line between the Trojan Horse and the work barge. "I'm going to sink it right to the bottom and kinda get the feel of it. Don't go away," he grinned.

"Have you got enough air in your tanks?" Ellen asked.

"Lots, enough for half an hour. If it looks good, I may even hook onto the truck and give it a tweak or two. Keep an eye on my signal float — if it goes under and pops back up again a couple of times, you'll know I've lifted the truck off the bottom."

The signal float was an empty bleach bottle, spray painted fluorescent orange, attached to a length of 1/4 inch nylon rope, laid down in figure 8's over two wooden pegs behind the board which served as his seat beside the air control manifold. The signal float line would pay off the vertically set pegs on its own as the Trojan Horse sank. Simply swinging his arm around behind his back, he could 'find' the signal rope immediately when he needed it.

With everything in readiness, John pulled his mask down over his face and put his own air supply hose in his mouth. He opened the air vent valve and the Trojan Horse began its descent. A few feet below the surface, John closed the air vent to check the descent, which was accelerating due to the increased water pressure on the outside of the bladders collapsing them and thus reducing their volume and the buoyant force exerted on them by the water. With the valve closed, the Trojan Horse seemed to slow, but it had passed the point where simply stopping the loss of air would bring it to equilibrium. The descent continued at an increasing rate. Unchecked, it would now plunge to the lake bottom. John rapidly cracked the air supply valve wide open, and heard the hiss of air in the delivery line from the barge. The bladders inflated quickly, and John was thankful for the air compressor's ability to supply plenty of air on short notice. "Love them CFM," he told himself, as the Trojan Horse's descent stopped. He closed the valve and waited to see what would happen. The lifting frame came to a halt some 30 feet beneath the surface, the pressurized air in its inflatable hull giving it a volume just sufficient to provide neutral buoyancy at that particular depth.

If he let out air, the bladders would decrease in size, and down they would go again. If he fed in air, they would expand and the Trojan Horse would rise. Juggling the air pressure in the bladders would clearly take careful watching. Cautiously he spilled some air.

It was difficult to gauge the rate of descent without a reference. The signal float rope! He swept his arm overhead and behind himself, and caught the rope. By how quickly it passed through his fingers, he could gauge his descent. "Helpful if we had another line, stuck to the bottom, for the trip back up," he mused. He felt the rope passing through his fingers begin to speed up. Quickly he closed the air vent valve, but as before, the descent continued. He opened the inlet valve, and seconds later his 'gauge' indicated the descent was checked.

By the time he reached bottom, he had the feel of the Trojan Horse to a nicety. The 'landing spot' was a few yards ahead of the truck. He let in air till the Trojan Horse stood about ten feet off the bottom, and then rolled off the seat and slowly flippered the Horse into a position over the front end of the truck.

He had to ascend further to bring his lifting cables to the correct height for connecting to the tow pin on the front of the truck frame. When he had it connected, he swam up to the deck of his inflatable beast and resumed his perch by the 'control console'. "Just like a submarine," he grinned to himself. "Always thought it'd be interesting to go down in a submarine, and here I end up building an 'open air' version!"

"Well, let's see if your figures were right, Johnny." He cracked the air supply valve and felt the Trojan Horse rise till it took the slack out of the cables below, then stop as if anchored. Air hissed in through the manifold and the fuel bladders filled, displacing more and more water, and in so doing increasing the lifting force on the cables below. Finally, he felt the frame begin to rise, lifting the 130,000 lb. ore truck part way from its resting place. He continued to let in air for a little longer, then closed the valve and swam down to see how the truck looked.

It was difficult to see in the murky water at the best of times, but now visibility was decreased by the mud stirred up as the truck's front end had come free of the bottom. But free it was. John Kelly could see that the front of the truck was now about five feet off the lake bed. For an exultant second he thought of swimming beneath the suspended giant's bulk, and as quickly rejected the idea.

He swam back to the control seat and spilled air. When the truck was back on the bottom, he disconnected the cables from the tow pin and started the Trojan Horse on its ascent.

At the surface, he gave a thumbs-up signal and motioned to Danny to ease the work barge close in to the Trojan Horse.

"Let's push it back to shore and moor it, then we'll call it a day," he said to his helpers when they had the lifting frame tied to the work barge and the long air delivery line back aboard the barge.

Chapter 29
WHEN THE HILLS ARE BLUE

An hour later John and Ellen were on their way back to Smithers.

"Did you tell Thatcher you'd picked the truck part way up off the bottom?" Ellen asked.

"Nope. Just told him we'd bring it up and beach it on Monday, and told him to get Mike Cliffmont and a Finning mechanic on site to witness the whole business. I told him Bob wanted to come out and see the beaching and the autopsy, too."

"How'd he react to that?"

"He wasn't keen about it, but he agreed. Cliffmont and the Finning man will hit the Smithers airport just before noon Monday, so Thatcher's going to lay on a chopper to bring them out here from Smithers direct, to save time."

"Wouldn't that be neat!" Ellen exclaimed. "I've never been up in a helicopter. Have you?"

"Couple of times. They are neat. The only one Thatcher could get for Monday was a 6-place chopper, so there'd be room for both you and Bob if you wanted to do that. How about if we go see the helicopter charter outfit at the airport tomorrow and see?"

"Okay. I'd really like that, if it worked out. But . . . will you need me in the morning at Granisle?"

"Nope. But I want you there in the afternoon."

John drove in silence for a few minutes, then said, "I think we're going to have some more snow pretty soon."

"How can you tell that?"

"When the hills look as blue as they did this afternoon, it usually snows in a day or so."

"For sure?"

"Pretty sure. We're due for it anyway. Snow usually comes by about the 10th of October up here, and by the end of the month it's here to stay."

"Can you turn up the heater, John? I'm cold."

John laughed, and glanced across the cab at her. "Say, you *do* look cold! I thought you were just making a joke because I said it was going to snow. Are you okay?" he asked, concerned, turning up the heater.

Ellen nodded. "I'm okay, but I guess I got kinda cold today after I got out of the lake. I probably should have got out of my wetsuit and warmed up at noon when I finished in the water. Ah, that feels good," she said, pushing her feet towards the heater outlet. In a few minutes the cab was warmer, and in a little while she dozed off. At Houston, John stopped and woke her just sufficiently to get her to drink two cups of steaming hot chocolate which he brought out to the truck.

"Well, boy, how'd it go?" Bob asked as he pulled John's door open almost before the Land Cruiser rolled to a stop in the yard.

"Everything is copacetic. We'll beach it Monday afternoon." John climbed out of the truck and closed the door quietly.

"What's the matter with Ellen?"

"She's okay, just sleeping. She got kinda cold today and she's a little done in."

They went around to her side of the truck and opened the door carefully. John shook her shoulder gently. "Come on, Ellen. We're home."

Ellen stirred groggily.

"Daylight in the swamp, kid!" said Bob.

John unhooked the seatbelt and lifted her out of the truck. At this she woke up and put her arms around his neck. "You want me to carry you into the house?"

"Why not?" she said sleepily, and dropped her head on his shoulder.

"Gosh, she weighs a ton!" he said to Bob.

"You're a beast," Ellen mumbled softly. She wished the house were a mile away.

They set her on the couch beside the fireplace and left her to 'warm up, wake up, or sleep around the clock' as Bob put it, tucking an afghan around her before straightening up and turning to John.

"Sure am glad to hear everything worked out okay out there, John," he said, clamping an iron palm over his shoulder.

"Don't tell me you've been worried . . . ?" John said in a bantering tone. He looked at Bob and saw all that could be said written plainly on his friend's face. "Hey! Don't be so free with your hands, old man," he said with a grin, winking at Doris, as he dug Bob in the ribs and clapped him on the back hard enough to fell an ox.

"Now, I want to go have a good hot shower and get into some clean clothes. Then I think I'll give Ailene a buzz, Doris, if that's okay?"

"Sure. Go ahead. Don't wake Ellen if you can help it. She must be really tired."

"Yeah, she's pretty beat."

"I'd ask you to put her in her own room, but it's nice there by the fire, and she looks so comfortable I hate to disturb her. You go ahead and call Ailene when you're ready to."

Late that night, snow began to fall and by 9 o'clock the next morning, a six inch blanket of dazzling white covered everything.

Chapter 30
EVIDENCE OF SABOTAGE

John heard the chopper before he saw it, and looked to the west in the direction of the sound. It was a 206L Bell Jet Ranger. It came in nose down, low and fast over the hill behind the townsite, whup- whup'ing flatly, and continued out over the lake before banking into a turn which brought it back towards the townside barge landing. The sound of its blades reminded John of a 3/8" slot drill in cast iron at about 300 rpm. The chopper slowed and John could see the pilot looking about to select a landing area. The chopper tipped nose up, and came to a halt in mid-air, then moved sideways and down, its rotor popping the air over the ear-piercing whine of the jet turbine engine.

The pilot cut his engine as the skids settled on the snow. The sleek shape of the cabin broke up as the doors opened. Ellen ducked, and ran out from under the slowing rotor blades towards John.

"Hi! How'd you like your flight?"

"Oh, it was just super, John! It was so *neat*! Thanks for suggesting that I come out with Cliffmont. I'd rather have come with you, till I climbed into that thing, then I was so excited, I forgot all about anything else. Oh, it's the greatest way to travel! It took us 28 minutes from the time we lifted off at Smithers Airport till we landed just now."

John smiled at her, enjoying her enthusiasm. "You liked it, eh?"

"I did. Uncle Bob got a big kick out of it, too." She kissed him in her exuberance.

"Kiss Thatcher. He's the one who laid on the chopper!"

"EEE-Yuck! I'd rather kiss a toad!"

"Well, suit yourself!" John laughed. "Let's get going and join the party. What's the mechanic's name?"

"Chuck Evans. He's nice. He was showing me photographs of his kids — triplets! Three little girls, five years old. Come on, let's go."

They went towards the boat dock where the others had assembled. John had put his gear aboard the Babine Mistress earlier and had his wetsuit on under a pair of padded coveralls. Introductions were quickly made and they headed out across the lake.

"Where will you beach the truck, John?" asked Mike Cliffmont.

"Right at the mineside barge landing. The bottom slopes out pretty gentle there and goes down to about 85 feet deep. They'll have the D9 and a couple of loaded ore trucks down there to bring it ashore, 'bout the time we get there with it."

Three quarters of an hour later, John climbed into his place on the Trojan Horse, opened the air vent valve, and disappeared beneath the surface. The descent went smoothly and the Trojan Horse was soon reconnected to its burden. John flippered back to his seat and cracked the air inlet valve.

Air hissed through the line and the bladders began to fill. As on Friday afternoon, the Trojan Horse was soon straining at its cables, and then the weight beneath it was overcome by the buoyant force exerted by the tons of water being displaced by the swelling bladders. The Trojan Horse rose relentlessly and John felt a slight lurch as the truck's lowest point broke contact with the bottom.

"Well, how about that, Kelly!" John grinned to himself. The Trojan Horse had the full weight of the truck now, and lifting capacity to spare. John cracked on more air and began easing his 'air powered submarine' towards the surface. Once they were on the way up, it was largely a matter of spilling air to keep pace with the water pressure, which decreased with decreasing depth.

When John Kelly's head broke water, he was about 30 feet from the work barge. As the log deck cleared the surface, John closed the air valves, pushed his mask up onto his forehead, and spit out his breathing tube. He pointed downward, then raised his hand, making an 'O' with his thumb and forefinger.

John spoke across the water to the mine manager. "Roger, can you stand the Babine Mistress off a ways to give Danny room to back up and circle around so he can take a tow line aboard from the front end of the lifting frame? We'll tow the truck around to the barge landing. When we get there, we'll nudge it in to shore till the rear wheels hit bottom, spill air till all its wheels touch down and then hook onto it with the D9 and bring it up on the Island."

In a few minutes the Babine Mistress headed for the barge landing with all but Ellen and John aboard. They stood in the wheelhouse of the push boat with Danny Mathias, looking at the shoreline receding on their right, and at the wake of the Trojan Horse.

A cheer went up from the watchers as the nose of '65' broached the surface of the lake. Then its front wheels, and finally the entire truck came ashore under the inexorable pull of the D9 and two ore trucks.

John Kelly hauled himself back aboard the work barge from his dive to release the Trojan Horse's cables from the tow pin, and to connect the landward tow cable.

As he removed his scuba tanks, mask, and flippers, he spoke to Ellen. "Ask Danny if he'd mind nosing this thing in against the barge landing slip long enough to let you go ashore, will you please, Ellen? I'll get changed in his wheelhouse and come ashore in a minute. I want to see what's what with 65."

John talked to Danny as he toweled off. They both agreed the salvage had worked pretty slick.

"What I can't figure out is how come nobody here at the mine thought of floating 65 up from the bottom that way," said John, pulling on his pants.

"Most white men aren't very bright."

"Yeah?" said John, sensing there was something more to come — Danny's Indian humour was slow and dry.

"Well, you stop and think about it for a minute, Keh-lly: before the white man came here, food was free, nobody paid any income tax, and women did all the work. Who could improve on a system like that?"

The two of them laughed together as John stowed his diving gear in his duffle bag. Then, setting the latter outside the wheelhouse door with his scuba tanks, John stuck out his hand. "Thanks for all your help, Danny. It's been a real pleasure working with you."

"You too, Keh-lly." They shook hands. John stepped out of the wheelhouse, slung the duffle bag over one shoulder, picked up the scuba tanks, and stepped from the bow of the push boat to the deck of the work barge.

He reached the group standing around #65, just as its cab door opened and the Finning mechanic leaned out.

"There's your problem, Mr. Thatcher," he said, holding out two objects in his right hand. "Somebody sabotaged your truck!"

"You're kidding!?"

"What the heck do you mean?"

"Sabotaged!?"

Chuck Evans climbed down from the truck cab. "Somebody sawed through the brake pedal arm right at the floor level till there was only about 1/16th of an inch of solid metal left. It was bound to go the first time somebody stepped on the pedal very hard. The rust is fresh from the time since the truck went in the lake, and you can see the hacksaw cuts — they're pretty uneven, so probably someone did it with just a blade rather than a blade in a frame. And they did pretty much the same thing with the emergency brake lever, except they cut it even thinner."

"But who . . . ?" Thatcher began.

"I don't know. You'll have to check out who was using or working on 65 on the shift before the accident happened."

"But who would do a thing like that?" asked Doris when they were all gathered around the table for supper later that evening. Ellen had flown back with the chopper, with mild urging from John, and Bob had driven back with John in the Land Cruiser.

Bob shook his head. "Who knows? They may never find out. Thatcher insisted they tear down the parts I worked on, more to save face than anything else. Boy, old Chuck sure showed those mechanics at the mine how to tear down a wheel hub in a hurry!"

Chuck blushed. "Ah, I've done so many of those I can do it with my eyes shut. I sure had trouble keeping a straight face when I pulled out the part you repaired for them, and handed it to Thatcher. 'What's the matter with the part?' he says. 'Nuthin,' says I. 'It's as good as when Bob Davidson fixed it for you.' "

"Well, you'll have to give the guy credit for a decent apology," said Bob.

"What did he say?" asked Doris.

"He just turned to Uncle Bob, and shook his head, and stuck out his hand, and said 'Mr. Davidson, we owe you an apology. I'm truly sorry about all this.'"

"I thought Ellen was going to kick poor old Thatcher in the ankle," laughed John.

"Well, I'm glad it's all over with for us," said Doris. "When will you collect the rest of the money from Babine Copper for the salvage, John?"

"Thatcher and I talked to the accountant before we left the mine. We worked out the current net book value of the truck at $328,000. They'll mail me and the credit union a letter tomorrow, authorizing release of the $35,000 to me."

"And what did Thatcher say to you, John?" asked Mike, burying his fork in a wedge of raspberry pie.

"He just said it was a mighty stiff price for less than a month's work, but that he appreciated the way it went. I told him he might look at it as a lesson in corporate good manners which could be quite useful to him in future dealings with local suppliers who go out of their way to do the mine a favour."

*   *   *

Tuesday, Bob and John were busy in the shop till late in the evening, trying to catch up on several jobs which had come in in the past few days.

Wednesday morning Ellen went into town to get mail and groceries, and came back quite excited. She came to the shop and went to stand beside John, who was milling a keyway in a shaft on the Garvin mill. He finished the cut, and flipped the overhead lever which cut the drive from the lineshafting to the machine. "Whatcha got, lovely lady?"

"A letter for you from Babine Copper Ltd."

John opened it. It was the promised authorization of release of the money held by the Smithers Credit Union, plus a cheque for various expenses John had incurred.

"Great! After lunch we'll go into town and go see about cashing this. $1500 of this one is for you, for a long, cold day Friday, and your help, Monday, too."

"But that's 50 percent over the amount we agreed on."

"Call it a bonus for nearly freezing to death Friday, and for advising me on what gear to buy, and teaching me to scuba dive, and so on. Anyway, that's what I charged Babine Copper for your services, and they never batted an eye."

"Well, thank you, that's really nice, John."

"Hey! What're you doing, kissing my best machinist during working hours!" Bob barked. He'd been working on some adjustments to the drive belts to the lathe. Ellen blushed deeply.

"I'm going. I just wanted to give John his letter from the mine." She fled.

Chapter 31
SURPRISE AT BEAR ISLAND

On the Saturday morning following the salvage, John and Ellen set out for Granisle again, this time to have a good look at the Fulton River spawning channels. In case they got another moose, John had emptied the rear of the truck, hosed it out, and had sorted out most of the gear which had been accumulating in the truck in the past several weeks. Non-essentials he left in the Davidsons' porch, to be re-stowed or otherwise disposed of later.

By 11 o'clock they had reached the Fulton River station and thereafter spent an hour talking to an enthusiastic Fisheries employee who gave them a most interesting tour of the entire facility. Eventually they repaired to the truck and tackled the lunch Ellen had packed.

As they ate, they talked, and the subject of shooting came up. Would she like to try shooting John's Springfield? Sure, but wouldn't it kick too hard for her? No, he would show her how to hold it properly, and the kick would not be severe, for the rifle was heavy, and she could additionally pad her shoulder by wearing John's jacket. Where could they do this?

"There's a place up past Granisle about five miles, where a little road goes down to the lakeshore, across from a rocky island about 500 yards off shore. It's called Bear Island. The shore is quite flat there. It'd be a good spot for a boat launch, and it's a good spot for shooting. The island makes an ideal back stop. And there's no danger of somebody getting into your line of fire unnoticed, 'cause you're shooting across open water."

At the conclusion of their lunch, they packed up, and made ready to head for the Bear Island landing. Before they started, John dug out a box of ammo from the glove compartment and transferred it to four steel clips which held five rounds each.

"What are those things?"

"They're called stripper clips. You stick a loaded clip into the little vertical notches for it that are machined into the Springfield's rear receiver ring, and push down on the top round. All five shells are stripped out of the clip into the magazine in about a second."

"Will we shoot with the scope on or off the rifle?"

"I put it on before we left this morning, 'cause I was thinking then of letting you shoot it. It'll be easier for you to shoot with the iron sights, at least at first. But I'll leave it on 'til we get ready to shoot. I don't want the scope rattling around loose in the truck while we're driving." He slipped two full stripper clips into each of his shirt pockets and started the truck.

"Is it much trouble to take the scope off?"

John shook his head. "Takes maybe 15 seconds, 30 to replace it. It's made to go on and off easy like that, being a target telescope."

When they neared their destination, John slowed down, watching for the little dirt road which abutted the main road they were on, at a point perhaps 150 feet above lake level, and which descended the hillside to a flat an acre or two in size. He found it and turned into it.

Ellen was speaking to him, and his attention was diverted towards her, such that neither of them at first noticed a battered pickup truck parked on the flat below them near the water's edge. They were part way down the road to the lakeshore before they noticed the truck, and a man standing close against the far side of the truck.

They had hardly spotted him when the windshield of their own vehicle disintegrated as a bullet cracked through the cab and tore out through the rear door of the truck. It had missed Ellen's face by no more than three inches, and she felt the shock wave of its passage an instant before they heard the crash of the rifle below them. John swerved the truck hard right, driving the front bumper into the soft cut bank above the road.

"Jumpin' catfish! What does that guy think he's doing!?" He wrenched open the door and stepped out of the truck. "WHAT DO YOU THINK YOU'RE DOING!?" he roared in a voice that could be heard a mile away. A second bullet shattered the driver's door window beside his shoulder, and went out through the roof of the truck.

"Ellen! Get out of the truck and get under cover. Get behind a tree or down behind a log. And MOVE!"

He leaned down and grabbed the Springfield from its place, and another bullet shattered the left rear side window. If he hadn't leaned forward at that precise instant, it would have gone through his chest.

Another shell smashed into the front of the truck as he leapt over the bank and took cover behind a large stump against which two downed tree trunks had lodged. Ellen was a split second behind him.

"Good girl, Ellen! Now keep your head down. Are you okay?"

"Yes — so far. What on earth is that guy trying to do — kill us?" She looked more angry than frightened.

"Looks that way. I'll put a bullet in his head if he doesn't cut it out. Listen: You keep your head down, no matter what happens. We may be pinned down here 'til dark. This is a good chunk of cover." He was stuffing shells into the Springfield as he spoke — with the Unertl scope in place he could not use the stripper clips. Quickly he unscrewed the steel lens caps from the scope, and began working towards a spot from which he could get a shot at the maniac down by the shore.

"Be careful . . . "

"Just keep that blonde head of yours down. It'll show up like a beacon."

He filled his lungs and raised his head slightly. "HEY! WHAT ARE YOU SHOOTING AT US FOR?"

As answer, another round crashed into the truck above him, to be followed an instant later by a muffled explosion as the gas tank burst into flames. In seconds, the truck was an inferno. They could feel the heat of the fire from their hiding place 30 feet away.

"Oh, John, your truck . . . !" exclaimed Ellen in dismay.

"Never mind about it — they're makin' new ones every day. I'm going to drill that nut . . . " Cautiously he poked the Springfield out between the two tree trunks where there was a gap between them, and yet the branches provided sufficient cover to prevent him being seen. Iron sights would be useless, for the branches that gave him invisibility would be in his line of vision. The Unertl provided a steel and glass 'tunnel' through which he could peer, unseen. He put his eye behind the scope and swept the lakeshore, picking up his target in a second or two. The Unertl's superb optics brought the scene 16 times closer. He judged the range to be about 200 yards. He could see a blue boat with a red hash mark on the bow drawn up to the shore beyond the pickup truck. He could also read the pickup truck's license number, which he repeated to Ellen three times.

"Memorize it," he told her.

The man, whom he could see quite clearly, had a box of ammunition open in his hands and was deliberately reloading his rifle, which was a slab-sided Remington pump action. 'Model 760 Gamemaster' he thought with a detachment that surprised him. He put the cross hairs on his man and waited, his finger off the trigger.

"Oh, John, what are you going to do? Don't kill him! Oh, this is terrible."

"I'm not going to kill him unless I absolutely have to. Better to wound him. Less trouble in the long run."

The truck continued to burn above them, its plastic, rubber, and other flammable synthetic parts fueling the initial gasoline fire.

John Kelly watched the man by the pickup truck below him. The man held the rifle pointing more or less in their direction.

"PUT DOWN THAT RIFLE OR I'LL BLOW YOUR BRAINS OUT," roared Kelly. A bullet crashed into the dirt a few feet to his left. "Fine, you like to shoot so much, let's see how you like it coming back," he muttered, putting the cross hairs on the upper forend of the maniac's rifle, which by the way it was now held, pointed skyward.

He took a breath, let it out, took another, let it half out, set his cross hairs exactly on the top end of the Remington's forend, and squeezed off the shot.

He heard Ellen's startled gasp, and rode the Springfield's recoil back, working the bolt and picking up his sight picture as he eased back into shooting position, all without conscious thought. Through the scope, he saw with grim satisfaction the results of his one well-placed shot. The man's rifle lay several feet from the truck, its forend shattered and the barrel bent. The man hung onto the side of the truck with one arm, obviously hurt.

John searched every area in his field of vision to see if the man had anyone with him, but evidently he did not.

"Well, that seems to have corrected his behaviour rather neatly," said John quietly. "Ellen, I'm going to go down there, and see what that guy's problem is. Stay here 'til I tell you to come down."

"STEP AWAY FROM YOUR TRUCK AND OUT IN THE OPEN WHERE I CAN SEE YOU."

The man stood where he was.

"MOVE, OR I'LL PUT A ROUND INTO *YOUR* GAS TANK."

Holding his right arm, the man shambled painfully away from the truck and stopped 20 feet clear of it.

John Kelly walked down the hill, his rifle, cocked and loaded, across the crook of his arm.

At a distance of some 40 or 50 feet from the other man, he stopped, eyeing him silently for a minute: 20-23 years old, 6 foot 2, and well over 200 pounds, shoulder-length black hair, greasy and unkempt.

"What seems to be your problem, mister?"

"I thought . . . I thought you were Paget."

"Nice of you to check so thoroughly. Are you hurt bad?"

"My arm's broken. What did you shoot at me for?"

"You don't seem to have a very well developed sense of fair play, do you? It's quite okay for you to nearly kill me and my friend, and burn my truck to a cinder, but I'm ever so nasty for shooting back."

The man swore at him under his breath.

"Lie down on the ground. On your stomach."

"I can't. My arm's broken."

"Try, sweetheart. I've got all afternoon." John Kelly kept his eyes on him the whole time. Finally the man was lying face down in the sand, his head turned to one side.

"ELLEN, COME ON DOWN HERE!"

She came running down the hill and arrived slightly breathless. John asked her to check the truck for keys, and anything of interest. She did so, and reported the keys were in the ignition, and several pieces of miscellaneous rope and a pile of sacking in the back of the pickup.

"Okay, grab the best piece of rope you can find. We're going to hobble this character."

She returned with a piece of half inch rope about 30 feet long, which she untangled as she came. "Good. Now then, Mister, we're going to make life simpler for all of us, so listen real close. When I tell you to, I want you to bend your left leg at the knee, so your foot sticks straight up. And then you better hold very still, 'cause this lady — who you very nearly killed a few minutes ago — is going to tie one end of the rope around your ankle. If you try any tricks, or try to kick her, or anything, I'll shoot you so quick you'll never know what happened. And I'd like the excuse to do it, so don't even twitch. You understand that real good?"

The man nodded.

"Say it in words — out loud."

"I understand. No tricks."

"Fine. Raise your left foot." The foot came up, its prostrate owner wincing as the effort hurt his broken arm.

"Good. Now hold very still. Ellen, put a nice snug bowline around that ankle." John Kelly's rifle was pointed right at the man's face. The bowline was in place in short order.

"Fine. Now drop your left leg and raise your right one. Same procedure: no tricks. Ellen, cut that rope off long enough to put a bowline on his right ankle, and to reach from one foot to the other when he's got one foot up and one down." He tossed her his pocket knife; she caught it, opened it and did as he instructed.

"Good. Now drop your right leg." The leg dropped.

"Okay. Ellen, tie that longer piece of rope to the middle of the one between his feet, so we'll have him on a leash."

When this was done she brought his pocket knife back to him. "Now what?" she asked.'

"Well, we've got to get this guy to town for some first aid. I suppose we could use his truck . . . "

"I wouldn't John. The police are going to be asking enough questions as it is. If you move his truck, you're 'disturbing the evidence.' I don't think you should touch his truck."

"You're right. Well then, let's all walk up to the road and flag ourselves a ride into Granisle. Come on Sweetheart, on your feet. Ellen, you hold his leash, and if he tries anything, yank his feet out from under him."

'Sweetheart' struggled to his feet, Ellen carefully keeping her distance.

"Okay, you know where we're going, so start walking. I'll be between you and the girl, so if you try to run for it, there'll be nothing in my way to prevent me shooting you. And have no illusions — I will."

"But my arm hurts . . . " the man whined.

"My heart bleeds for you. Let's go."

They started across the flat and up the narrow dirt road toward the main road. Their progress was slow because the injured man's hobbles impaired his progress. Ellen gave him just enough slack to let him walk without restraint by the leash, but was ready to jerk it up short if need be.

It took about ten minutes to reach the main road, where they stood about waiting for a vehicle. It was about fifteen minutes before they heard one coming. Ellen had relaxed her vigilance somewhat and when John turned his head in the direction of the sound, 'Sweetheart' saw his chance. He whirled, struck her in the stomach, and grabbed her neck in the crook of his good arm. "Now then, fella, drop the rifle or I'll break her neck." They were three steps apart, Ellen between them.

"All right . . . " Ellen gave him a look of . . . he could not read her thoughts, but he tensed, and in that instant, he saw her raise her right foot, and stamp it down hard, scraping the length of the man's shin with the edge of her shoe, and coming down hard on his instep. It was meant to surprise and hurt, and it did both. At the same instant, she bent forward as far as she could. In the blink of an eye, the 9-1/2 pound Springfield turned end-for-end and the side of the butt stock caught the man a crashing blow full on the side of the head. John Kelly felt the solid connection of walnut with bone through his right hand on the grip of the rifle, and the man crumpled, sprawling, Ellen with him, though his arm no longer choked her. John caught her to her feet and held her upright with one arm around her shoulders. "Are you okay?"

She nodded, whitefaced, fighting for breath. "Thanks. Oh, my throat! What a brute — he's as strong as a bear. Boy! You sure hit him — I could feel it shake him all the way to his knees."

"I shoulda hit him twice as hard . . . "

A pickup truck with two men in it had pulled to a stop beside them just as he finished speaking. "What's going on here?" asked the driver, rolling down his window.

"This chap tried to kill me and my friend when we started driving down towards the Bear Island landing. We jumped out of the truck, which he managed to set afire — I guess he hit my gas tank. Anyway, I shot his rifle out of his hand, and busted his arm in the process."

"What's the matter with him right now?" asked the second man in the truck.

"He grabbed her when I turned my head, when I heard you fellows coming. I caught him on the side of the head with the butt of my rifle and changed his mind. Can you give us a lift in to the cop shop in Granisle?"

"Sure. Let's throw him into the back of the truck. We'll give you a hand." The two men piled out and came around to where the unconscious form lay.

"Hey, you've caught yourself an interesting fish!" said the second man. "Do you know who this is?"

"No, I never bothered to ask him."

"Well, its Jimmy Fredrickson."

"The truck operator? The one that was drowned?" asked Ellen. "The very same. What was he doing down there?"

"Don't know. He had a boat pulled up against the shore. I didn't ask him any details about his business."

The passenger of the pickup duo looked up sharply, checked himself, and said, "Well, let's chuck him in the truck and get him into town. Bill, you take his feet and we'll take his shoulders." He looked at John as he spoke.

John handed Ellen his rifle and in a minute or two the unconscious Jimmy Fredrickson was none too gently arranged in the back of the truck.

In spite of invitations to the contrary, Ellen insisted on riding in the back of the truck with John. When they were underway, she turned to him. "Oh, John. I'm so sorry. I should have been paying attention . . . " She was close to tears.

He shook his head. "Don't worry about it, Ellen, it's not your fault. Everything's fine." He glanced at the butt of his rifle. "Boy, I caught him good with that one, eh? He's sleeping like a baby."

He put his arm around Ellen's shoulders and pulled her close against him. It helped brace them both against the swaying of the truck, and they stayed that way for the rest of the trip.

"You're safe and that's the main thing. You did real good, stomping on his shin like that, and diving over that bank after me. Most girls would have sat there screaming hysterically, and if you'd done that, you might be in that truck right now, burned to death." She leaned against him, glad of his protective arm around her. The effect of the last 3/4 of an hour was beginning to hit her, brought home perhaps more than anything John's last words.

"What about your truck?" she asked after an interval.

John shrugged. "Ultimately, the government's motor vehicle insurance scheme will cough up the current market value — it's a 1978, so they won't give me the price of a new one. I'll have to make up the difference between that and whatever I decide to buy. This creep should have to pay the difference, but that could take months. Actually, when it comes down to it, he should have to pay back the whole shot. It was no accident!"

They talked about that for a little longer, then John looked at her. "You know, I keep thinking, there's something familiar about that guy in this truck. Not the driver, the other one. We've seen him before someplace, but I can't remember where. You know who he is?"

She shook her head. She had in fact paid little attention to either of the two men.

John Kelly began to unload his Springfield, putting the four remaining live rounds back into the stripper clip. He took the Unertl's lens caps from his pocket and blew them off before replacing them on the scope. He looked at the rifle thoughtfully, then grinned at Ellen. "You never even got to try it at all, did you?"

When the truck pulled up at the RCMP office, John went inside and a minute later came out with a Constable who looked into the back of the truck.

"That's him alright! We'll call the first aid man to come down here and fix him up. Then I guess they'll take him into the hospital at Burns Lake." He looked at the owner of the pickup. "Can you wait till the first aid man gets here, or do you want him out of the truck right now?"

"I'd just as soon be on my way . . . Ed here wants to go pick up his girl in Houston."

Ed nodded. "I might as well head for the bunk house right now. You want a hand unloading Fredrickson?"

Bill shook his head. "We can manage. Off you go, Ed, we don't want to interfere with your love life."

Ed cracked an ugly smile, revealing a row of dirty, uneven, smoke-stained teeth. Whoever his girl friend was, she was welcome to him, Ellen thought.

Bill lowered the tailgate of his pickup. They pulled the unconscious man out feet first, and laid him on the wooden sidewalk of the RCMP office. John and Ellen thanked him for the lift and he drove off.

"Now then, Mr. Kelly, we'll need to get a statement from you. You, too, Miss. Will you both come inside, please?"

When they came to the point where John had asked the man why he'd shot at him, and John said: " . . . he said, I thought you were Paget", the Constable looked up sharply from his note taking.

"Did you say *Paget*? Paget's the guy who was with the guy who drove you in here! Ed Paget. He's a shovel operator at the mine. When he's not working, he's in trouble of one sort or another, as often as not."

"Well, I don't know anything about that, but it strikes me I've seen him before, somewhere . . . "

"Say! I know where we've seen him," said Ellen. "He pulled in beside where we were parked at the restaurant, the day you put your proposition to Thatcher about salvaging '65'. He was driving a green Toyota Land Cruiser exactly like yours. Don't you remember? You said there was a guy with good taste in vehicles."

"That's it! That's why Fredrickson would have thought I was Paget, 'cause the trucks are identical."

The Corporal nodded. "There's some connection, and knowing Paget, I'll bet he's on his way back to Bear Island right now. Come on, let's go . . . " He turned to the other officer, who'd been taking down John's statement. "You can stay here and hold the fort, Sanders. I'll drive up there and see what's what. Is that first aid man coming or not?"

"He should be here any minute. Go on; I'll take care of that side of things."

It took just four minutes to cover the five miles from Granisle to the Bear Island landing turnoff in the RCMP squad car. When they nosed down the road to the landing, there was a dark green Land Cruiser parked near the pickup truck. A man was wrestling with some heavy object at the back of the Land Cruiser, the rear doors of which were open.

The Corporal flicked a switch on his radio and picked up the handpiece. When he spoke, the loud hailer on the roof of the police car spoke for him:

"STAND AWAY FROM THE GREEN TRUCK, AND STAND STILL."

It was Paget, all right. He let the object he was struggling with fall to the ground, and stepped back a pace or two from his truck. The police cruiser edged past the burnt-out hulk of John's truck, which nearly blocked the road, and worked its way down the hill. The RCMP officer got out, as did his two passengers.

"Well, Ed, what are you up to now?"

*   *   *

" . . . Anyway, Paget spotted the rock when he was running the shovel in the pit one day, the week before '65' went in the lake. He and Jimmy Fredrickson lifted it into Jimmy's ore truck and Jimmy was supposed to dump it back of the pit. . . "

"But he didn't," Ellen took over the explanation being presented in Bob and Doris' living room. "He was mad at Paget, 'cause the last time they found a 'pocket' of crystal in the pit and sold it, Paget had kept too big a share for himself to suit Jimmy. Besides that, *this* rock was worth a whole lot more than anything they'd ever found before! Jimmy decided to double cross Paget and dump the rock somewhere else . . . "

John took over. "Then he ran his ore truck into the lake to make it look like he'd drowned, for Paget's sake. The cut-off controls in the cab were just to make it look as though somebody else had messed around with the truck, and poor Jimmy was the victim, instead of the perpetrator, of an accident. The shirt we found

228

snagged to a tree near the shore the day Ellen went down to retrieve the body, that was just more of Fredrickson's own handiwork."

"But how did he get off the island?" asked Doris. "Nobody could swim two miles in Babine Lake!"

"They figure he must have holed up on the island till that night, and snuck onto the barge in the dark. There was a freight truck off the island late that night and he may have been hiding in one of the piles of big tires being sent out for recapping — they send out whole truckloads of tires regularly to be retreaded. Anyway, he got off the island and disappeared. The truck he had at Bear Island today is registered in Kamloops in a name they're still checking out. The boat they don't know about yet. It could have been bought or stolen anywhere — Tahtsa Lake, Ootsa Lake, Germanson Landing, Fort St. James — anywhere. My voice is giving out, Ellen. You tell it."

"Okay. Eventually, Jimmy Fredrickson came back to get the rock. We just happened along after he'd got it into his truck at Bear Island landing. When he saw the Land Cruiser, he figured it was Ed Paget, and grabbed his rifle, and started shooting . . . "

"But what was so special about this rock they were after?" asked Bob.

"You should have seen it! They run into pockets of rock crystal in the pit from time to time. The shovel operators are the guys who spot them, because they're right there looking at the muck pile when they're digging and loading the ore into the trucks. Anyway, these pockets of crystal are usually just a mass of clear quartz crystals, some the size of a match head, some half as big as a banana. Usually there's some iron pyrite — which looks like gold — or some native copper. The whole thing can be quite beautiful. The shovel operators are usually the boys who see them, and they grab them. Usually they break them up and give them away. But sometimes they sell them. That's what Paget was doing. He sold them to a character he knew in Prince George, who'd take them to a curio shop in Jasper, in the Rockies, to be sold to tourists."

"But how much would they get for a mess of crystals? Surely not enough to try to kill for it!?" exclaimed Doris.

"That's true, most of the time. They'd get 50 bucks, maybe 75. But this one was different. You should have seen it! The police are holding it now, for evidence, but eventually it'll get back in the hands of Babine Copper. You should have seen old Roger Thatcher when he saw it. I thought he'd faint! Or drool!" laughed Ellen.

"Well, come on girl, tell us what was so special about it!" growled Bob.

"Well, it was a pocket about the size of a football, maybe a little bigger. It had the usual assortment of crystals, but they were all different colours, blues, and reds, and greens, and purples, even orange. And there was a great big slug of gold — not iron pyrite — real gold, at least the size of your fist, or bigger, and then flecks of gold shot all over the crystals, like the gold had come in as steam, almost, and condensed on the crystals. Oh, it was enough to make your eyes pop!"

"Sure made Thatcher gasp, I'll tell you," laughed John. "Man, when he came down to the RCMP office and saw it, I bet his pulse rate must have tripled in about two seconds flat."

"What do you suppose it's worth? Will they crush it and take the gold out?" Doris wanted to know.

"No, and if you saw it, you'd know why. Thatcher told us on the way out here that they'll probably write to a lot of the big natural history museums in Washington, New York, Toronto, Paris, London, etc., and invite their geological curators to bid on it. Or they might auction it, or sell it to a private collector. Or they might get it appraised and then donate it to the Royal Ontario Museum and take a big tax write-off on it. Any way they slice it, he figures it's got to be worth a half a million easy, maybe a lot more.

"My goodness, he'd appreciate you recovering something like that for them! It's no wonder he drove you out here himself!"

Ellen snorted: "You're darn right he appreciated it. He appreciated it a lot more than just enough to drive us out here, though! He told John to go into Smithers on Monday and to pick himself any vehicle he wanted, and to have the dealer's sales manager phone the mine — they'll pick up the tab right now for whatever he wants, short of a Rolls Royce, and John can reimburse Babine Copper by whatever he gets from the insurance on his old truck, when he gets it."

"I guess we'd have to concede Roger Thatcher is not so bad after all. That strikes me as a pretty handsome offer," said Bob. "What sort of vehicle will you get?"

"Oh, I suppose I'll get another Land Cruiser, but it sure isn't going to be a green one! They're too dangerous! Ellen says I should get a blue one, so it'll match her navy blue ski jacket and her navy blue pants, and her navy blue skirt."

"I never said anything of the sort. All I said was that if I were buying a new car, I'd get a blue one. I think navy blue is a sharp colour."

Much later that evening, when they had gone to bed, Doris said quietly to her husband, "Would you care to place a small bet for or against John's new truck being navy blue?"

"Not if they make 'em in that colour." He turned over, and with a well coordinated hunch of his shoulders and a twitch of his leg pulled the blankets out at the foot of the bed. Having thus got a little slack in the system he wrapped the sheet around the top of his head like an old Russian grandmother, and promptly went to sleep.

Doris sighed. For 40 years she had tried to tuck the blankets in sufficiently tight that he could not pull them out. Never once had she succeeded in all that time.

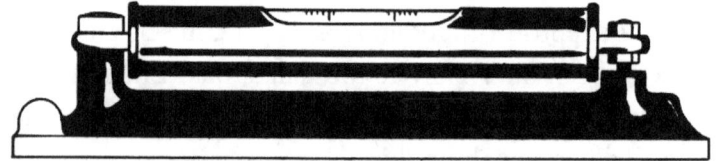

Chapter 32
SNOWSTORM

The weather worsened in the week that followed. Bob and John worked long hours on the firewood mill and by Saturday night it was well along.

At six o'clock Saturday night Bob suggested they take the rest of the week off. After supper, John had just stretched out for a nap when the phone rang downstairs. Doris' voice floated up the stairs moments later. "John, it's for you." He padded barefoot down the stairs and took the receiver.

"Hello. Kelly here."

"John, it's David Bellemeau calling from St. Joe . . . I'm sorry I haven't been able to get back to you 'til tonight, but here I am. Couldn't do no better."

"That's okay. Your wife said you'd been called away on short notice. What can I do for you?"

"Well, John, I was up in Ottawa a while back, and I saw that steam deck winch model of yours in the Museum of Science and Technology. You're a professional model builder, are you not?"

"Yes."

"Have you ever seen a magazine called MODEL ENGINEER"

"Yes."

"Have you seen any recent issues?"

"I've seen up to about the middle of August of this year."

"Do you recall the series on the Bentley BR2 rotary engine, by that chap in Australia — oh, what's his name?"

"Yes. I thought it was quite a project. I can't put my finger on the name of the guy either, right this minute, but I know the article you're talking about."

"Well, John, could you build an engine to that design?"

"Yes. That wouldn't be a problem."

"How about something a little different?"

"What have you got in mind?"

"Could you build me a model of a Pratt & Whitney nine cylinder radial?"

"I'd need drawings, or something pretty close to it. What sort of model do you have in mind — an exact scale museum class job, or a working model just patterned generally along the lines of the prototype?"

"I want an exhibition job, as close to the prototype as is practicable, but not intended to be run. Actually, I want two identical engines. Would you be willing to tackle that sort of job?"

"Yes, if you're prepared to foot the bill, but I'm gonna be blunt and brutal with you, Mr. Bellemeau: it's a big job, and I don't mess around — it's cash up front for a big chunk of the work, and only a rough estimate as to total cost. And work stops when the money's been gone through."

"I wouldn't expect you to touch it on any other basis. Listen, John, I have to go up to Tuktoyuktuk for a few days. I'd like to meet you so we could talk this thing over in more detail, face to face. I've been looking at a map. Could you meet me in Prince George if I arranged to stop over there on my way to Tuktoyuktuk? I'd get into Prince George on the evening flight from Vancouver."

"Well, I suppose I could do that . . . "

"Fine! Now, I'm not asking you to regard this as a sales trip, to be done on speculation. I realize you're talking about a 500 mile round trip, and two days time. I'll wire you $500 on Monday morning, if you'll meet me in Prince George that evening. Is that fair enough?"

"That'd be fine, far as I'm concerned. Let me just speak to my friend here for a minute — we're in the middle of building a firewood cutting mill. . . " He spoke to Bob briefly, not covering the receiver. Bob just waved his hand and said, "By all means, go."

"Okay, I'll see you in Prince George Monday evening. Where do you want me to meet you?"

"I've got a room at the Inn of the North. How be if we meet there for supper about 7:30?"

"Sounds good. You want me to stay overnight so we can talk further Tuesday morning before you take off for Inuvik and Tuk?"

"Yes. I can have my secretary make a reservation for you at the Inn of the North if you want."

"All right, that'd be fine, Mr. Bellemeau. You can wire the $500 to me care of the Smithers Credit Union, in Smithers. I'll be on my way to Prince George when they confirm receipt of it. It's a five to six hour trip, so they better not be late getting it . . . "

"I understand. We'll see to that from this end. I'll see you in Prince George at 7:30 Monday night at the Inn of the North. And when you get there, make it *David*, not 'Mr. Bellemeau', okay?"

"Okay, David. See you Monday evening, and lookin' forward to it."

He put down the receiver.

"What was that all about?" asked Ellen, who'd been curled up by the fire with a book.

"That was the Mysterious Man from St. Joe . . . " He proceeded to fill them in on the call.

"Oh, that sounds like a super project!" Ellen was delighted for him, as were Bob and Doris.

"Well, it's not an accomplished fact yet. When I've had a look at the whites of his eyes, I'll feel better, but he sounds okay, and if he's for real, it'd be a neat project."

The credit union called Monday at noon and John was on his way to Prince George within a half hour. It was a beautiful sunny day, and the road was largely free of snow, in spite of the bad weather of only days before. At the last minute, Ellen had given him a bag of chocolate brownie cookies, ('. . . don't start on them till you're on your way home . . . '). He pulled into Prince George an hour early, checked into the Inn of the North, and at a quarter past seven, enquired at the desk for David Bellemeau and rang his room on a house phone. Five minutes later Bellemeau stepped from the elevator and approached John in the lobby. He was a big man, with a head of white hair and a friendly, but business-like manner. John liked him right away, and over a steak dinner, learned something of his background and his wishes with respect to the proposed model commission.

He was connected with the oil industry, owning a company which manufactured oil field drilling equipment. He had grown up in

236

Hartford, Connecticut and as a kid of seven or eight had hung around the Pratt and Whitney shops, and had actually seen the #1 prototype R985 Wasp run up on unofficial tests before the official tests witnessed by the U.S. Navy. During WW II he'd been a Navy fighter pilot, in Wildcats and Corsairs, both powered by more advanced Pratt and Whitney derivatives of the Wasp. After the war, he'd ceased to fly actively, but never lost his admiration for the Pratt and Whitney radials.

"Man, we loved those engines — what a power plant they were!" he enthused, sipping coffee after the meal.

"I've often thought I'd like to have a model of the P&W Wasp engine, then I got to thinking, if I had one made, one of my two sons'd someday end up with it, and the other not, so I decided to get two made at the same time. So about a year ago, I started making enquiries as to who might make such a model, and got exactly nowhere until last month, when I had to go to Ottawa. I saw your work in the Museum there, and I talked to the curator. He couldn't find your address, but he remembered you lived out on the west coast. I figured Vancouver was the most likely place to start with, so I got busy on some telephone enquiries, looking for a John Kelly who built models, and about the 18th J. Kelly in the Vancouver phone book, I got your tape recording, so I left my number to call back, and your friend, Mrs. Larsen, called us Monday morning. Funny how you can track down a needle in a haystack when you put your mind to it."

John nodded. "'Tis. I have to do that sort of thing often enough myself. I get a kick out of it, actually."

The talk turned to drawings and where to locate same.

"I'll look after that, unless you've got a set on a string already?" said John.

"No, you look after that. And exact choice of scale. I want an engine something like so." His hands formed a circle about ten inches in diameter.

"What about the electrical system? Do you want working magnetos and so on, or . . . ?"

"No, just the external details, plus correct wiring. But I want the mechanical guts of the engine complete, or as complete as you can make them, though."

The talk went on over a delayed dessert of pie. Lousy pie, in comparison with Ellen's, John noted to himself.

It was fairly late when they finally retired to their rooms for the night. John was up early the next morning, and having slept on the discussions of the night before, made some notes and added some questions before going downstairs to meet Bellemeau for breakfast at eight. Bellemeau's plane was due to leave at noon. It would take him on to Fort St. John, and Whitehorse in the Yukon, where he'd overnight before a long DC3 flight to Inuvik, then by chartered plane to Tuk.

As they were finishing their breakfast in the hotel's coffee shop, John heard himself paged: "Mr. John Kelly. Please come to the reception desk. Mr. John Kelly. Long distance telephone."

He excused himself and walked from the coffee shop to the reception desk where a clerk handed him the phone.

"Hello. Kelly here."

"John. Bob. Can you bring us back a set of 5/8-18 taps? We're gonna need them on this firewood mill."

"Sure. Will do. Anything else?"

"Yeah — don't be too long getting back. I don't like the weather reports. There's supposed to be a big storm comin' down from Alaska. Looks fair to dump about two feet of snow on us."

"How's Hudson's Bay Mountain look?"

"Bluer'n Ellen's been since you left. There's snow a-comin' boy!" In the background John could hear Doris saying, "Now, Bob, you be quiet!" and Ellen's stage whisper, "Oh, don't tell him about that, Uncle Bob."

He could imagine her blushing furiously, and smiled to himself.

"Okay. I'll be home in time for supper, so don't eat my share, or it'll be taps for you, and they won't be 5/8-18 either, old man."

He hung up, and as he did so, his smile faded. What had Ellen meant? "Don't tell him about *that*?" About what? Or had she meant, 'Don't say that,' and phrased it poorly due to embarrassment? He shrugged . . .

He went back to the coffee shop, where David Bellemeau was working on a final cup of coffee. "Sorry about that. Bob just wanted me to pick up some taps he needs before I head back to Smithers."

"No problem, John. Looks to me like we've about covered everything, so there's no sense you hanging around to entertain me till my plane leaves at noon. Why don't we say goodbye now and you can get your taps, and be on your way?"

"Okay, David. It's been a pleasure meeting you, and I'm looking forward to this job. It's gonna be a real treat, as well as a challenge." He shook hands with the older man as he spoke.

"I'm glad I was able to find somebody who'd tackle it, and I appreciate you coming out here yesterday to discuss it, . . . and I've enjoyed meeting you too, John."

They parted, and John went up to his room to phone around to locate a set of 5/8-NF taps.

A set of 5/8-NF taps is usually not that hard to come by, but in Prince George, that particular day, none were to be had. After several phone calls to various industrial suppliers, he finally had what he wanted, but he'd have to wait till the noon flight from Vancouver: the supplier's Vancouver store would send the taps by courier to the Vancouver airport, and " . . . poof, nuthin' to it."

He looked at his watch. 9:20 a.m. Nearly five hours to kill. No sense digging up Bellemeau again.

He got some hotel stationery and drafted a letter to Pratt and Whitney, before checking out of his room. He drove to the public library, on Dominion Street, where he spent some time locating the Company's head office address, and the names of several key personnel, including the president.

Browsing in the Engineering section of the library, he located a book entitled, 'The Pratt and Whitney Story', and was soon engrossed in the story of the Company and its development of the various P&W radials, from the 9-cylinder Wasp, through the 14 cylinder Double Wasp, 18 cylinder Wasp Major, and the mighty 28 cylinder 'corncob' — the R4360.

The next time he looked at his watch it was 1:45. The plane, hopefully with his taps on it, would be landing in 22 minutes. He bought a bun and some sliced ham in a delicatessen, and headed for the airport. The temperature was now noticeably lower than earlier.

He need not have hurried: the flight was an hour late due to minor mechanical problems which had had to be corrected in Kamloops. By the time the 737's wheels hit the tarmack in Prince George, it had begun to snow — tiny, dry flakes.

Another 20 minutes passed before the air express bag was sorted, and in short order thereafter the package was signed for, and disappeared into a pocket of his parka. He was soon on his way back into town, and after a brief stop for fuel, pulled onto the Yellowhead Highway, glanced at his watch, and settled down for the 230 mile drive to Smithers. It was now nearly 4 p.m. and the early northern winter dusk was already upon him.

"Home in time for supper? Not likely, Kelly," he said to himself. Call it 9 or 10 p.m. if he was very lucky. And with this snow, it might well be much later.

Before he reached Vanderhoof, it was obvious it was going to be *much* later. It was now full dark, and snowing hard. Five inches of new snow blanketed the highway, and the only consolation one could find in the biting cold was that the snow was dry, and therefore not as slippery as it would have been if the temperature had been closer to freezing. It was, he found out when he stopped in Vanderhoof, nearly 25 below zero Fahrenheit. And dropping.

He scraped wind-packed snow from the front of the truck, particularly the headlights and the windshield. He decided to call Bob so they wouldn't be worrying about his late arrival, but when he tried, the phone was busy. Well, he'd try again at Fort Fraser, which was about 20 miles further along.

Starting out again, he reviewed his meeting with Bellemeau and was satisfied. He'd get his letter off to Pratt and Whitney tomorrow to start the process of scaring up drawings . . . The thought of drawings brought Ellen to mind. He reached over to the passenger seat where he'd put the bag of cookies she'd sent with him, found it, and ate one. He found a note in the bag, and turned on the overhead courtesy light to read it.

> "John: Hope you've had a good trip so far,
> and good luck in your meeting with Mr.
> Bellemeau.
>
> Don't eat all these cookies at once! See you
> when you get home. Love, Ellen."

He flicked off the courtesy light and tucked the note into his shirt pocket. 'Love, Ellen'. He turned the phrase over in his mind.

241

"You know, Kelly," he mused. "Bob's arm isn't going to be in a cast indefinitely. Nor is Doris' leg. One of these days you'd better bite the bullet and have a talk with Ellen."

This train of thought was interrupted by a set of headlights surmounted by a pair of flashing yellow lights coming into his field of vision. As the vehicle passed, he saw it was a tow truck, with a terribly smashed and snow-packed car behind. The sight turned his thoughts to the immediate situation, and he began to review the hazards.

It was snowing heavily, therefore the road was treacherous, one could easily lose control of the vehicle and go off the road, which might mean simply into the ditch, or down a 150 foot embankment. There was little traffic on the road, which was okay so long as one had no trouble. But if one went off the road, how long might it be before one's erring tracks in the snow were noticed? Or, what if the tracks were obliterated before another vehicle came by? It was cold, and getting colder. Off the road, injured — poof — nuthin' but a piece of frozen meat, by the time they'd find you, Kelly. Or you might hit a moose crossing the highway — two frozen meats. Or you could doze off and 'fail to negotiate a curve' as the phrase goes . . . frozen meat again. The hazards were real enough, and this did not by any means exhaust the possibilities.

"Okay, Kelly, you better first make darn sure you stay awake. And you can start by keeping an eye peeled for signs of any other traveller in trouble . . . " The phone was dead when he tried it at Fort Fraser, and he went on again. He considered the wisdom of laying over at Fraser Lake: well, if he could get in touch with Bob, and if there was a vacancy at a motel . . . on the other hand, if not, and if it got no worse, why not push on? "Let's see how it looks when we get to Fraser Lake," he told himself. "In the meantime, get this beast into four wheel drive . . . " He stepped on the clutch, and reaching down, eased back on the lever which engaged the drive to the front wheels. Immediately, he could feel the effect on the truck's handling. He twitched the wheel carefully right, and then left. The truck responded more surely. "Good — shoulda done that 50 miles back."

He missed the sheepskin seat covers he'd lost in the green truck. He had ordered a new set, but they would not be available for some weeks. In the meantime, he had borrowed a wool blanket from Doris.

He liked the new truck. If anything, it handled better than the old one Fredrickson had caused to burn up. Ellen had been right about blue as a colour choice; it looked fine. He and Bob had gone into Smithers on Monday and bought it, and they had spent two evenings going over every accessible bolt and nut. Everything had been shipshape.

His world had shrunk to the truck cab, and a small lighted cavity produced by his headlights in the black void ahead. The snowflakes seemed to rush into this lighted cavity from all sides, and disappear with a swoop at the edges of his windshield. The effect was mildly hypnotic. The road was now virtually obliterated, except for the tracks of other vehicles, and these now formed one lane in the center of the highway, widening into two passing sets of tracks whenever an oncoming vehicle forced each driver to ease over to his own side of the road. One didn't stop or slow, one just eased over into 12 to 15 inches of virgin snow, and plowed back into the track again as soon as the other vehicle had passed . . . Luckily, there were very few other vehicles on the road.

The phones were as useless at Fraser Lake as in Fort Fraser, and there were 'no vacancy' signs at all the motels. "Well, it's only eight miles to Endako — and not much chance of a room there . . ." and so it proved. No room, and the phones dead.

And at Burns Lake, 35 miles further on.

At each stop, and sometimes out on the highway, he broke away the wind-packed snow which built up on the front of the truck and threatened to mask his headlights entirely.

He was within five miles of Topley when he jerked forward in his seat and what he saw made him downshift twice, rapidly. A medium-sized car was nose-down over the snow-drifted highway shoulder. The tire tracks were quite fresh, but wildly confused . . . There was a dark form on the opposite side of the road. He rolled to a stop behind the stricken vehicle, switched on his hazard lights, and got out, glad of his parka, wool pants, and insulated boots. Man, it was cold!

He peered into the car. A form lay slumped in what remained of the front seat. The entire front end of the car was demolished, the windshield smashed to smithereens. He leaned in the opening where the windshield had been. "Hey! Can you — are you alive?"

There was a moan. "Ohh, my arm." The voice was filled with pain. He wrenched open the driver's door and leaned in.

"What happened? Can you move? Is it just your arm?"

"A moose . . . Ohh, my arm is broken — I'm okay otherwise, I think." It was a woman's voice.

"Look, I'm going to try to get you out of here. I'll get you into my truck and take you back to Burns Lake, to the hospital."

John Kelly knew as well as anyone not to move an accident victim without knowing the extent of the injuries, and preferably not without the requisite first aid training — "well nuts, man, the preferred and the requisite you ain't got tonight, and by the time they get here, this lady could freeze to death." He worked an arm around her back and with a " . . . hang on, this may smart a little . . . " he eased her into a sitting position. "How's that? Not so bad as you thought, eh?" The woman nodded. There was blood on her face.

"Now, put your good arm around my neck, or grab my parka, or something, so I can get you out of the car and onto your feet."

"I'll try," she said weakly.

"You do that lady, or you like to freeze to death," he thought grimly. However, he said, "Okay, let's do it. Come on. Hang onto my coat as hard as you can. Now, easy, back we go. Now, can you put your foot out of the car?"

And so, by degrees and careful stages he lifted and talked the injured woman onto her feet, up to the road, and back to his own truck. After helping her into the passenger seat, he climbed in the driver's side, and began to turn the truck around. When his headlights crossed the highway, he saw again the dark form he'd noted as he pulled up, and now it moved. "Oh no, it's still alive . . . " he groaned. "Look lady, I know you're hurt, and I'm gonna get you back to Burns Lake as fast as I can, but I gotta see to that moose."

He got out of the truck again, and walked cautiously toward the downed animal. Its rear legs — one was grotesquely bent — appeared to be paralyzed, and its back was probably broken also. It would have to be put out of its misery. John wished fervently that he had his Springfield in the truck, but he had not yet had time to rig, in it, a duplicate of the arrangement for its unobtrusive storage which he had had in the green Land Cruiser, and so he had reluctantly left it at Bob's.

His mind cast over the possibilities: cut its throat (too dangerous); park the truck on its windpipe (too slow); clobber it — with what? An axe. Yes! No — the axe he'd bought to keep in the truck was too short. For this, one would need to be on one's feet and ready to jump out of the way, and a powerful swing would be required. . . Maybe in the woman's car? He hurried back to the truck and spoke to the woman. No, there was no axe in the car. She was certain. A shovel? Nothing.

The wind brought him the sound of a large diesel engine being geared down. He stepped to the front of the Land Cruiser and waited. In a minute the snowy darkness was pierced by the headlights and running lights of an eighteen-wheeled freight rig. John swung his arm up and down at his side in an arc. He heard the trucker gear down and begin to slow, saw the truck lights blink acknowledgement of his signal.

John ran up to the cab on the driver's side, reaching it as the window several feet above his head rolled down.

"What's the problem?"

"Lady hit a moose. I'm gonna take her to the hospital in Burns Lake. The moose is still alive. Have you got an axe?"

"Yeah, I got a fire axe."

"Will you loan it to me for a minute?"

The trucker had opened the door and climbed down to the ground. "Watcha gonna do?"

He was a short, stocky, partly bald man with a barrel chest and arms as thick as some men's legs.

"Can't leave that moose there with a busted leg and all messed up, to freeze to death. Besides, where it is, another vehicle could hit it."

"So what you want an axe for?"

"To put it out of its misery. Unless you've got a rifle? Once it's dead, if you'll give me a hand, we can roll it off the road."

"You wanna kill a moose with an axe?"

"Look chum, it's probably 40 below. I've been here ten, maybe 15 minutes. I'm cold. I'm tired. I gotta get an injured lady to hospital. Yes, I'll kill the moose with your axe, if you'll get it outta your truck and give it to me. If you want to see how it's done, you can watch, or no, as ever you please." John's usually patient nature had been somewhat strained by the exchange.

"Okay, Mister. Better you than me." The driver pulled himself back up to the cab of his truck and emerged in short order with a fire axe with a 36 inch handle.

"Perfect!" breathed John.

"What you think the cops're gonna say about you killing a moose like that?"

"I don't much care what they say. Nor will that moose. If you see any cops, you can ask 'em." He headed for the moose.

She lay on her side, her front legs stretched out. With heavy heart, John positioned himself slightly in front of her, his feet apart, and swung the axe experimentally. Mercy demanded there be no error. Bad enough that it had to be done this way at all.

"I'm sorry, old girl, but it's the best thing I can do for you." He swung the axe up level with his right shoulder and fixed his eyes on a spot in the middle of her forehead. The axe flashed down, and drove deep into its mark. The cow lunged half way to her feet and instantly collapsed again, in pain no more. John heard a retching sound behind him.

He put the axe down, and reached for a foreleg, to roll her over and off the roadway. The next instant, he was knocked sprawling.

"Ya shoulda waited!" said the trucker, helping John to his feet. "You okay?"

"I guess so. She must have struck at me when I touched her leg. Man, she like to knocked my hand off! Let's give her half a minute." John rubbed his left hand, and flexed it carefully. It hurt, but everything worked . . .

"Okay, let's see what we can do here," the trucker grunted, and grasping both front legs, rolled the moose onto her back and tipped her over. A weak stomach he might have, but his arms and chest were something else again. Even as John moved to help, the trucker grunted again, and the moose rolled unceremoniously over the snow-blanketed shoulder of the road.

"Thanks," said John, picking up the axe and wiping bits of hair, bone splinters and nearly frozen brains and blood from the blade.

The trucker took it and stuck out his hand. "No problem. Like I said fella, better you than me. I doubt I coulda done it."

They shook hands.

"Sorry I was a little short with you a minute ago," John said.

"Forget it. I gotta be getting on my way. I'll see ya, fella."

"Okay — thanks — don't get into the sugar[11]."

"You too, buddy."

The trucker revved his idling diesel and started on his way west again as John Kelly cut a semi-circular track in the center of the highway, and headed east, back towards Burns Lake. The injured woman took her misfortune like a brick. She was a local resident, on her way back from Burns Lake where she'd been visiting her daughter, to her own home in Houston. She had been, she told him, a

---

11 A common north-country parting shot in winter, meaning: "don't get stuck", or "don't go off the road into the snow."

resident of the area since 1927, when she'd arrived as a girl of three with her parents, who had built and operated a sawmill to supply ties for the railway, and lumber to the local farmers. She and her husband now ran a building supply store in Houston.

Just as they entered Burns Lake, the woman remembered her car keys, which neither she nor John had thought to take from the car.

"I'll have to speak to the police about killing that moose after I drop you at the hospital. They'll have somebody on the highway and they can radio to them to pick up your keys for you. I 'spect you won't need them tonight anyway. With that arm, they'll probably keep you in until tomorrow."

An hour later, John walked out of the Burns Lake RCMP Detachment office. The thermometer by the entrance said 38 below zero Fahrenheit. His hand throbbed. The doctor at the hospital had said it'd be okay — soak it in hot water. It was now shortly after 10 p.m. and here he was pulling out of Burns Lake for the second time. At the rate he'd been going it'd be 3/4 of an hour to Topley, half an hour to Houston, 3/4 of an hour to Telkwa, and the best part of another half hour to Bob's place. That meant it'd be . . . 1:30 a.m. by the time he got to Bob's. Call it 2 a.m. Fatigue had taken the edge off his thinking to such an extent that he had passed Decker Lake, five miles out of Burns Lake, by the time he had this sorted out. He fumbled around on the seat for Ellen's cookies, and found them, crushed in the bag; the woman had sat on them! Well, squashed or no, he would eat them now.

Chapter 33
BITING THE BULLET

He refueled at Houston, and by the time he eased off the Highway at Smithers, he could hardly have given his name correctly. The storm had abated somewhat, but there was at least 18 inches of fresh snow to plow through for the four miles to Bob's place. Somehow he made it without going off the road, which was unmarked and almost obliterated.

The porch light was on for him. At the kitchen door he let himself in with his key. Quietly, he closed the door behind him. It was 2:30 a.m.

From the living room, where a single light glowed beside the fireplace, came Ellen's startled voice: "Oh, is that you, John?"

"Yes. What are you doing up at this hour?" he asked, surprised, but speaking slowly. He had been awake 21 hours. The ten hours since he had left Prince George seemed to have put lead weights on his tongue.

In a moment she was beside him, helping him out of his coat, pulling out a chair for him, helping him take off his boots. All the while she was speaking quietly: "I must have drifted off to sleep. Oh, I'm so glad you're home! I was worried, when you didn't get here for supper. Did you have trouble on the road? You must be exhausted."

"I had to wait in Prince for the taps Bob wanted, and . . . I'm sorry, Ellen, I'm pretty beat. Can I tell you about it in the morning?"

"Of course — but you're all right?"

"Just tired."

"Can I get you something to eat? I can have it ready in a few minutes."

"No thanks, Ellen. I just want to get some sleep. I'll be okay in the morning."

"Did you have supper?" ,

"No. I just had the cookies you sent with me. A lady sat on most of them . . . "

"What do you mean?"

He raised his hand in a gesture of dismissal. "It's too complicated. I'll tell you all about it in the morning."

"Okay."

He stood up, and she helped him do so. It was then he saw the tears in her eyes, brimming, ready to spill. He came full awake. "What's the matter, Ellen?"

"I . . . I was worried for you. Uncle Bob said you'd be all right,and told me to go to bed, but I couldn't. I kept thinking of all the things that could happen . . . and . . . and" She dissolved, burying her face on his chest, her arms tight around him.

He rocked her slowly from side to side, and stroked her hair gently. "If that's all that's troubling you, you shouldn't be crying. I'm home, safe and sound."

"I know, but . . . " she sobbed quietly.

"What's the matter, Ellen? Let's go sit down for a minute or two." He sensed there was more bothering her than she'd let on.

"No, it's . . . I'm okay . . . You're too tired to talk . . . " but she let him lead her into the living room.

"I'm not too tired to listen, if you want to talk about something. Now come on, what's the matter?" He sat down, and she beside him.

"I'm sorry, John. It's late and you're ready to fall asleep on your feet . . . but . . . well . . . " she twisted around, and picked up three items from the little table beside the couch.

"These came in the mail yesterday."

"What are they?"

"A letter from Toronto; I can have my old job back. And an air ticket. They want me to come right away, or as soon as I can. And . . . this . . . " she handed him the third item, a somewhat homemade-looking card. Neatly inked on the front were the words, 'WE'D LOVE TO HAVE YOU BACK, ELLEN!' Inside, it had been signed by at least two dozen people, obviously her former coworkers. "I don't know what to do. It'd be anti-climactic to go back, and I was so tired of that job, and that office. The people were nice, but it was the same old routine, day after day, . . . but, I haven't been able to find a job out here . . . "

"If ever there was a time, Kelly," he told himself, "when you'd better strike while the iron is hot, it's now."

"Listen — will you stay here for a minute, and let me get something from my room? I'll be right back."

When he came back, he handed her a small, blue box. Across the top, in darker blue, was embossed a single word: 'BIRKS'. It is a name universally known across Canada from the Atlantic to the Pacific, and Ellen's eyes opened wide when she saw it.

"Don't open it for a minute, okay?"

She nodded, silent, her heart racing.

"Do you remember when we were driving out from Prince George, when you told me about your mom and dad being killed? I said I understood how you felt. I said, 'I know, because I've been there,' or something, and when you asked me who, I didn't answer you?"

"I remember. I felt very bad, because I shouldn't have asked."

"You had every reason to ask: I invited the question. It's not something I find very easy to talk about, but I brought it up and I should not have left you feeling embarrassed. That was rude of me, and I'm sorry."

She turned a little more toward him then, put her open right hand on his left cheek and pulled his head closer to her. She kissed him, and said very softly: "It doesn't matter, John. I felt bad I'd asked because I could see it was something you couldn't talk about. And anyway, you've been so nice to me ever since the first time I spoke to you on the bus."

"Well, I'd like to tell you about it now, if you'll let me." He opened his right hand and turned it so the light fell on it. "See that thin white scar? . . . "

He told her the whole story then. At the end, she wept for him.

"When I was in Vancouver on that Saturday I asked you to arrange as a stopover for me when you fixed up my reservations for the trip to Frisco . . . well, I had a long talk with Ailene about a lot of things that day, you not least among them. And I brought that little blue box back up here with me. It's been stored away in a locked trunk in my basement ever since Janet was killed . . . open it, Ellen, if you will."

She raised the hinged lid of the little box. Within, on a pad of royal blue velvet lay a diamond engagement ring and a matching wedding band. Tucked into the lid was a small square of paper, on which, in a neat engineering hand, was lettered:

> You have been to me
>
> All gentle things and kind,
>
> And made my heart forget
>
> The bitter stone.[12]

She stood up, pulled him to his feet, put her arms around his neck and laid her face against his cheek.

"Do you like them? If you'd rather choose a diff . . . "

She reached up and put her hand to his lips. "John, there isn't an engagement ring nor a wedding band from here to Halifax, or from Tuk to Yucatan, that I'd rather have. They're lovely — just beautiful."

"Will you marry me, and come back to Vancouver with me?"

"Nothing in the world could make me happier."

"I've been wanting to ask you for quite a while, but the right occasion never seemed to come along. I wouldn't have thought this'd be the ideal time, but I guess it'll have to do, eh?"

"It's a fine time." She freed herself, or more accurately, let go of John, took the card from Toronto, and tore it in half.

"John?"

He looked at her.

"Most girls like to be kissed when they get engaged," she said very softly.

---

12 Adapted from a poem by Jehanne de Mare, and cut from an unknown publication some years before I was born. GBL.

"You're not afraid of turning into a frog?"

"Not a bit."

He kissed her. Quite thoroughly.

"Let's see how that engagement ring fits," he suggested afterwards. He sat down, and pulled her gently onto his knee. It was when he tried to put the ring on her finger that she noticed that his left hand was swollen, and nearly blue.

"Oh, whatever happened to your hand?" she asked, all thought of the ring gone in a split second.

"It's nothing. I'll tell you about it tomorrow," he hedged.

"Were you in a fight?" she asked, in a voice so filled with concern he almost burst out laughing.

"No, I wasn't in a fight, Ellen. I just got my hand bashed 'cause of being in the way when I shoulda been a bit smarter. It's alright. Does the ring fit?"

"Yes, it's perfect! See?" She held out her hand for him to see. He took her hand in his and squeezed it, then kissed her again.

The fatigue came back on him then like a door slamming in his face. "Ellen, I love you very much, and I know this is a heck of a thing to say at a time like this, but I'm tired. I've just gotta get some sleep. We'll tell Bob and Doris everything in the morning, okay?" "Okay, John."

"And if you can't sleep tonight, you can think about the wedding. When and where, and so on, and where you'd like to go on our honeymoon. Now, I'm off to my trundle bed as fast as my hairy little legs'll carry me. Good night, my lovely lady."

"John?"

"Yes?"

"Could we go to San Francisco for our honeymoon? I'd love that."

"Then we will. Good night, Ellen."

"Good night, John."

He stopped once more, two steps further up the stairs. "That was a pretty good pun, Ellen."

"Pun? Did I do a pun?"

"From Tuk to Yucatan. Tuktoyuktuk — Tuk to Yucatan. Very good."

"Go to bed. You're delirious."

"I have reason to be . . . "

*   *   *

It was sometime after ten the following morning before John was heard stirring, and in due course, he came downstairs washed, clean shaven, and none the worse for his trip. Bob had much earlier betaken himself out to the shop, with orders to be called when John got up.

When John came into, the kitchen, Ellen put her arm around him and said, "I couldn't wait till you got up to tell them."

"Tell them what?" he asked, with a look of utter puzzlement.

"That we're engaged!"

"Oh, my gosh! I wasn't actually sure it was for real — I thought maybe it was just a nightmare after that drive in the storm and all. Did I really ask you to marry me last night?" he asked, looking at her straight faced.

"Yes, you did!" she laughed, pointing to the engagement ring on her left hand.

"Took so much out of him to ask you, he doesn't even remember, and sleeps in till nearly noon to recover from it," teased Bob.

He found himself more or less mobbed then, Bob's handshake and back-slapping being the most noteworthy, but no warmer than Doris' congratulations.

"I'll get you some breakfast," Ellen said, giving John's left hand a squeeze.

"Oww," he gasped, wincing involuntarily.

"Oh, your hand, I forgot. I'm sorry — did I hurt you?" she said contritely.

"No, it's okay," he said, rubbing it ruefully.

"What's the matter with your hand?"

"Oh, it's nuthin'," he said, not wanting to go into details about the killing of the moose, for Ellen's sake.

"He was brawling in a haunt of vice in Prince George," Ellen said, flouncing off toward the stove.

"I was *not* brawling in Prince George, nor was I in any haunt of vice, as you so delicately put it, except inasmuch as the Inn of the North may be, or the Prince George public library. I got kicked by a moose!"

Bob shot him a look of rank disbelief.

There was no way out then but to tell what had happened, which he did while Ellen made him a pile of pancakes.

Bob got himself a plate and began stealing John's pancakes, then Doris began stealing bites from Bob's plate. Finally Ellen set places for herself and her aunt, and mixed more batter.

"If anybody wants anything to eat at noon, they'll have to fix it for themselves," she warned good naturedly.

Chapter 34
A SECRET UP HER SLEEVE

That evening, Ellen asked John if she could have some of her belongings shipped out from Toronto to his house in West Vancouver.

"Certainly. But how'll you get the stuff packed, unless you go down east and do it yourself?"

"I'll phone my brother in Kitchener. He'll pack it all up and crate it. There's my writing desk, and some china, and clothes and so on . . . "

"Well, whatever there is, you just tell your brother to ship it out here, freight collect, to John Kelly. Give him my address and Ailene's phone number. If it gets to my place before we get there, Ailene'll come up and unlock the house and they can put the stuff inside, any place she tells 'em. We'll straighten it all out when we get home."

"Okay. That'll be perfect, John."

Ellen had a secret up her sleeve which she had no intention of disclosing to him at this point. The next day she phoned both her brother *and* Ailene during the afternoon, while John and Bob were out in the shop. Her things would arrive in West Vancouver before her and John did, if all went according to her plan.

She was somewhat apprehensive, as she dialed Ailene's number, about the sort of reception she would have there. However, she need not have worried, and within the first minute of the conversation she understood why John Kelly had liked her instantly when he had met her as Janet's mother.

"John told me a lot about you when he was here on his way back from San Francisco. He certainly thinks the world of you, Ellen."

"Well, he's very fond of you too, Mrs. Larsen. He was showing me that walnut tool chest you gave him. It's beautiful!"

"Now don't you call me Mrs. Larsen. You call me Ailene, or Mom if you like. And when he showed you that toolbox, did he tell you that about two months before I gave it to him he'd spent three full days putting in all new copper plumbing in my house? I'll bet he didn't . . .

"No, he didn't mention that . . . "

"Well, you'll just have to learn to live with that side of him. Half the truth, most of the time, and always the same half — what somebody did for him, not what he did for the other fellow."

As they said goodbye, the purpose of the call having been dealt with, Ellen had said, "Gee it's going to be nice to have a Mum again."

Chapter 35
MACHINIST'S MATE FIRST CLASS

"Well, I guess the truck oughta be warmed up by now . . . We better say goodbye and be on our way."

"Goodbye. Have a good trip home."

"Goodbye, Doris. We will. Thanks for everything!"

"Thanks for all the help, both of you."

"Best holiday I've had in years, Bob," John said as they shook hands. "Don't either of you come outside. Man, 52 below zero and it's hardly December yet!"

He gave Doris a hug while she was squeezing Ellen's hand tightly and then they were off. Ellen turned to wave again as she climbed into the truck.

It had snowed during the night and although the country was locked in the grip of a savage cold spell, the day was clear and bright. The wedding had been very small, conducted in the Davidsons' living room by a minister friend earlier that morning. The whole thing had been a blur for John, except for two things: Ellen was now his wife, and he had never seen her look so happy, nor so pretty, since the day he'd first spoken to her on the bus.

"We just have to stop in Smithers to pick up the tickets for our trip," said Ellen, settling herself.

"Okay. Tell me again how you set up everything for that."

"Next Monday we fly down from Vancouver to San Francisco. We have a room reserved at the Hyatt Regency there. I think it's far too expensive for the likes of us, but you said to, so I did. Anyway, we stay in San Francisco for four days. Then we rent a car and drive to Phoenix, Arizona. That'll take us about two days. We'll spend about two days in Phoenix. While we're there we must see the Desert Botanical Garden. It's supposed to be the foremost one of its type in the world. And there's a mineral museum we'll have to see too, particularly since we are such experts at finding nice examples of spectacular mineralization!"

"Where do we stay in Phoenix?"

"We take what we can get, no reservations made. When we leave Phoenix we rent another car, and we drive north to Flagstaff and on in to the Grand Canyon, where we spend a day. My brother went there two years ago and he told me we should be able to see about everything we'd want in one day. We'll stay at Grand Canyon Village for one night. I didn't reserve a room for us there because our schedule may get out a bit by that time. We can phone ahead and set that up before we leave Phoenix. From Grand Canyon we go on to Salt Lake City, seeing Bryce Canyon and Zion Canyon on the way. We drop the car and fly home from Salt Lake. We'll be back just in nice time for Christmas."

"Sounds like a pretty nice trip. But no matter where we go, or what we see, there's nothing to top this part of B.C., is there? Just look at the snow and the mountains and everything. Man, it's beautiful!"

"It is. It's just glorious. Everything looks so sharp and clear and sparkly-new."

After picking up the air tickets, they were on the way again, heading east on the Yellowhead Highway. They drove in silence for a few minutes, then Ellen spoke.

"Say, I know what I meant to ask you . . . What were you and Uncle Bob so engrossed in Tuesday evening while Auntie D and I were working on the wedding cake?"

"You remember that fat envelope with all the British stamps on it that you brought home from the post office Tuesday morning?" Ellen nodded.

| "Well, that was a set of drawings I ordered from a guy called Tinker, in England. You remember a couple of days after I got back from seeing Bellemeau you got a money order for me in Smithers and sent it off to N.W. Tinker, 123 Spinney Crescent, Beeston, Nottinghamshire? You were chuckling over the address at the time, and said it sounded so typically English?"

"Sure, I remember. What were the drawings for?"

"A tool and cutter grinding jig. I've been on the lookout for a small, used tool and cutter grinder for a couple of years now, and they just never seem to surface very often. Tinker advertises from time to time in MODEL ENGINEER. When I was in Vancouver in October I looked through some back issues till I found his address, and sent off to him for information. When it came, it looked good, so I sent for the drawings, which came this past Tuesday."

"And?"

"It looks real good. Bob and I went through all the drawings and figured it out. It'll do everything I want a tool and cutter grinder for, and it's simple to build . . . there's just one casting required — actually two identical castings, which are machined just slightly different, and the rest is duck soup — simple parts, only a couple of them to particularly critical limits, and very few in all. You set it up beside an ordinary bench grinder, which I've already got."

"So you're going to make one?"

"No, I'm going to make two, one for me and one for Bob. It won't take any longer to round up the materials for two than one, and it won't take much longer to build two than one, either."

"When are you going to do all this?"

"As soon as we get back from our honeymoon. The next few months are going to be pretty busy, from the look of things — two Tinkers, and the dividing head, and then the two Pratt & Whitneys." The air tickets, which Ellen had placed on the truck's dash board, fell to the floor at this point.

"Make sure we don't loose those," said John, as she retrieved them and tucked them into her purse.

"We won't. I'll keep everything organized for you."

"I know you will. As a matter of fact, it has crossed my mind more than once how much simpler things'll be for me from now on, having you as my wife . . . "

"How so?"

"Well, you can do all the bookkeeping and the drafting, and when I need a third or fourth hand in the shop, you can be my machinist's helper."

"I want a better title than that!" said Ellen.

"What do you have in mind?"

"Well, how about 'Machinist's Mate, 1st class'?"

"Sounds fair enough to me."

Chapter 36
HOMECOMING

They pulled into John's driveway late the following evening. John parked the truck and a minute later, having unlocked the front door and pocketed the keys, scooped Ellen up and carried her over the threshold.

"When I left here in September, I never thought I'd have to do *that* when I came home!" he grinned, kissing her before setting her down. "How about a quick tour of the premises before I unload the truck?"

"Okay."

They went through the whole house hand in hand. It was a comfortable place, not large, with a view out over English Bay and the city. They found a bowl of fresh flowers on the dining room table, and another in the kitchen. One was from Ailene, the other from John's parents and brother in Nova Scotia. "Probably arranged for through Ailene," said John.

When they went downstairs, they found four crates, one large, and three smaller ones, at the foot of the stairs.

"Looks like your stuff's got here ahead of us!"

"Oh, I forgot to tell you! Ailene phoned three or four days ago to say it'd just been delivered. You and Uncle Bob were in the shop at the time. Auntie D and I were so busy, getting the house cleaned up and everything, I guess it slipped my mind."

"Well, I'm glad it's here and in good shape. Your brother knows how to do a first class job of crating, I must say."

"Oh, that's nothing! Wait'll you see my writing desk. You'll have to tell me where I can put it . . . "

"*You* can decide where you want to put it, Ellen. It can go in the living room upstairs, or wherever you like. Come on, let's have a quick look at the den."

Although directly beneath the living room, being one storey lower, the den had a lesser view out over the city. A drafting machine on a portable drawing board sat on a large desk placed against one wall. A sofa, a chair, and two bookshelves occupied the other end of the room.

"This room is nice and cosy in the winter, with the fireplace, and like the whole basement, it's always cool and comfortable on even the hottest days in summer."

"Oh! This is so nice!" exclaimed Ellen. "Could we put my writing desk in here?"

"Certainly. One other change I want to make is to move that bookshelf into the spare bedroom upstairs."

"Oh? Why do you want to do that? It looks good there . . . "
"Well, we're going to need the space for your wedding present — to wit, one only piano, which we are going to start looking for tomorrow."

"Oh, John, that'd be lovely!"

"Now quit kissin' me and let me get that truck unloaded before I show you my workshop, okay?"

"Okay. I'll help."

*   *   *

"There. That's our winter meat supply!" said John closing the deep freeze on Moose Number 2. "Now come on, and I'll show you the shop."

Chapter 37
FINAL SURPRISE

John pushed open the door to his shop, flicked on the lights, and ushered Ellen into the room ahead of him.

Against the wall opposite the door was a workbench, with a Wilton machinist's vise at one end. On the wall behind were hung numerous hand tools on a pegboard rack. Ranged along the wall to her left as she entered were two cloth draped machines on welded steel stands. On the right side of the room, shelves blanketed the wall from floor to rafters. On the latter were hung face plates, a steady rest, a Myford metric conversion banjo, a machete, rolls of abrasive paper of various grades, welding torches, and various sizes and lengths of cold rolled steel, brass and aluminum bar stock, drill rod, and a host of other items appropriate to such a shop. There was an empty space on one rafter where the Springfield would go.

John flicked on a 4-foot fluorescent light above one of the cloth draped machines. "This is my lathe," he said, carefully removing the cover. "It's a Myford Super 7."

"Don't you ever use it?" Ellen asked with a smile.

Not only the lathe was clean: here, as throughout the whole house, you could have eaten off the floors.

"Sure, I use it. But I also look after it properly. If I should live so long, I expect to be using it when I'm 90."

"My dad had an old South Bend lathe, but it wasn't in anything like as nice condition as this. He said it was still good and accurate, but it looked well used," Ellen said.

John nodded, moving over to the other machine, which he uncovered, while Ellen continued to look at the lathe. He reached up and pulled the fluorescent light over to a point midway between the two machines. The noise of its movement startled her.

"I'm sorry. I didn't mean to scare you. The light is hung on a track of curtain I-beam, so I can move it to wherever I need it, over either machine, or over the bench," John explained.

"This is my milling machine. You remember that day we went up to Smithers Landing and you were asking me about my shop? I told you how I'd wanted to get a shaper, but the one I wanted — the 7" South Bend — went out of production, and then I found this thing? I never even knew they made a knee-type mill this size till I saw this one. I took one long look, and bought it. It's from Taiwan, but it's a really good machine."

Ellen ran her finger over the silk smooth surface of the 6 x 24 inch table of the vertical mill.

Like the lathe, it was as clean as though it'd never been used. Her finger left a mark in an invisible coating of thick oil on the surface. "Starrett Ml oil," John said, producing a short length of toilet paper for her to wipe her finger.

"Where did that come from?" she asked in surprise.

"Reflex action, I guess," grinned John, pointing to a roll of toilet paper on a dispenser under the lathe's chip tray.

"And if you had a shaper, where would you put it?"

"Right there by the door."

Ellen nodded, and after another look about her, and a thoughtful pause, she smiled at John and said, "Well, with or without a shaper, it's a nice shop. My dad would have been tickled pink to see it. Now, will you do me a favour?"

"Sure," said John, replacing the cloth covers on the two machines.

"Will you open one of those crates for me tonight?"

"I'll open them all, if you want."

"No, just one. I'll show you which one, it's marked."

She led him from the shop, and looked at the three smaller crates.

"This one," said Ellen definitely, pointing to a '#3' on one of them.

"Okay. What's in it?"

"You'll see. All we need to open it is a wrench. When Ed makes a crate for something, he bolts it all together."

John glanced at the bolts, went into the shop, and returned with a six inch adjustable wrench. In short order the crate dissolved into a top, four sides and a bottom. Whatever was in the crate was surrounded with an enormous quantity of crushed and tightly packed newspaper.

John went off to the garage and came back with a large cardboard box to put the newspapers in. With all the newspapers removed, they were confronted with a lumpy object tied around with an old cotton sheet. At this point, Ellen put her hand on John's arm.

"John, I want to tell you something. Sit down on the stairs for a minute, okay?"

John sat down, puzzled. Ellen sat beside him, and put her arm around his shoulders.

"After my parents were killed, my brother and I decided to sell whatever of Dad's tools Ed couldn't use. There was the lathe and a lot of machinist's hand tools. Naturally, if I'd know then that I would meet and marry you, we'd never have sold any of it. But I didn't and we did, and that can't be helped. But there was one thing neither of us could bring ourselves to sell, even though Ed couldn't use it.

"I . . . , we . . . well, when you asked me to marry you, and I guess even before that maybe, I knew exactly what I wanted to do with it, so I phoned Ed and told him. He agreed and . . . well . . . this is sort of a wedding present for you from me and Ed, and my Dad, too, in a way. I know he'd have liked you, and would have wanted you to have this thing. Now shut your eyes again for a minute while I take that sheet off it, and tell you to open your eyes, okay?"

"Okay." John closed his eyes. Ellen got up from where she sat beside him. She pulled off the sheet and wads of newspaper within, which she'd instructed her brother to include to disguise the shape of the item.

"All right, open your eyes."

John opened his eyes, and found himself looking at the most exquisite small power shaper he'd ever seen. He was speechless.

"It's not a 7" South Bend. It's only got a 5" stroke, but it runs as quiet as a little mouse, and it is superbly accurate."

"Oh, Ellen! That is fantastic! Where on earth did your Dad ever find that?"

"He didn't find it. He made it!"

John's head turned from the shaper to Ellen so fast it almost made a complete revolution.

"Your Dad made this?!!"

"He did. He found a gear in something that was being scrapped at work, and he got to looking at it, and decided it'd be the perfect bull gear for a shaper. So he designed one around the gear, made the patterns, and got castings made. He did all the heavy machining at work, and made the small parts at home, or during lunch hours."

John squatted down beside the shaper. "That is something else! I would sure have liked to have been able to shake your Dad's hand! Look at that! It's got a variable automatic crossfeed, and everything!!" There was no mistaking the delight in his voice.

And indeed the little shaper "had everything": scraped and frosted working surfaces, polished brass ball handles, graduated micrometer dials, variable stroke, and more. The exterior was painted a soft blue, while the inside of the table casting and the main frame casting were painted bright red.

John stood up, and put his arms around Ellen and hugged her. "That's the most wonderful wedding present in the world, next to yourself. Thank you very much, Ellen. You, and Ed, and your Dad. "

"Well, if you like it, it's exactly where it belongs: in this house. There's a steel stand for it, and all the tools that go with it, in the crate with my desk. But it's late now, John. We've had a long drive today, and we're both tired. Let's leave it for tonight. There'll be time enough tomorrow to uncrate the desk and get the shaper set up in the shop."

John nodded, reluctantly. "Yeah — I guess so. Man, that's a neat little machine, Ellen!"

Ellen draped the cotton sheet over the shaper. "There, it's covered up, just like the lathe and the mill. It can sleep there on the floor for tonight — which is something I don't intend to do," she added with a twinkle in her eye.

Appendix A: GRANOLA

4 cups rolled wheat flakes
1/2 cup brown sugar
3/4 cup wheat germ
1/4 cup coconut
3 tbsp. sesame seeds
3/4 cup sunflower seeds (or nuts)
1/2 tsp salt (if seeds or nuts unsalted)
Blend all the above in a bowl

In a saucepan, heat together and stir till bubbly
1/3 cup salad oil
1/2 cup honey
1 tsp vanilla

Then mix thoroughly with dry ingredients so that all the dry
ingredients are coated.
Pour onto a cookie pan (this recipe requires two cookie pans) and
place in a 325°F oven for 15 minutes, or till brown, stirring two or
three times.

Appendix B:
CHOCOLATE CHEESECAKE

Crust

1-1/4 cups crushed chocolate wafers
1/4 cup butter
Combine and press into an 8" round pan

Filling

Soak 1 envelope gelatine in 1/4 cup cold water. Heat if necessary and then cool.

Blend:　　　　8 oz. cottage cheese
　　　　　　　4 oz. cream cheese
　　　　　　　1 cup sugar
　　　　　　　2 tsp. vanilla

Add 3 egg yolks, one at a time, then 6 squares semi-sweet melted chocolate.
Beat first, then add 3 egg whites and 1/4 cup sugar.

Whip 1/2 pint whipping cream and add the gelatine, then fold into the chocolate mixture.

Pour into pan and chill.

www.ingramcontent.com/pod-product-compliance
Lightning Source LLC
Chambersburg PA
CBHW060902250626

47159CB00008B/2843